ALSO BY MAGGIE SHIPSTEAD

Great Circle

Astonish Me

Seating Arrangements

You Have a
Friend in 10A

You Have a
Friend in 10A

MAGGIE SHIPSTEAD

ALFRED A. KNOPF   New York

2022

Some pieces originally appeared in the following publications:
"Acknowledgments" on BuzzfeedNews.com (November 15, 2017);
"The Cowboy Tango" in *VQR* (Fall 2009) and subsequently collected
in *The Best American Short Stories 2010*, edited by Richard Russo
(Houghton Mifflin Harcourt, 2010); "Lambs" in *Mary Review* (2016);
"You Have a Friend in 10A" in *Tin House* (2011); "In the Olympic Village"
in *Subtropics* (Winter 2012); "Angel Lust" in *Electric Literature* (May 22, 2013);
"The Great Central Pacific Guano Company" in *American Short Fiction*
(Spring 2012); "La Moretta" in *VQR* (Fall 2011); "Souterrain" in *Guernica*
(December 1, 2015); and "Backcountry" in *VQR* (Winter 2017).

Library of Congress Cataloging-in-Publication Data
Names: Shipstead, Maggie, author.
Title: You have a friend in 10A / Maggie Shipstead.
Description: First edition. | New York: Alfred A. Knopf, 2022. |
"This is a Borzoi book"—Title page verso.
Identifiers: LCCN 2021041037 (print) | LCCN 2021041038 (ebook) |
ISBN 9780525656999 (hardcover) | ISBN 9780525657002 (ebook)
Subjects: LCGFT: Short stories. Classification: LCC PS3619.H586 Y68 2022 (print) |
LCC PS3619.H586 (ebook) | DDC 813/.6—dc23
LC record available at https://lccn.loc.gov/2021041037
LC ebook record available at https://lccn.loc.gov/2021041038

This is a work of fiction. Names, characters, places, and incidents either
are the product of the author's imagination or are used fictitiously.
Any resemblance to actual persons, living or dead, events,
or locales is entirely coincidental.

Jacket illustration by Toby Leigh
Jacket design by Kelly Blair

Manufactured in the United States of America
First Edition

For Rebecca Gradinger

CONTENTS

You Have a Friend in 10A

The Cowboy Tango

WHEN MR. GLEN OTTERBAUSCH HIRED Sammy Boone, she was sixteen and so skinny that the whole of her beanpole body fit neatly inside the circle of shade cast by her hat. For three weeks he'd had an ad in the Bozeman paper for a wrangler, but only two guys had shown up. One smelled like he'd swum across a whiskey river before his truck fishtailed to a dusty stop outside the lodge, and the other man was missing his left arm. Mr. Otterbausch looked away from the man with one arm and told him the job was already filled. He was planning to scale back on beef-raising and go more toward the tourist trade, even though he'd promised his uncle Dex, as Dex breathed his last wheezes, that he would do no such thing. Every summer during his childhood Mr. Otterbausch's schoolteacher parents had sent him to stay with Uncle Dex, a man who resembled a petrified log in both body and spirit. He had a face of knurled bark and knotholes for eyes and a mouth sealed up tight around a burned-down Marlboro. He spoke rarely; his voice rasped up through the dark tubes of his craw only to issue a command or to mock his nervous, skinny nephew for being nervous and skinny. He liked to creep up on young Glen and clang the dinner bell in his ear, showing yellow crocodile teeth when the boy jumped and twisted into the air. So Dex's bequest of all forty thousand acres to Mr. Otterbausch, announced when a faint breeze was still rattling through the doldrums of his tar-blackened lungs, was a deathbed confession that Dex loved no one, had no one to give his ranch to except a disliked nephew whose one point of redemption was his ability to sit a horse.

It was true that Mr. Otterbausch rode well, and because he liked to ride more than anything else, he quit his job managing a condo building at a ski resort, loaded his gray mare Sleepy Jean into a trailer, and drove up to pay his last respects. By the time the first rain came and drilled Dex's ashes into the hard earth, Mr. Otterbausch had sold off most of the cattle and bought two dozen new horses, a breeding stallion among them. He bought saddles and bridles, built a new barn with a double-size stall for Sleepy Jean, expanded the lodge, and put in a bigger kitchen. When construction was under way on ten guest cabins and a new bunkhouse, he fired the worst of the old wranglers and placed his ad.

Sammy showed up two days after the man with one arm. She must have hitched out to the ranch, because when he caught sight of her she was just a white dot walking up the dirt road from the highway. His first impulse when he saw she was only a kid was to send her away, but he was sympathetic toward the too-skinny. Moreover, he thought the dudes who would be paying his future bills might be intrigued by a girl wrangler in a way they would not have been by a man with a pinned-up sleeve who tied knots with his teeth. Mr. Otterbausch maintained a shiny and very bristly mustache, and his fingers stole up to tug at it.

"Can you shoot?" he asked.

"Yeah," she said.

"How are you with a rope?"

"All right."

"And you ride good?"

"Yup."

He dropped a saddle and bridle in her arms and showed her a short-legged twist of a buckskin, a bitch mare who had recently not only thrown Mr. Otterbausch but kicked him for good measure, leaving a boomerang-shaped bruise on his thigh. When Sammy pulled the cinch tight, the mare flattened her ears and lunged around, her square teeth biting the air until Sammy popped her on the cheek. The mare squealed and pointed her nose at the sky, then stood still. Sammy climbed up. The mare dropped her head and crow-hopped off to the right. Sammy tugged the reins up once and drove with her seat and sent the mare through the gate into the home paddock. In five minutes, she had her going around like a show pony.

"Hang on there a minute," Mr. Otterbausch said. He went and threw some tack on Sleepy Jean, rode her back to the paddock, and pulled open the gate for Sammy. "Let's try you without a fence. Head down the valley." Mr. Otterbausch pointed toward a horizon of dovetailing hills. The buckskin cow-kicked once and then rocketed off with Sammy sitting up as straight as a flagpole. Her long braid of brown hair thumped against her back. Sleepy Jean was plenty fast, but Mr. Otterbausch kept her reined in to stay behind and observe. Sammy rode farther back on her hip than most women, giving her ride some roll and swagger. It was a prickly, gusty day and the buckskin was really moving, but Sammy didn't even bother to reach up and tug her hat down the way Mr. Otterbausch did. By the time they got back to the home paddock, both the horses and Mr. Otterbausch were in a lather.

"You want the job?" he asked.

Sammy nodded.

"How old are you?"

She hesitated, and he guessed she was deciding whether or not to lie. "Sixteen."

This seemed close enough to the truth. "You're not some kind of runaway are you? You should tell me so I can decide if I want the trouble."

"No one's coming to look for me."

"Where're your folks?"

"Wyoming."

"What do they do there?"

"Chickens."

"They won't have the cops after me for kidnapping?" Trying to set her at ease, Mr. Otterbausch chuckled. The girl did not smile.

"No sir."

"Just a joke," Mr. Otterbausch said. "Just joking."

Sammy lived in the lodge until Mr. Otterbausch had a cottage built for her in a stand of trees off the east porch, on the far side from the guest cabins and the bunkhouse. He'd hoped when she was transplanted to another building she would be less on his mind, but no such luck. All day he was mindful that she might be watching him and considered each movement before he made it, choreographing for her eyes a performance of strength while he moved bales of hay or of grace as he rode out on Sleepy Jean in the evening. He tried to stop himself from wringing his hands while he talked to her because an old girlfriend had told him the habit was annoying. Every night his imagination projected flickering films of Sammy Boone onto his bedroom ceiling: Sammy riding, always riding, across fields and hills and exotic fantasy deserts, always on beautiful horses, horses that Mr. Otterbausch certainly didn't own. He liked to imagine what her hair might look like out of its braid, what it would feel like in his fingers.

Sometimes he allowed himself to imagine making love to Sammy, but he did so in a state of distracting discomfort. The bottom line was that she was too young, and he wasn't about to mess around with a girl who had nowhere else to go, even though she had a stillness to her that made her seem older, *old* even. He told himself he loved her the way he loved the wind and the mountains and the horses, and it would be a crime to damage her spirit. Plus, she showed no interest. She treated Mr. Otterbausch and the wranglers with a detached man-to-man courtesy. Sometimes she could even be coarse. She called the stuck latch on a paddock gate a "cocksucker," and she told a table of breakfasting dudes that the stallion had "gone out fucking" one Sunday in breeding season. When she ran into Mr. Otterbausch, she never talked about anything beyond solid concerns of trees, rocks, water, and animals. If he tried to ask her about herself, she gave the shortest answer possible and then made herself scarce.

"You have any brothers or sisters?"

"Some brothers."

"Where are they?"

"Don't know. Got to check on Big Bob's abscess. Night, boss."

TEN YEARS PASSED this way. Sammy stayed skinny but muscled up some. She started to go a little bowlegged, and her forearms turned brown and wiry. The dude business worked out well. Mr. Otterbausch made enough money to keep improving the ranch a bit at a time and also to put some away every year. Out on a ride he found a hot spring bubbling beside a creek, and he dug the pool out bigger, lined it with rocks, and put in a cedar platform for the dudes to sit on. Dudes, it turned out, loved to sit in hot water, and the sulfurous pond drew enough new business that he added three more cabins and built a shelter way out on the property's north edge for use on overnight treks. The guests called Sammy a tough cookie, which irked Mr. Otterbausch, as when anyone said the distant, magnificent mountains were like a postcard.

Since the beginning, Sammy'd had the job of taking the best old horses up to a hillside spot called the Pearly Gates when their times came and shooting them in the head. The place was named for two clusters of white-barked aspens that flanked the trail where it opened out into a clearing. Mr. Otterbausch guessed that Sammy got on better with horses than people, and he figured she gave them a proper goodbye. When the wranglers saw Sammy come walking back down from the hills, they knew to keep out of her way for a while. She left each carcass alone until it was picked clean enough, and then she went back and nailed up the skull on one of the pines around the clearing if it hadn't been dragged away somewhere. Not many horses were lucky enough to go to the Pearly Gates. Most of the ones who came in from winter pasture lame and rickety were sold at auction and ended up going down to Mexico in silver trucks with cheese-grater sides, bound for dog food. But worthy horses came and went over the years, and their skulls circled the clearing past the Pearly Gates like a council of wise men.

Mr. Otterbausch went up there sometimes to get away. He would sit beneath the long white skulls and look up through the aspens' trembling leaves at a patch of sky. The dudes paid the bills, and he knew they had as much right as anyone else to enjoy this country, but some days they seemed as profane a blight on the land as oil derricks or Walmarts or fast-food billboards. They strutted around, purposeful and aimless as pigeons, staring at the mountains and the sky and the trees, trying to stuff it all into their cameras. Wherever he was, Uncle Dex must have been royally pissed off.

Usually Sammy rode out alone when she wasn't with the dudes, but Mr. Otterbausch was happiest when he could make up some excuse for the two of them to ride together. Around dusk, after the dudes and the horses had been fed, he would seek her out to check on this or that bit of trail or retrieve a few steers that he had purposely let loose the night before. Those evenings, when the sky was amethyst and Sleepy Jean's mane blew over his hands as they loped along, it seemed that his longing and the moment when day tipped over into night were made out of the same stuff, aching and purple. While they hunted around for lost steers, he talked to her, telling her all his stories, and she listened without complaint or much comment, though sometimes she would ask "Then what?" and he would talk on with new verve. He worried that she would fall in love with a dude or with one of the wranglers, but she never seemed tempted.

He wanted to believe it was self-restraint that kept him from falling on his knees and begging her to love him, to marry him, at least to sleep with him, but during the rare moments when he told himself he must, if he did not want to spend the rest of his life in agony, confess his feelings, he knew the truth was that he was afraid. She was a full-grown woman now, not some helpless girl. He was afraid she would leave, afraid she would laugh, afraid he would not be able to survive all alone out on the blinding salt flats of her rejection. He might have gone on that way until he was old and gray, but when Sammy had been at the ranch for almost ten years, Mr. Otterbausch called the girlfriend he kept in Bozeman by Sammy's name one too many times. "God damn it!" she shouted, standing naked beside her bed while Mr. Otterbausch cowered beneath the sheets. "You have called me Sammy for the last time, Glen Otterbausch! My name is LuAnn! Remember me?" She grabbed her breasts with both hands and shook them at him. "LuAnn!"

He drove home, tail between his legs, and took a bottle of whiskey out on the front porch. The sun was dropping toward the hilltops where he had first ridden with Sammy, and he sat and looked at it. He didn't actually like whiskey, but it seemed to fit the occasion and was all he could scrounge from the two guys who happened to be in the bunkhouse when he stopped by. The dudes came in for dinner and then were herded off to campfire time. After the lodge fell quiet and the sky was fading from blue to purple, Mr. Otterbausch went over to Sammy's cottage and knocked on the door. Her dog, Dirt, barked once and fell silent when she said, from somewhere, "Dirt, hush up." She answered the door in her usual clothes, except she was barefoot. For a moment, he stared at her pale toes, which he'd never seen before. Then he looked beyond her, over her shoulder, saw a rocking chair with a Hudson's Bay blanket on it. A skillet on the stove. He caught the smell of fried eggs. Dirt sniffed around his boots. The dog had simply appeared one day, walking up the dirt road like Sammy had, and she had acted like she'd been expecting him all along. Because Dirt was shaped and bristled like a brown bottlebrush, the joke with the wranglers was that Mr. Otterbausch had turned one of his old mustaches into a dog for Sammy.

"Boss?" she said. One hand was up behind her head. She was holding back her hair.

"Sorry to disturb, but I've got a favor to ask. Mrs. Mullinax—you know her? the lady from Chicago?—says she left her camera up on the lookout rock. I said I'd ride up and check, and I was

wondering if you'd come along. Two eyes better than one and all.
Or I guess it's four eyes. Better than two." He laughed.

"It's getting dark."

"We'll be quick."

"All the guys are busy?"

"It's campfire night, and C.J. and Wayne went to town." Still
she hesitated, he hoped not because she sensed his nervousness or
smelled whiskey on him. "I thought you could take Hotrod. Give
him some exercise."

"He don't get enough exercise with all that fucking he does?"
But she shut the door in his face, and when she came back out her
hair was in its braid and she had on her corduroy jacket with a
woolly collar. "Dirt, you stay," she said.

Mr. Otterbausch was drunker than he thought and had to hop
around with his foot in the rawhide stirrup before he could pull
himself up in the saddle. As soon as he did, Sleepy Jean spread her
back legs and lifted her tail to squirt some pee for Hotrod, who
flipped his upper lip up over his nostrils and let the scent bounce
around his cavernous sinuses.

"Slut," Sammy said to Sleepy Jean, reining Hotrod away from
her.

On the lookout rock, with the valley dark below them and the
stars coming out to one-up the small twinkling lights of the lodge
and outbuildings, Mr. Otterbausch waited for the perfect moment,
the moment when Sammy was standing with her hands on her
hips and saying disgustedly, "I don't see any damn camera," and
he swooped in and got her by the braid and kissed her hard on the
mouth. She hauled back like she was going to punch him, but she
remembered not to punch her boss right when he remembered to
let go of her braid—soon enough but a little late. He fell to pieces

with apologies and tried to drop down on his knees to beg her to forget the whole thing but somehow tipped back onto his butt instead, and then he figured as long as he was down there he might as well go whole hog.

"Sammy," he said, looking up at her dark shape, "I'd like to give you the ranch."

"What?"

"The ranch. I'd like it to be yours as well as mine."

"What for?"

He began to sense he'd made a wrong turn, but he was too drunk and panicked to do anything but press on. "Well, I'd like to marry you. We could run the ranch together. It'd be yours too. Wouldn't you like that?"

She kicked a rock that went rattling down into the darkening valley. "You think you can buy me with the ranch?"

"Of course not."

"I don't want it."

"Don't want what?"

"The ranch."

He felt a hopeless burst of hope. "But you do want . . . the rest?"

She waited for a minute before she answered, and he felt so nervous he thought he might faint. But she said quietly, "No."

"You're sure? You're not being stubborn? I didn't mean it like a bribe. I swear, Sammy. I meant I'd give you anything." Behind them, Sleepy Jean, tied to a tree, squealed at Hotrod, who was tied to another. Mr. Otterbausch tried to stand up but sat back down. He found he was wringing his hands.

Hotrod whuffed at Sleepy Jean and pulled and pranced at his tree. Sleepy Jean squealed again, lifting her tail. Sammy took a step back from Mr. Otterbausch. "I just don't love you," she said. "I wish I did, but I don't. It's one of those things. I've thought about it. I've tried to get myself to, even, because you're the most decent man I know and you'd treat me good, but I'd feel like a liar."

"I don't mind," said Mr. Otterbausch, raising his voice over Sleepy Jean's.

Sammy whirled around on the mare. "God damn slut horse, stop your yelling!" She stepped close to Hotrod and, as she was pulling his cinch tight, she said, without turning around, "I'm real sorry." She untied the stallion, punched his neck when he made a lunge for Sleepy Jean, climbed on, and rode away. Mr. Otterbausch sat and watched the moon rise huge and yellow from behind the horizon. He felt woozy, exhausted, tremulous, like a survivor of a terrible collision. He did not know whether he was more afraid of Sammy leaving the ranch or of her staying. Eventually he rode down and finished the whiskey and avoided Sammy pretty well for three months, after which time everything went back to normal and stayed that way. More years went by. He loved her and tried to conceal that he loved her; she pretended not to notice.

HARRISON GREENE WENT OUT to his uncle's ranch once he was very certain his marriage was over. He was a man of great patience, a bird-watcher and a fly fisherman, and the ink on the divorce papers had to dry for a whole year for him to be certain he was really divorced, even though by then Marjorie had already been living with Gary-the-Architect for eight months. So he gave up the lease on his sad bachelor apartment, sold most of his possessions, and drove west, pulling his horse Digger in a trailer, Illinois unrolling in his side-view mirrors. Harrison made his living from larger-than-life paintings of animals and birds. They were perfect down to the last follicle. His life, lived slowly, had eventually bored Marjorie beyond her tolerance, which is why he was surprised that she chose to shack up with Gary of all people, a man who sat in a cantilevered house and made silent, minute movements with his pencil while, across town, Harrison made silent, minute movements with *his* pencil.

"I think she's really gone," he said to his uncle on the phone.

"Well, yeah, you think? Ha ha ha," Uncle Glen said. Harrison remembered why he had never particularly cared for Uncle Glen. The man was annoying.

"She's moved in with this architect," Harrison continued. "I don't know. Anyway, I was thinking, it might do me good to come out to your place for a while. I'd pay, of course."

"No need for that. No need at all. Do you still paint?"

"Yeah."

"Maybe you can make a few paintings for the lodge. You still have that horse?"

"I thought I'd bring him along."

"He's a beauty. If you wanted, you could just pay me with that horse. Ha ha ha."

"Ha ha ha," said Harrison.

"All right. Call when you're coming."

The first thing Harrison saw when he drove up the road was a woman riding an ugly Appaloosa. Her braid and the shape of her waist gave her away as a woman, but she rode like a man, back on her hip. When the Appaloosa let go a series of bucks, dolphining up and down along the fence, she slapped him lazily back and forth across the shoulders with the reins and sent him streaking off at a gallop. As she passed, she tipped her hat to Harrison.

"Who's that girl?" he asked his uncle after he had settled Digger in the barn.

"What girl?"

"The one on the Appy out there."

"Most people don't spot her as a girl right away."

"There's the braid."

"Don't go telling Sammy she rides like a girl. Ha ha ha."

"She doesn't. Anyway, women ride fine. It's not an insult."

"You don't remember Sammy?"

"I've never seen her before."

"Sure you have. She's been here fifteen years. Guess you didn't notice her when you had Marjorie with you."

"I don't see why I wouldn't have."

Uncle Glen took him by the arm and turned him away toward the lodge. "You're in here. Next to my room."

Right away Harrison started tagging along on Sammy's rides, bringing up the rear in a gaggle of dudes but never losing sight of her hat and her braid beneath it. At first she paid him no notice, but he waited and after a couple of weeks he knew she must have at least gotten used to him because when he rode off to investigate a birdsong, she would whistle for him up the trail. Once she dropped back beside him to say Digger was the best-looking horse she'd ever seen, and when he offered to let her ride him she said, "Yeah? Serious?"

"Sure. Why not?"

"The Otter hogs all the good ones."

Harrison had a lot to say about Uncle Glen. How he laughed at his own jokes, which weren't even jokes. How he had a habit of saying something to your back as you turned to leave a room. How he was so jumpy that Marjorie had called him human itching powder. How Harrison longed to rip that preposterous mustache from the man's face. But he said, "I'd think he'd want you to ride them."

She looked alarmed. "Why?"

"Because you're a great rider."

She seemed relieved. She shrugged. "The Otter rides good, too. They're his horses. Marty, sit up straight there," she shouted at a dude in a bolo tie who was drooping back in the saddle. "No potato sacks." The dude looked back over his shoulder, wounded, and she trotted up to the front of the line.

Harrison found with the passing days that Sammy was staking a larger and larger claim on his thoughts. He rode with her as much as he could, and in the evenings when he went out in the paddocks with his sketchbook, he found himself only half concentrating because he was listening for her footsteps behind him. She often came out to see what he was drawing. Sometimes he sent her out on Digger, and it was a glorious sight. He made sketch after sketch, and afterward she would say "That was all right" and rest a hand flat on the horse's neck, leaving a print in his sweat. At night in his bed with Uncle Glen's snores coming through the wall, Harrison filled imaginary canvases with Sammy and Digger done in big, loose brushstrokes, more active and alive than his usual Audubon-gets-huge stuff. Having something other than Marjorie to think about was welcome. There was nothing in Sammy to remind him of Marjorie. Marjorie was beautiful. She had delicate wrists and shoulders, and her veins showed through her skin like the roots of baby flowers. Sammy was strong and awkward with weathered skin and a braid too long for a woman her age. Marjorie was busy and jumpy, a jingler of change and a tapper of toes, which made it pretty rich that she called Uncle Glen hyper. She had never sat all the way back in a chair in her life, and she undercooked everything out of sheer impatience. Sammy, on the other hand, might have been reincarnated from a boulder. Marjorie would laugh and laugh and laugh, and her laughter was like birdsong. Sammy's laugh was the sound of air being let out of a tire.

Uncle Glen, it became clear, was nursing a crush of his own on Sammy. God only knew how long that had been going on. Long enough that his feelings, which Sammy clearly did not return, seemed to have congealed into some notion of ownership on the old guy's part. He was always popping up wherever they were, making strange non-jokes that only he laughed at, rubbing his paws together and staring at Sammy. When he could, he'd ask Harrison to do him a favor and ride out to check the fence line at the far edge of the property while Sammy took dudes in the opposite direction, or he'd send Harrison into town to buy a bucket or a sack of bran mash or some such when Sammy was due back in from a ride. After Sammy started riding Digger, Uncle Glen complained suddenly of an arthritic hip and turned the choicest of his horses over to Sammy. He'd watch her ride from the porch with a glass of something clear sweating on the arm of his chair.

Sammy must have known that the boss had a thing for her. If she felt anything for him, it stood to reason that they would have gotten together years ago. Maybe they had. Maybe Sammy broke it off but Uncle Glen was still carrying a torch. Anything was possible. Harrison examined Sammy for traces of an attachment to Uncle Glen—it would be unsporting to interfere with a long and fraught lead-up to love—but he detected only practiced tolerance in her treatment of him. Once, from the window of Digger's stall, he had watched Sammy as she stood with her arms folded on the home paddock fence looking at the horses. Uncle Glen came up beside her and folded his arms on the fence too. Their hats bobbled as they talked, and Sammy pointed down the valley. Uncle Glen looked, but at the side of her face instead of where she was pointing. Then Glen scooched a few inches closer to Sammy and then a few more, until their sleeves were touching. After a moment, Sammy inched down the rail, away from the insistent brush of Glen's plaid shirt.

But Glen closed the gap, and Sammy retreated, and like two halves of one caterpillar, they made their way down the fence, about four feet in the twenty minutes as Harrison watched. Their hats kept bobbling the whole time, and he supposed they weren't even aware of their slow tango.

Harrison found his uncle in the ranch office, sitting at his desk paying bills. "I'm going to take Sammy into town tonight," he announced. "To go dancing."

Uncle Glen ran a finger through the condensation on a glass that sat on his blotter. "Sammy would rather die than dance. If you knew her, you'd know that."

"There's no harm in asking," Harrison said. "If she'd rather, we can just sit in a bar."

"Go ahead and ask then. But be careful she doesn't kick you in the teeth. Ha ha ha."

"I didn't need permission. I was just telling you as a courtesy."

As Harrison turned away, his uncle said, "She's a dead end. Better men have tried."

"What men?"

"Just some guys here and there."

"What do you mean 'better'?"

"Just she doesn't seem to want all that."

"All what?"

"All I'm saying is she's had other offers, and she's turned them all down."

Harrison brought a sketch of the dog Dirt to Sammy's door. Dirt was ancient and blind now, running low on teeth, and Harrison drew him like that, floppy-lipped and milky-eyed.

"It looks like him," Sammy said when she saw it. "Ugly old geezer." She held the paper carefully, balanced on her fingertips.

"It's your night off, isn't it? Let's go get some drinks."

She glanced up at him, her hand creeping over her shoulder to her braid. "Fine," she said. She shut the door in his face and came out again in five minutes. She looked like she always did, but he smelled something that was neither dust nor horse and might have been perfume.

In town, they found two barstools at Jed's Antlers. She ordered whiskey, and Harrison followed suit. They sat and watched a few couples dancing the two-step to a band that played in jeans and boots on a shadowy stage in the corner.

"I've never been here," she said.

"All these years? There wasn't anyone you'd let take you out?"

She snorted.

He said, "Uncle Glen would have been up for it."

"What makes you think that?"

"Look at him. Always sniffing around you like a guard dog, growling at people like me."

She shook her head. "The Otter's all right. He's a good boss."

"Some people say that I'm too slow about things. But old Glen's been biding his time for, what, twenty years?"

"Fifteen," she said. She caught herself and scowled.

"You'd think he'd get it together to try something on you."

"You know what," she said, looking him in the face, "I owe the Otter real big, and he could have tried harder to make me pay him back, but he never did."

"Are you off men in general or just the ones around here? You'd be doing me a favor to say."

Her hand went up to her braid. "I guess just the ones round here."

"Why did you say you owe him?"

"He helped me out when I was young and didn't have anyplace to go."

"Why didn't you have anywhere to go?"

"You know. Sad story." She examined her whiskey. "What about you? You got a sad story?"

She had never asked him anything personal before. He knew it was unfair, but he felt intruded upon. "I guess," he said. "Not the saddest in the world. My wife left me for an architect. That's why I came out here. She said I was too deliberate. No, she said I was boring."

"Sounds like a bitch," Sammy said.

"She was. Sometimes."

"I guess I meant the situation." She lifted her glass at the bartender.

"Not that things were perfect," Harrison said. His drink was only half gone, but the bartender, without asking, topped it off. "She moved in with the architect, this guy Gary. God knows she can't stand to be alone. She acts like only unlovable people are alone." He thought for a moment about what he had said and then nodded in agreement with himself. "Yeah," he said. "That's right."

Sammy watched the dance floor. He wondered if she was listening, but she said, "Seems to me some people are alone because it's easiest. That don't seem so different from finding an architect because that's easiest." She sipped. The whiskey was cheap and went down like a buzz saw, but Harrison wouldn't have guessed it to look at her. She didn't grimace at all.

"What's your sad story?" he asked. He had been playing with a matchbook, but he dropped it and touched her wrist lightly with his fingers. He felt the way he did sitting on a barely broken horse—one wrong move and she would bolt.

"There was this architect who broke my heart," she said, staring him down. "Lives in Chicago. Name of Gary."

It took him a second to realize she was joking. He felt off-balance, something he did not relish. "Very funny," he said.

She smiled into her glass, pleased with herself. He pushed his uncertainty away. "Your turn," he said. "Sad story. Lay it on me."

She hunched a little and pulled her braid over her shoulder so she could hold its end. "Not too much to tell. A mean dad, mean brothers, mean boyfriend I ran off with, and then he left me. I couldn't go home. The Otter gave me a job. That's it."

"That's not it. There's more."

"That's it as far as you're concerned right now. No offense."

"Oh, none taken," he said. He emptied his glass and clunked it on the bar. "Well, I think there's only one thing to do, and that is to dance." He stood up and held out his hand.

"I don't dance."

"Sure you do." He took her hand.

"I don't know how," she said, yanking it back.

"Sammy, come and dance." He stood waiting until she got up, as hangdog and reluctant as a kid heading for the principal's office, and when they were on the dance floor he put one arm around her waist and held her against him so tightly that sometimes only the tips of her boots grazed the floor.

"I wish I owned a skirt," she whispered.

They drove back in silence, weaving a gentle, drunken serpentine over the empty road. In her cabin he had their clothes off while old Dirt was still thumping his tail and rolling his milky eyes around. She said, "It's been so long I might as well be a virgin." She did not cry out, but she clutched his shoulders so tightly that he did.

———

IN THE LODGE, staring at his barren bedroom ceiling, Mr. Otterbausch listened to the emptiness of his nephew's room. He had heard the truck drive up and their footsteps on the gravel. Now there was nothing but the coyotes yipping in the hills. Mr. Otterbausch, alone in his bed, joined in the silent chorus of the unloved.

SAMMY WAS SORRY the Otter was angry, but there was not much to be done about it. He was working her like a dog, sending her out with the dudes, sending her out again as soon as she got back. She knew the method: When Hotrod got bad, she'd gallop him down to jelly legs to get his mind off the mares. But it was no good. She'd never be too tired to go to bed with Harrison Greene. "That was all right," she said to him every time, resting her hand on his stomach. This business of being happy was something so long forgotten that she'd forgotten she'd forgotten. She was happy enough on a horse, but that was over as soon as her boots hit the ground. She hadn't been happy with a man since before Davey started being a bastard, which was a while before he drove away while she was in a truck-stop bathroom outside Boise. Truth be told, in the six months or so before Harrison had shown up, she'd started to think maybe she should get it over with and marry the Otter. The Otter had been nice to her for half her life. She owed him, and she didn't want to leave the ranch. When she was younger, she'd still thought she'd leave eventually. She'd thought she wouldn't mind being alone forever. She'd thought lots of things. Then the years piled up and she got set in her ways, and the Otter was one of her ways. Sometimes, usually on their dusk rides, she wondered, for the millionth time, if she could prod her gratitude to him into something more. But Harrison came along and reminded her that people couldn't help who they loved.

Sammy had never had to share her cabin with anyone, but Harrison was so slow and still and quiet she didn't mind him. It was like having a new piece of furniture that painted pictures. He taught her how to fly-fish when they could get away from the Otter and take Harrison's truck down to the river. He cooked for her. It was only when she asked him questions that he seemed to freeze up and get irritated. Then he'd either go off somewhere or he'd kiss her and squeeze her to change the subject. So she stopped asking him things.

The summer passed, and in November, after the last of the dudes had gone and the first snow had come, Harrison took Sammy by the hand and told her he had to go away to visit some people.

"Like who?"

"Like my mother for one. And Marjorie for another. We have some things to settle. Small things. I have to take care of some business too, about some paintings."

"Are you coming back?"

"I plan to, yeah." But he was freezing up.

"You plan to?"

"That's what I said."

"Don't do me any favors."

"I'm being honest. I plan to come back."

"You mean that?" Stop pushing, she told herself. Let it be.

"I do, but nothing's ever for certain."

"Only that I'll be sitting here in the snow with the Otter, waiting. Feeling like an ass."

"What happened to stoic Sammy?" He pulled her to him and kissed her cheek, then held her at arm's length, by her shoulders. "You stay here where you belong. Take good care of Digger."

She pushed him away. "Have a good fucking trip, Harrison." She tipped her hat and walked off.

He left that day. For a while he called regularly enough, but she wasn't any good on the phone. She wanted to ask him when he was coming back, but she wouldn't. He called less and less. She had never minded winter much, but then she had never been cooped up with an angry Otter before. Most of the other wranglers were off on winter jobs in Arizona or Texas. Just slow-minded Big Georgie was left in the bunkhouse, probably settling in for a long talk with his balls. What made things worse was that, back before Harrison left, Sammy and the Otter had gone after a wound-up steer, and Sammy hadn't been paying close attention and let the steer go careening at the Otter. Sleepy Jean took a funny step getting out of the way and tweaked a foreleg. Walking back to the lodge, the Otter said, "You're getting sloppy, and we both know why, and I'm embarrassed for you."

Sammy was riding, and the Otter was walking, leading Sleepy Jean. The dents in the top of his hat looked like an angry face. "That horse is too old for cutting work and you know it," she said.

"I hired you because I thought you'd be tough like a man, not get all moony-eyed the second someone pays you some attention."

"Someone tried to give me a whole ranch once."

That shut him up, and until Harrison left he mostly glowered at her from afar, leaning like a Halloween decoration against the porch posts and blowing clouds of vapor into the cold air. Usually in winter the Otter was a nuisance but not a menace. He'd show up at her door with Chinese checkers or some other game with lots of small pieces that inevitably ended up in the floorboards when the Otter nervously overturned the whole thing. This year, though, once they were alone, he started picking fights with her, bounding at her through the snow like a pissed-off ferret, wanting to give her shit about the water troughs or some feed he said she'd forgotten to order. His window stayed lit into the early morning, probably because he was up drinking, and she never saw him on a horse.

He spent a lot of time in Sleepy Jean's stall, wrapped up in an Indian blanket, reading a book. The horse didn't look good. She was an old girl to begin with, but her bum leg had made her crooked everywhere. Swaying around her stall, she looked like she was thinking, "Oh, lordy, my back. Oh, my aching knee." Her skin was as thin and fragile over her bones as rolled-out pie dough. Sammy brought her an apple, and the horse was working on it with her yellow teeth when the Otter's voice came from behind her. "Heard from your boyfriend?"

He knew she hadn't. "We don't do well on the phone," she said, not turning.

"Now that's dedication."

"More like a challenge." Sammy held her palm through the bars of the stall window for Jean to lick.

"A challenge?" The Otter came up alongside her.

"Harrison thinks everyone is as patient as he is."

"Bet you really miss him, ha ha ha. Bet you wish you weren't here with me."

Sammy flared up, tired of the sight of his sallow drunk's face, and said, "Yeah, and what about it?"

He smiled at her, showing teeth. The rest of him was going to hell, but his mustache was still as sharp and shiny as a sea urchin. "Patience is a virtue," he said.

Indeed Harrison's leaving seemed to have been the starting pistol for a relay race of misfortune and bad feelings. There was the ugliness with the Otter, and then the wolves got a steer right out of the home paddock, and then Sammy hurt Big Georgie's feelings by laughing when he said he wanted to learn to ride so he could ride Digger someday, and poor old Dirt kicked the bucket in the second week of December, right next to his dinner bowl. Sammy cried because the ground was too hard for her to get a shovel in, and she had to put him in the deep freeze. Harrison's drawing of Dirt was too much for her, and she took it down from above the fireplace. Everything was so grim that when the knock came at her door on the first sunny day they'd had in a while, she opened it thinking the devil himself might be on the other side. It was the Otter.

"There's a big snow coming," he said.

"Yeah?" She waited for him to say something about how the snow would probably delay Harrison, ha ha ha.

"It might last a week." He ran a hand over his face, pushing all the broken pieces around. "Jeannie's not doing well. Four more months of winter, at least four. She won't get better in the cold. I thought about trailering her over to the vet's, but the roads are bad, and she wouldn't like standing in the truck that long." He blinked his red eyes at her. "She's old anyway."

"She's a good old girl," Sammy said cautiously. The Otter was talking to her like he had in the days before Harrison. Back when he loved her, was how she thought of it, though she knew he must still love her or else he wouldn't be so miserable. The winter was harsh, his horse was dying, and his love was scummed over with booze and jealousy.

"So," the Otter said, mustache quivering, "I need you to take her up to the Pearly Gates before the big snow. I think she can walk it now. I'd hate to wait and then have to have her hauled away. She should be up there."

Sammy nodded. "Dirt died. I put him in the deep freeze."

He looked past her into the cabin as though for Dirt. "Poor old boy."

The walk to the Pearly Gates was slow. Sammy picked the best route she could, but still Jean ended up skating on ice a few times. The horse walked on a slow three beat, bobbing her head. "Well, Jeannie," Sammy said, "thank you for all your good work at the ranch and for taking care of the Otter and all. He's always liked you best, even though he had better-looking horses. Not that you're ugly, you're just kind of rough, you know? But you're a good cutter, and you were damn fast. I don't know what the Otter would have done without you. He's going to feel pretty lonely now, especially because of me. I wish you could stick around to keep him company."

Sammy never liked shooting horses. When it was over and Jeannie's knees had given out, first the front and then the back, and she had fallen down in the snow like someone who was just so tired, Sammy sat with her back against the horse's, looking up at the skulls crowned with little snowdrifts. The sky through the trees was a hard winter blue. She thought about the Otter down in the lodge, and she asked someone, maybe the skulls, to send Harrison back soon.

She found the Otter in the dudes' game room with his glass and his bottle, sitting beneath a huge portrait of Sleepy Jean that Harrison had finished before he left. Jean looked old and tired in the painting. A cue leaned against the billiard table and the balls were out on the green felt. Sammy switched on a lamp.

"Leave it."

"Okay." She came closer and stood leaning against the table.

"Don't say how she was a good old girl and how everything has to die because I know."

Sammy said nothing.

"And don't go stapling her skull to some tree or turning her rib into a scepter or whatever it is that you do. Fucking nonsense. I don't know why you had to make that place all mystical or whatever it is. You can leave Jeannie be. You've done enough."

"I haven't made it anything. It's where I go shoot horses when you tell me to, and if you want to do it yourself, you go right ahead. I thought I'd check on you, but I see you're fine. Good night."

"He's not coming back," he said as she turned away. "Lover boy's gone back to his wife but is too big a coward to tell you."

"He wouldn't have left Digger."

"But he'd leave you? You're admitting that? He'd leave you but not the horse."

"Aw, shut up. I know there's no way in hell he'd leave Digger. Fuck all else."

"Sammy, Sammy. He left the horse for you. As payment. Just like he left those for me, for services rendered, ha ha ha." He pointed at a stack of three canvases turned to the wall. She crossed the room slowly, aware of her boots compressing the carpet and the sound of the Otter's breathing, his ratter eyes following her. The first painting was of Digger, the second was of her riding Digger, and the third was of her alone, sitting in the grass. "To be clear," the Otter said, "he left them for me, not for you."

She touched her own image. She could feel the texture of the canvas through the paint. "I'm sorry," she said.

"For what?" He was leaning forward, gripping his glass.

"That I love him and not you." She let go of the painting and walked out of the room.

The big snow came the next day. Shut in her cabin, she wondered what the Otter's next move would be. It was ten days before the sky snowed itself out and the roads were passable enough for her to drive into town. She told herself she was getting away. She liked the sound of that, getting away, like she was going to Hawaii or Mexico and not just drinking beer at Jed's Antlers and watching people dance the two-step. She ate potato chips in a motel room by herself; she went to the movies; she bought a new coat. By the time she drove back to the ranch, she was in a forgiving mood. Poor old Otter had gotten his heart broken and never had it set right. One of her brothers had an elbow that had healed wrong and looked like he had a lump of cauliflower under the skin. The Otter's ticker must resemble lava rock by now, brittle and full of holes. She would invite him to play Chinese checkers.

But first thing when she got back she went out to the barn to check on Digger and found his stall empty.

Big Georgie scratched his head and leaned on the fork he'd been mucking with. "Well, yeah, he's not there cause Otter put him on the truck."

"What truck?"

"The auction truck."

"No," Sammy said. "Digger. The big, good-looking horse that's usually in this stall."

"Yeah, I know." Georgie nodded and kept on nodding. "The big horse. Arn came and had the truck all loaded up with the kibble horses, and then the Otter threw the big horse on there at the last minute. Did he get sick or something? 'Cause he looked good to me. He's going to think he's at the wrong party."

The Otter would not open the door of his bedroom no matter how hard Sammy pounded and kicked on it.

"I swear you better be swinging from a beam in there! Do you think nobody else was ever sad? Do you?"

There was only silence from the other side. Every time she

thought she heard a rustle or the tinkle of ice, she charged the door with the worst her fists and words could do, but it was solid oak and would not budge.

"Well," Georgie said when she went back out to the barn and grabbed him by the woolly lapels of his sheepskin jacket, "I reckon they said the auction was tomorrow, and that was yesterday. So," he said, frowning, "I guess it's today."

As Sammy drove, burning up the road toward Billings, she did two things. First, she prayed, or really begged, for some luck. Just some god damn luck this one time. Second, she reached over and flipped open the glove compartment, feeling for the thick white envelope that she had been checking and rechecking the whole way. She wedged the envelope lengthwise between her thighs and, darting her eyes back and forth between the road and the bills, counted yet again. Six thousand dollars. All she had. It had to be enough. She needed it to be enough. Who would pay six thousand dollars for a few sacks of dog food besides her? Please, she thought, squeezing the envelope like a rosary, please give me some luck here.

The auction was in a low brown clump of livestock sheds. Sammy had to stop twice at gas stations to ask where to go, and at the second one the driver of a big stock truck said to follow him. In the paddocks she saw a brown patchwork of swaybacked horses with shaggy, shit-crusted coats. In the auction hall, every horse they brought out made her pulse race, but it was an hour before they brought out Digger. The crowd murmured. Tall, handsome Digger didn't belong with the broken-down nags that the packers' men were buying for chump change with lazy waves of their numbers. He didn't belong in this parade of the dead. He lifted his head and showed the whites of his eyes and the insides of his flared nostrils to the crowd. Veins stood out on his head and neck, ran down his legs like tributaries of a mighty river.

· "Well, I don't know, folks," said the auctioneer. "Not the usual horse, let's not start at the usual number. I'm asking five hundred."

Sammy lifted her number up and held it there in her trembling hand while the bids went up and up. She held hers like a torch.

"Six thousand one hundred," said the auctioneer. Sammy's arm wavered. He pointed at her. "I have six thousand one hundred." He pointed past her. "Do I hear two from you, sir?" Someone over Sammy's shoulder must have nodded, because the auction-eer said, "I have two and I'm looking for three, do I have three?" Her arm stayed up until six thousand seven hundred, buttressed by whatever had held Sleepy Jean on her feet for a few seconds after the spinning piece of lead lodged in her brain. Then that trem-bling force let go, and her number fell to her knee. "Sold! For six thousand seven hundred and fifty, and, gents, I think that's both a record high and a bargain. Good for you, sir."

Sammy sat. The men led Digger off the block and brought on another nag. "I'll start the bidding at fifty dollars," said the auc-tioneer. For the first time, she hoped that Harrison would never return. Then she was seized by the wild thought that he must have been the one who bought Digger. He must have found out and come back. She stood up. No one was standing except her and the man who won. She could not see his face. He was a hat and a pair of hands in the shadows, the number thirty-one held down at his side. He stepped into the dusty light, and she saw across the empty seats and scattered hats that it was the Otter. He looked at her with his face twisted around his mustache in an expression of deepest remorse. His sad otter eyes glittered at her, and she felt an answer-ing cry of pity as rough as anything she'd ever felt at the Pearly

Gates. Poor Otter who failed at revenge and bought back his heart, lava rock or not, at the last minute. Even if she'd had a million dollars in her envelope, the Otter would have found a way to outbid her because only the Otter wanted that horse more than she did. She looked at him while the next sad-sack horse got pulled out to the block, and he looked at her, and they wondered what was to be done.

Acknowledgments

I HAVEN'T SEEN Ivy in nearly a decade now and haven't spoken to her in longer. Really, there was only the briefest window when we were anything akin to friends, back in the first days of graduate school, before I made the surprisingly consequential misjudgment of supposing that because she kissed me once she would again. For some years she crossed my mind only rarely, if at all, though now, as I while away the final days before the publication of my debut novel—plagued by anxiety, yes, but also aswim in preemptive nostalgia for these last hours before I will become An Author, for better or for worse—she flits through my thoughts with increasing regularity. In fact, it might not be unreasonable to posit that Ivy, or at least the version of her that is trapped, Persephone-like, in my psyche, is as intrinsic to the book as its very binding. Sometimes I think I wrote it for her.

The opening line goes like this: "Frankly, I'm only a joke because I decided to be." I intended to establish tone and voice, of course, but I was also responding to something, possibly the last thing, Ivy said to me, although I am not sure she will recognize it as such, or if she'll even read the book. I have thought of having my publicist send a copy to her agent and request that it be passed along, but in the end I would rather she find her own way to it. There was, early on, some discussion of asking her to blurb the book, as she has made a success of herself and I was rash enough to let slip that we were acquainted, but I managed (barely), with some vigorous backpedaling, to quell my publisher's excitement and forestall what would have been some intolerably mortifying and in all likelihood unsuccessful forelock-tugging. In any event, my narrator, the writer D. M. Murphy, both does and does not believe what he says—re: jokes and our universal status as same— since he is (drum roll, please) *unreliable*. He is also, incidentally, me. But, at the same time, not.

The Canon According to D. M. Murphy, a novel by D. M. Murphy, is to be released this Tuesday—released, finally, from the cardboard ova in which its thousands of incarnations are currently incubating in stockrooms and warehouses around the country, released into the hands and minds of this reading public I've heard so much about. It's a kind of birth, this.

There's more to be said about Ivy, but, as that word, *birth*, beckons irresistibly toward an origin story, I find I am compelled to digress briefly into the many births, many beginnings of D. M. Murphy. So. In the corporeal sense, I entered the world on April 11, 1980, via C-section, at Hart County General Hospital, up near the tip of Michigan's bemittened middle finger, not far from where Hemingway spent his boyhood summers. I was Daniel Manitou Murphy on my birth certificate, Danny to my parents, Dan at school. (Yes, I intend the Nabokovian echo.) My middle name is a folly of my mother's, albeit one I long ago embraced, and has as its referent a pair of islands in Lake Michigan: North and South Manitou, forested oblongs that, according to legend, were the Great Spirit's memorial to twin bear cubs drowned while swimming after their mother to shore. Why my dear genetrix would bestow on her infant an epithet belonging to another mother's dead offspring remains something of a mystery, but nonetheless I have always liked the name.

My father was an orthodontist before he retired, and my mother worked as his receptionist until they divorced, though I decided long ago that my literary alter ego should have no mother. She ran off, or possibly died. I left the details murky, but that maternal absence is fundamental to the character.

When, five years ago, I first queried my agent (Fitzy, to friends) and sent him one of my D.M. stories, he wrote back, "The satirical elements of this are sharp and at times quite funny, but right now the story's self-awareness isn't developed enough. If you can get there, though, the results might be very interesting."

This took me by surprise as I hadn't meant the story to be satirical at all, and I did not pursue the correspondence.

At the time I was living in a part of Brooklyn that serves as a kind of voluntary gulag for writers, where gloating shoptalk is the lingua franca and attendance at dull, squeaky-microphoned barroom readings the nightly obligation, and though I wanted few things more than an agent then, I could not yield to the idea of D.M. as a comic foil (nor did I grasp the eminent exploitability of the literary world's appetite for the subversion of self). The character as I'd envisioned him was an embodiment of artistic struggle. Through him, I would take the boredoms and frustrations of my own life and from them spin the golden floss of literature, which, properly stitched and woven, would seduce my readers into feeling my own emotions as profoundly as I did. I saw myself as conducting an experiment in radical empathy, and to strip D.M. of his dignity and make him into a figure of fun seemed both a failure and, worse, a betrayal.

Two years passed, two more trips around the sun while I toiled in obscurity, and then, one blossom-wreathed spring morning, as I waited for my then girlfriend Elinor's yoga class to end so we might brunch (I had somewhere entered that phase of bourgeois adulthood in which one is obliged to use *brunch* as a verb), I watched through a studio window while rows of women, legs spread, bent to press their hands to the floor, lifting their spandex-clad asses in my direction. I knew they were not offering themselves to me and, in fact, that I was being a creep, but still I couldn't help but imagine going from one to the next, pollinating. As they transitioned to Warrior II, I imagined the consequences that would befall a man careless enough to articulate this passing fancy to his girlfriend. The poor lustful fool would fight to pull the argument from the realm of the emotional to the philosophical; he'd cling too tightly to a rational defense of the harmlessness of fantasy, the value of honesty. A whole narrative fell into my mind, delivered unto me by a dozen or so muses in Lululemon.

I texted Elinor a rain check on brunch, went home, and banged out a first draft. (*I turned down other plans 4 u. Next time more warning plz,* she replied, though she was appeased by a meager bunch of bodega roses.) Within the week I'd sent the story to a literary journal that had been previously impregnable to my charms. The editor's acceptance email praised my wit and ruthlessness, and though I felt a twinge at his description of D.M. as a "jackass," I was generally well pleased. I mailed a paper copy of the issue to Fitzy with a note that began, "I don't know if you remember the work I sent you two years ago, but . . ." Insert here a misty montage of phone calls and emails and old-school boozy lunches, and today he resides deservedly at the top of my acknowledgments page. *Fitzy of the eagle eyes and hollow leg, you saw D.M.'s potential before I did.*

Speaking of acknowledgments, there is one person who does not appear in mine but perhaps should, as I have her to thank for suggesting the notional possibility of my vocation. I mean Miss Giles, my sixth-grade teacher, whose knee-length corduroy skirts and patterned tights dominated my pubescent erotic reveries. In the fall of '91, she cooked up the idea that our class should, over the course of a school year, write novels. Perched on a stool at the front of the classroom, knees crossed and cheeks fetchingly flushed, she talked earnestly about character and suspense and scene, and every month we each slipped a new chapter between the cardboard covers of our books in progress. The other kids never seemed to think about their books except when due dates drew nigh, but I mulled mine over near constantly: while I rode in the car or played left field or sat in front of the television with my father, watching the anodyne sitcoms he favored. I became crabby and secretive— "dreamy," as my mother put it.

"It must be hormones," I heard her telling my aunt on the phone. "I thought boys weren't supposed to be like this."

I went outside and hit a tennis ball against the garage door again and again, raging at her misapprehension that I was under the thrall of something so common and sordid as puberty and not, as I was, possessed by beings and stories I'd discovered while bush-whacking through the wilds of my own mind and spirit.

My best chapter followed the protagonist, a boy named Buck from Chicago (a place I had visited twice and found both terrify-ing and thrilling, a decadent and transgressive Cockaigne compared to my small, staid hometown), as he had braces installed by his orthodontist father. I had recently undergone said procedure myself, but whilst I had endured in gape-mouthed silence, Buck went abruptly berserk and bit off his father's index finger. I was proud of the cliffhanger ending and my rendering of the spurting blood, but what Miss Giles praised were details I'd borrowed from life: the bright, hostile lamp poised on its steel arm above Buck's face; his father's hairy, overhanging nostrils and invasive, latex-covered fingers; the maddening winching together of his dentition. Miss Giles liked the chapter so much that she ascended her stool at the front of the room, crossed her knees, and, one heel popping idly in and out of a clog, read the whole thing aloud to the class.

A more nimble writer than I would find a subtle way to mark this moment as formative, even primal, the ur-accomplishment that would forever lie beyond the green light at the end of the dock. But I will say only this, openly and bluntly: The sound of my own words issuing from the mouth of a pretty woman brought me ecstasy such as I had not known life might contain.

"You have a real talent for writing," Miss Giles told me when she handed back my book. As I turned toward that word—*talent*—like a sunflower toward Helios, she added, "Maybe you'll be an author when you grow up."

"I really want to be," I said.

"I should probably ask for your autograph now, then." She smiled and squeezed my shoulder, triggering a puny, childish erection mercifully concealed by the mille-feuilles of wood pulp and laminate that were my desk. At the end of the day—I cringe at the memory—I handed her a sheet of lined paper with my signature carefully inked in the empty middle.

LET US SKIP that Rabelaisian era known as adolescence and hop jauntily to my twenty-fifth year, when I, Daniel Manitou Murphy, received my acceptance letter to a master of fine arts program in fiction writing. This particular program was not my top choice, nor, frankly, my second or third, but I was offered a quite nice fellowship and the opportunity to teach undergraduates and an excuse to live for two years in the Rocky Mountains, where I'd never been but where I thought I might become an intriguingly rugged version of myself. The biggest draw, though, of course, and the reason I'd applied in the first place, was that Baker Forge taught there. Baker Forge! Hero of my youth. Stubble-faced, denim-swathed pillar of literary manhood. Author of *Onioning* and *You Only Ever Know What You Already Knew* and a staggering abundance of terse but heartbreaking short stories and, of course, the much-lauded Reginald Banksman trilogy. (Though, I will regretfully own, I've come to conclude the trilogy is a mite overrated.)

When the fateful letter arrived, I was living in Chicago, the siren metropolis of my childhood that, once I began my freshman year at the University of Chicago, had quickly ceased to impress me as anything other than a disappointing gray hive of unfashionable Midwesterners. After graduation I had stuck around out of poverty and baffled inertia, living in a cheap walk-up with a guy named Gerard who'd served with me on the editorial board of our college literary magazine and had since become a paralegal, which I thought of as a woman's job. I brooded continually over moving to New York, but at the time I lacked the courage, which made me ashamed. I worked in a downtown bookstore. I wore corduroy blazers with pocket squares and tried to improve the customers via esoteric suggestions. "Try this," I might say to the matron asking for a good book-club book, handing her a copy of Gaddis's *The Recognitions,* my arm straining at the weight. "There's a great deal worth talking about in there."

If she asked what it was about, I would say, "The elusive nature of truth."

The night of the acceptance letter, to celebrate, I goaded Gerard into joining me on a bender, starting with shots at our local dive and then moving, at my insistence, in a taxi I paid for, to the lobby bar at the Four Seasons. As the waiter set down a silver tray containing three kinds of bar snacks, I said to Gerard, trying not to slur, "I feel like I'm living that moment in a short story, the one you're supposed to write toward, after which nothing will ever be the same."

"I think," said Gerard, who had also applied to MFA programs but had not been accepted, "that moment is supposed to come when the character realizes something. The realization is what changes things." He grabbed messily at the wasabi peas. "Epiphanies are internal, not circumstantial."

"Right," I said. "Exactly. That's what I'm saying: I've *realized* nothing will ever be the same. All of a sudden my future's just like"—I chopped at the air a few inches in front of my face—"right here."

"Must be nice." He opened the cocktail menu and made a show of recoiling from the prices.

"It's on me, man," I said, and when Gerard didn't protest, I added, "I insist. Let's blow some of that sweet fellowship cash. Next year when you get in somewhere, you can return the favor."

I see now, of course, what a tiresome poseur I was and how little I knew or understood of life and art, but one of my problems has always been that I can never identify and avoid, in the moment, behavior that will come across as dickish or insufferable. I can, however, thanks to my self-critical nature (a volatile witch's brew of blessing and curse), almost always identify my mistakes in retrospect, sometimes just moments too late, and so I live with the constant feeling that I have been tied to a post on the beach and left to face an endlessly incoming tide of shame. Though I have learned to harness the latent power of such a reliable inflow and channel it productively through the guise of D. M. Murphy, the sensation of self-recrimination remains unpleasant.

For example, I already regret the dedication I chose for my novel—"To Life"—but it has been printed thousands of times and cannot be undone. I regret that my author photo depicts me against a brick wall, eyebrows arched, in a shawl-necked cardigan, not that any of these things—wall, eyebrows, cardigan— are inherently offensive per se, but taken together they render the photo derivative and betray my hopes for consequence. I feel, sometimes, an unease when I am making such a choice, but always my ego overrides it, blinding me to a predictable outcome. This is a process I have tried and failed to subvert and so am forced to dwell with, as though with a less than ideal roommate. I regret thanking, in my acknowledgments, the authors who "paved the way for this work," none of whom I've ever met or corresponded with and most of whom are dead. *Thank you, Italo Calvino. Thank you, Roberto Bolaño. Thank you, Paul Auster. Thank you, Virginia Woolf.* (My editor urged me to include a woman, and Woolf *is* extraordinary.) *Thank you, Diderot.*

That night in Chicago, I felt smugly certain that Gerard would never get into an MFA and would go on being a paralegal forever. Then the following year he was accepted into the program that had been my first choice. *Do I feel a pang of jealousy?* I wrote in my congratulatory email. *I confess that I do, though also I believe I have wound up in the right place, for me, for now.* But, as it happened, he went to law school instead, and from what I can glean from Facebook, he is rich and happy in his Lake Forest mansion with his three small children and blandly beautiful trophy wife. (I present his carefully curated family images—the figures in them, as Barthes says, "anesthetized and fastened down, like butterflies"— ostensibly as evidence of his rosy contentment, though I know full well that everyone is a flimflam artist on social media. I myself am one. Lately I've been posting every scrap and snippet about *The Canon* to create an impression of hubbub. I confess I have retweeted compliments. I have described myself, without cause, as "humbled," though, honestly, what should one say?)

I remember the luxurious heft of my glass at the Four Seasons, how I waved it around as I told Gerard I would quit my job the next day, just walk into the bookstore and say fuck it to everyone and everything, since now *I* was going to be the one writing the books. *I* would be the one they put out cheese cubes for and plastic cups of wine. ("I'm really happy for you, man," Gerard said.) Someday soon I would be staying in hotels like this, paid for by my publisher (ha), and I would sit at the bar nursing a dram after a packed reading or a symposium of some kind, and a beautiful woman would sit next to me, and we'd get to chatting, and when she asked, I would say *I'm a novelist,* and all women want to have sex with novelists.

This is not true—I know that much by now—though something in me, not the best part, rebelled at the idea of embarking on the publication of *The Canon* while still attached to Elinor. "So," she'd said with some bitterness when I ended things a month ago, "you want to be free to fuck your groupies? You think you're going to *have* groupies?" I told her that wasn't it at all. Truly I don't expect to be flocked by randy, MILFy book-club ladies or star-fucking MFA students or effervescent chick-lit writers, and I tried my best to explain to Elinor how the issue was more that, at last, after years in the wilderness, I have found myself at a bustling crossroads of possibility. I am living a moment I believe I am obligated to savor and explore to the fullest. What I wanted to make most clear, I said, was that none of this was meant as any denigration, as she had been nothing but lovely and supportive, and I would be forever grateful to her.

She, too, is in my acknowledgments, near the end. *Thank you to Elinor, who always believed.*

I'm afraid I behaved badly that night with Gerard, though I cannot help but murmur puny excuses having to do with youth and perhaps an excess of excitement during a rare and long-sought moment of vindication. My memories are clouded by alcohol and time, but I know I spouted on a bit and interrupted and self-aggrandized, and by the end Gerard wasn't saying much. The atmosphere did not improve after the bill arrived—unasked for, but maybe I was getting a tad boisterous—and revealed that his two whiskeys were thirty dollars each. We'd walked home in silence.

Lying on my futon, one foot on the floor to ground myself against the spins, I thought again about how I was like a character in a short story, how this was the moment when everything changed. Why not follow that to its logical conclusion? Write what you know, they said, so why not write about what I knew best, which was being myself and being a writer? At the same time, I could explore thorny questions about fiction and reality—the elusive nature of truth, really. Here occurs another birth, of a sort: I would write both *as* and *about* a writer named D. Manitou Mur-

phy. The name was distinctive, I thought, even intriguing. Satis-
fied, I was drifting off to sleep when it occurred to me to that the
character would then be addressed by other characters as Manitou
Murphy, which sounded like the appellation of a Native American
detective or an Upper Peninsula fur trapper or possibly an Irish
manatee. No, D. M. Murphy was better, I decided. Stronger.

Even before then, when my writing career was utterly nascent,
autobiographical elements had already found their way into my
fiction. The story that got me into my MFA was a blunt and roughhewn piece, not uninfluenced by the work of Baker Forge, derived
from the historical facts of my parents' breakup: how my mother
had left my father when I was thirteen, not for another man or
because my father was cruel to her or for any reason other than, as
she put it, she "imagined a different kind of life for herself."

The crucial difference between her old and new lives, as far as
I could gather, mostly had to do with hobbies, as she immediately
sought out and was hired for another receptionist job (this time in
a law office) but also started making pottery and became a docent
at the lighthouse museum and a volunteer at the animal shelter.
She gained weight and doubled down on her earth mother-ish sar-
torial proclivities, and she appeared untroubled by the fact that, for
his part, my father had been thrown into the deepest of melancho-
lias. Unable to bring himself to hire a new receptionist, he allowed
his office to fall into disarray. Seemingly unconcerned with being
a cliché, he subsisted off frozen dinners and cans of Budweiser and
slept in a recliner while infomercials flashed blue over his slack
features. I was obligated to visit him in this squalor, to watch game
shows and eat from cartons of moldering Chinese leftovers while I
seethed inwardly at my mother, who had inflicted this plight upon
me. But all she would say by way of apology was "He's a smart
man. He could figure out how to cook and clean if he wanted to."

In my application story, the mother character took up with a man who built sailboats and who eventually left her for someone younger, throwing her into despondency. It was a cruel narrative but one I understood better than the reality, which was that, twelve years after the divorce, my mother was still alone but, she insisted, content. She had been the one, in fact, after that first terrible year, to step in and hire my father a new receptionist, a cheerful and competent and pretty-enough young woman who coddled him back to life and married him eight months later and immediately bore him another son: one family, in its mitotic splitting, yielding a new, superficially identical family. I suspected my mother had known she was choosing a replacement wife as well as receptionist, and I was embarrassed for my father, for how he had allowed her to expose the lack of depth or nuance to his preferences, his needs.

One month into Baker Forge's fall semester workshop, D. M. Murphy made his debut appearance in a short story: "THE FAWN" by D. M. Murphy. It was eighteen pages long and had as its premise the writer D. M. Murphy's frustration that no one would publish his challenging and unorthodox work. (Alas, I made sure to include secondary characters who told D.M. his work was not only challenging and unorthodox but necessary.) To blow off steam, he went hunting and shot a doe, who, when she fell, revealed a soft and speckled fawn. D.M. left the dead doe and instead slung the fawn over his shoulders and carried it out of the mountains and raised it on a bottle, but after he was betrayed by the woman he loved, he slit the fawn's throat and butchered and ate it. The final paragraphs leapt forward in time, to when D.M. had become a revered novelist. The betrayer-woman attended one of his readings, and they had a stilted and poignant conversation. "You always could tell a story," she said to him.

The way Baker ran workshop, which is more or less standard, was that first he would ask the writer to read a page or two from the work, and then everyone had to find something to compliment about the piece. In this way, a spongy layer of praise was deposited to cushion the criticism that came next and was to be endured by the author in silence. For the first five minutes I jotted down (with a nibbed pen, in a hardcover notebook) praise for my muscular descriptions of nature and for the shocking reveal of the fawn and for the authority of my voice. Through this, Baker sat back in his chair, hands folded over his small potbelly, nodding along.

I still wasn't used to seeing him in person. His face was more lined and his mustache more gray than in the black-and-white headshots that occupied the entire backs of hardcovers I'd bought at used bookstores in high school, but there was an unexpected twinkle about him, a leisureliness and casualness, as though life were one long sundowner hour spent on a cabin porch, spinning yarns in good fellowship. A few years before, to mild scandal, he had left his wife for a student, a vastly younger woman, a lithe and freckled hippie type with blond dreadlocks and unshaven armpits and tattoos of lotus blossoms and Sanskrit phrases. I saw her around town sometimes and regarded her with great curiosity, this groovy ingenue who'd stolen Baker Forge's heart. Among the men in the program, more than one conversation revolved around what she must be like in bed, and our ultimate consensus—that she must be, in short, unusually uninhibited—carried tones of both praise and condemnation.

After the compliments died down, Baker said in his gravelly voice, "All right. That's what's working. So. What should Daniel think about when he revises this story?"

I held my ludicrous pen over the creamy pages of my expensive notebook, unnerved that no one had praised the daring move of inserting a version of myself into my fiction, and here, after so much prattling, we return at last to the raison d'être of this monologue.

Ivy's voice, low for a woman's, cut through the silence. "It's a little up its own ass, isn't it?"

She was sitting directly across the table and staring down at the manuscript, one page lifted distastefully between thumb and forefinger.

I'd met her at the very beginning of orientation, Ivy. While we sat around playing getting-to-know-you games, I made a painstaking evaluation of her heart-shaped face, glossy black hair, slender figure, pert breasts, and small gold eyebrow ring. I followed this with a point-by-point comparison to the other women, and by the end of the day I had deemed her the hottest girl in the program, a preference that made me feel daring and cosmopolitan, given that she was Filipina, one of only three minority students. I struck up a friendly conversation (my habitual diffidence did not, for once, impair me, since the program's small size made chatting natural and inevitable), and when she registered interest in the fact that my lodgings abutted a network of mountain trails, I invited her for a hike. I kissed her on that hike, and she kissed me back, and when I tried again later, she demurred, saying she didn't want any complications while she was settling into the program.

In the weeks between the kiss and the workshopping of "THE FAWN," I had been careful to be cordial and respectful and a handful of times invited her for a friendly drink that she twice accepted, and only once did I wheedle her about when she might be open to complications. She had laughed and put me off in a way I see now was meant to be discouraging in a permanent sense, but, in the moment, I was sure we would eventually find our way to each other and said as much, eliciting an eye roll that I then lightly and teasingly scolded her for.

I glanced down the workshop table at Baker, assuming he would be a natural ally since his most famous character, Reginald Banksman, was both a hunter and clearly his own alter ego, but Baker, under the pretext of stroking his mustache, was hiding a smile. "There might be a more constructive way to phrase that," he said.

"I don't know," Ivy said in a tone that did not actually suggest uncertainty. "The narrator spends three pages moaning and groaning about how no one will publish his fiction and how it's all a conspiracy and how his genius is being, like, nefariously ignored by this cabal of narrow-minded lit-journal idiots who we're supposed to believe are jealous or something, but, as a reader, I can't help but think—Occam's razor—probably his writing just isn't very good."

"I have to say I agree," chimed in another girl, Kendra, who was in her late twenties and on the fat side and aggressively alternative, with cat's-eye glasses and dyed red hair and lots of colorful tattoos and the wardrobe of a celibate witch. "Like there's nothing about this character that suggests to me he's even capable of writing something worth reading. He has no perspective, you know? Also, slightly unrelated, but I think when violent animal death is a plot point, you really have to earn it, otherwise it seems like a cheap way to manipulate people into feeling something."

"To me, the lack of perspective is what's interesting about D.M., though," said Fred, a fellow first-year I'd been hanging out with. "He's like an outdoorsy idiot savant. He's completely baffled by human emotion, but he's also roiling with it."

Ivy jumped back in. "What I meant before, I guess, is that the story treats this deluded, silly, kind of horrible person with dire

seriousness. So maybe the real problem is that the 'narrator' "—
she made air quotes with her fingers—"is a little too far up *his*
own ass."

"Hmm," said Baker, his face now a study in neutrality. "Anyone
else?"

After the workshop, the tradition was that the two writers whose
work had been critiqued would choose a restaurant for dinner, and
after that everyone would go to a dark, sticky-floored bar with a
depressing jukebox and get drunk as cheaply as possible. Usually
I relished the camaraderie, but on that evening, what I wanted was
to go home to my tiny A-frame I could afford only by editing college essays online and to get obliterated while watching a DVD
and maybe some porn. But, determined to be a good sport, I went
out with the rest of my cohort, ate my burger with a wounded air,
and allowed my fellow workshoppers to buy me drinks.

"Don't let it get you down or throw you off," said Fred, handing me a well bourbon. He had a bushy brown beard and had once
worked at a lumber mill, a detail that, for a while, I contemplated
adding to D.M.'s backstory, never imagining that D.M. would one
day wear shawl-collared cardigans, live in Brooklyn, and take yoga
classes in the forlorn hope of getting laid. "Not everyone in that
room is going to be your reader," Fred went on. "I think the key is
to filter out the opinions that fundamentally don't matter."

"It's pretty shitty to publicly tell someone they're up their own
ass," I said, looking across to where Ivy was standing at the bar and
chatting with a red-faced, white-bearded faculty poet, a notorious
drunk and lech who wore safari shirts and was always identified
by all three of his names: Harold Tyson Slaughter. She laughed at
something Harold Tyson Slaughter said, and he reached out and
rested one hand on top of her head. She lifted it off and gave it a
high five before setting it on the bar.

"Yeah," Fred said, nodding amiably. "But the criticism might not feel so personal if you didn't, you know, name your character after yourself."

I gestured in Ivy's direction with my glass. "She likes Lorrie Moore, and Lorrie Moore's clearly always writing about herself. God forbid she should have a coherent critical rubric."

Another guy, Garth, joined us. He was a poetry student who'd been in the army and gone to Iraq and wrote exclusively about his experiences there, which I'd heard from the other poets in his workshop made his work difficult to critique because no matter how unassailably technical their quibbles, he would just mumble that that's how it *was*.

"What are you guys talking about?" Garth said.

"Lorrie Moore," I said.

He pretended to choke on his PBR. "Fuck," he said. *"Why?"*

On our hike, when I'd asked what had made her want to be a writer, Ivy had said, without hesitation, "Lorrie Moore." We were sitting on a boulder most of the way up a mountain, taking in the view and talking about writing, as writers will. "My parents split up when I was fifteen and already all sorts of messed up, or thought I was," she said. She wrapped her arms around her shins. "I was going out with an older guy—he was like nineteen, so scandalous—and he worked in one of those used bookstores that are really overstuffed, with the books crammed in every which way, and one day this little skinny spine caught my eye, and it said *Self-Help*. And I was like, that's exactly what I need." She laughed. "I thought it would be some actual self-help book. Thank god it wasn't. It saved me."

"I used to work in a bookstore," I said.

"Yeah? Did you save anyone?"

I thought of Gaddis with some doubt. "I'd like to think so. How did *Self-Help* save you?"

She lay back on the rock, looking at the sky, her hands folded just above where her shirt had ridden up to expose a narrow strip of belly. She said—I'm paraphrasing—that the stories had helped her understand that adults were just people, too, that they fucked up all the time without meaning to or knowing why and that her parents were peering out of their bodies with the same pervasive and permanent confusion as she was peering out of hers. She felt included by Moore's second-person *you* voice, recognized by it, and, reading, she'd experienced a burst of delighted (if queasy) suspense about her life: everything she would do, the myriad ways she would fuck up. She'd felt awe at the scale of the cumulative experience of all people, the living and the dead, which in aggregate was as vast and unfathomable as the universe itself.

"Chicks dig Lorrie Moore," said Fred.

"My girl doesn't really read," said Garth, "which sometimes is annoying but mostly just makes things easier. One less thing to fight about." For a minute we stood there in silence, the three of us tall and bearded and in plaid shirts, bobbing our heads to the Radiohead track emanating from the jukebox, staring into our drinks.

I looked at Ivy again, who was still at the bar. Harold Tyson Slaughter was tapping her forearm with two fingers as he talked. I said, "She's not going to fuck Harold Tyson Slaughter, is she?"

Garth swung around, made a spectacle of surveillance, swung back. "Probably. It's the whole reason these guys teach. Look at Baker's little Birkenstock babe."

"I think H.T.S. probably also needs the money," Fred said.

"Just so you know, Lorrie Moore's not always writing about

herself," came a voice from behind me. Kendra was sitting in a booth with two second-years, her chubby hands wrapped around a pint of beer. "You're assuming that because her fiction is so convincing. But some people are capable of actually inventing characters. That's kind of the point. And, no, Daniel, Ivy's not going to fuck Harold Tyson Slaughter. He's being a creep, and she's being polite."

"I just find Moore solipsistic and twee," I said. "That's all."

Sitting on that rock, I had told Ivy about my own parents' divorce. I'd told her how lonely and sad my mother's life seemed, even if she said she was perfectly happy—a claim that for some reason angered me. My distaste for the narrative she'd assigned herself had, unforgivably I suppose, driven me to neglect and avoid her. She and I had nothing in common, I told Ivy. She wasn't at all literary or intellectually curious, though neither was my father, whose life I found equally unbearable in its bland domesticity. He sponsored his new son's Little League team, the backs of their blue jerseys emblazoned with "Murphy Orthodontics." His wife festooned their house with signs bearing faux-playful drivel like "In This Kitchen We Dance" and "Keep Calm, It's Almost Wine O'Clock." Friday was the day for going out for ice cream, and Sunday was the day for church and televised sports, and all of my father's days, to my mind, were occasions for despair, as he progressed steadily and contentedly and compliantly toward death.

"I don't know how not to be contemptuous of them," I confessed. "Their lives have no *heft*."

She sat up and gazed over the sweeping coniferous prospect below. "Have you written about that?"

"About what?"

"About that feeling of not wanting to judge someone for being ordinary but doing it anyway. It could be interesting. I think our worst qualities bear investigating, you know?"

"I guess, although I don't think I'm judging so much as observing."

"Why do you think your mom's sad even though she says she isn't? I think I'd want to believe the happier version."

"Honestly, it's less that I really think she's sad and more that I think what she's chosen for herself is sad."

"Why?"

"I don't know, maybe I think it's pathetic to claim to be more fulfilled by dogs and cats and pottery classes than a marriage and a family."

"Maybe she's glad to not have to tend to anyone." She looked at me. "Is it that you're angry at her for being happier without your father?"

"I don't know. I hope not. Maybe." I saw Ivy wanted to be right, to help, and I said, "Are you secretly a shrink?"

She smiled, showing teeth, and I thought of the word *incandescent*, an obvious but apt descriptor. "I'm a shrink sent here to infiltrate the writers. To study their neuroses."

"Thank god I met you," I said. "One hike and you've diagnosed me."

She peered grandly down her nose, said with mock hauteur, "Indeed you are lucky to have met me."

"Indeed," I said. I leaned over and kissed her then, those full, soft lips. After a moment she pulled back. One hand, palm out, warded me off, but gently. When we were back down the mountain, parting ways, I tried again, but the hand came up more quickly and firmly; she angled her face away. Off-balance, leaning forward, I felt as though I were falling through a ghost of her, of what I had thought she would be.

Kendra, in the bar, gave me a long look through her cat's-eye spectacles. "And yet," she said, "for some unfathomable reason, Lorrie Moore is famous, and you're not."

"Lorrie Moore's like a million years old," I said. "So she has a head start." I knew immediately that this was neither true nor a good riposte, and Kendra saw that I knew and smirked. I turned back to my friends.

"Fuck Lorrie Moore," Garth said. "Like really."

Harold Tyson Slaughter was still at the bar, but Ivy had moved to a booth. When I next looked for her, she was playing pool, and Harold Tyson Slaughter was still at the bar, squeezing the upper arm of a poet girl while he talked at her. After that the place got crowded, and I lost track of Ivy until closing time, when it dawned on me that both she and Harold Tyson Slaughter were gone.

"She went home with him," I said to Fred. "I knew it. Didn't I call it? Didn't I?"

Fred steered me out the door. "Naw, man. I think she just went home."

"Girls like that . . ." I said. "Girls like that . . ." I didn't finish the sentence. I didn't yet know what I wanted to say. I'd had the idea Ivy would approach me at some point during the evening to clear the air, perhaps even to apologize, but because she had kept her distance, I concluded she was ashamed of herself. I believed she was a sensitive, reasonable, and insightful person, so if she was ashamed she must have had good reason to be, and so by the transitive property, I decided she had endorsed my right to be angry at her.

I paced my tiny living room, nursing a nightcap along with my grievances. The small concessions she had made—to hike with me, to engage in intimate conversation, to kiss me even for a moment, and she *had* kissed me—now struck me as traps. She had been inviting me to misunderstand, to overreach, but it hadn't been enough for her that I'd humiliated myself with my unrequited overtures. No, she'd needed to make sure the whole workshop saw me as she did: as unworthy.

A dawn alpenglow was pinkening the mountains by the time I sat at my typewriter. (In those days, when efficiency occupied a lower tier in my hierarchy of priorities than aesthetic purity, I worked on a tomato-red Selectric.) Keys pistoning with a magnificently satisfying rat-a-tat, the first lines of a story clattered out of me: *In my youth, before the publication of my first novel, I knew a girl who'd once let someone put a needle through her eyebrow and who went to bed with a dirty old poet. I believe she did this not because she was, as an uncouth soul might say, wanton or whorish but because she was seeking, with the reckless foolishness of the young, some confirmation that being desirable and being of consequence were one and the same.*

WHEN MY MOTHER DIED a few years later, I was sitting beside her and holding her hand, and this seems to me the best thing I have ever done. I don't mean there was anything heroic about my presence or that I exceeded the bare minimum of basic decency, but this was the event I had most feared my entire life, and I didn't run from it. I was thirty and at my most despairing even before her terrible diagnosis, after which she lived only a few months, as shocked as a person being hit by a bus, just slower. "You have been the joy of my life," she told me in the hospital, amid the bleeping machines, and the only thing I could think to say was that I was sorry. She didn't ask for what.

My father attended the memorial with his wife (no longer so young and cheerful) and their son (a shambling teenage doofus with a wispy mustache), and when he shook my hand, he said,

"She would never go to the doctor. It drove me crazy. She just took those herbs. This could have been avoided. Do you go to the doctor? Promise you'll go to the doctor."

Thank you to my late mother, who taught me to imagine different lives. I wish she had known I would write a book.

The worst thing I've ever done was turn in that story about Ivy and Harold Tyson Slaughter to the workshop. I called her Fern in it, and him Trevor Byron Stranger. I made her a poet of middling talent and vapid beauty who, having been spurned by, yes, the writer D. M. Murphy, throws herself at the old poet. I made Trevor Byron Stranger red-faced and white-bearded and safari-shirted. I wrote what I thought of as a bravely lengthy and unflinching sex scene that detailed Fern's unkempt pubic hair, her groveling displays of submission, the way his small penis and protuberant gut limited their choice of positions, her orgasm while he instructed her to finger her own backdoor. That's the word I used: backdoor. (*Now who's up her own ass?* I thought as I wrote it.) A subsidiary confession: I had to pause in the middle of writing the scene to jerk off right there at my Selectric.

Baker Forge, the day my story got workshopped, entered the room late and sat without speaking for a moment, smiling distantly, before he took a pair of reading glasses from the pocket of his denim shirt and commenced flipping through my manuscript. "Would you please read—"

Ivy interrupted. "I have a section I'd like him to read."

Baker regarded her over his glasses. "All right," he said finally. "Dealer's choice."

"Start at the top of page twelve," she told me. "I'll tell you when to stop."

The sex scene was three pages long and took about five minutes to read. After I'd read the first page, I hesitated, but when Ivy only looked at me and waited, I felt, out of both deference and defiance, that I had no choice but to go on. In my peripheral vision I could see her across the table: very upright, radiating hatred. Only after Trevor Byron Stranger had achieved his cartoonish climax with much all-caps grunting and dirty talk did she say, "Stop." A hot and rigid silence hung over the room. I stared down at the words I'd written.

When I said I might have written *The Canon* for Ivy, what I meant was that, perhaps, ever since that workshop, I've been writing toward a magna mea culpa, punishing D. M. Murphy on the page as I'd once tried to punish her, using that fool D.M. as both acknowledgment of my sins and atonement for them. I hope this book will bring me worldly success, of course, but I also hope its publication will serve as a catharsis of sorts and usher in an aftermath of tranquillity.

There was no ceremonial offering of praise in that workshop; in fact, there was no discussion at all. Instead, Baker made a show of studying the manuscript, then said, "With this one, we'd better start at the beginning." He cleared his throat, leaned forward, and read, "In my youth, before the publication of my first novel, I knew a girl who'd once let someone put a needle through her eyebrow and who went to bed with a dirty old poet." There was a pause. "It's hard to imagine a more insufferable opening line," he said, "but let's read on."

He went on, sentence by sentence, page by page. The classroom had a large picture window that framed a pleasant view of blazingly autumnal aspens, and I gazed out into the branches, my notebook unmarked as Baker calmly dismantled my story and laid out its component parts for all to see: fragility, arrogance, cruelty, self-indulgence, falseness, pretension. Among my most egregious crimes he counted my penchant for simultaneous prurience and prudishness. "Why say 'backdoor'? Why say 'went to bed'?" Baker asked the room. "Why flinch? If you're going to go there, just say *asshole*. Just say *fucked*." The sun dropped lower, casting a golden glow over the table, the scattered papers, the water bottles and coffee cups, the other writers. Ivy, her back to the window, wore a luminous halo.

Thank you to Baker Forge, for keeping me honest. I added that line to my acknowledgments a dozen times and deleted it just as many, wrung my hands and tossed and turned over whether to include it. Ultimately, I left him out.

"A good story assumes the reader is smart," Baker said, tossing the spent carcass of my manuscript on the table. "This story assumes the reader is stupid." He looked around the room. "Okay. That's enough." He picked up the day's second submission. "Oliver, would you read to us from page nine, please."

After class, as I was fleeing from the building, Ivy jogged up beside me. "Hey," she said. When I looked at her, she said, quietly, "You're a joke and you don't even know it." I flinched away, and I don't think she ever spoke to me again, not directly.

If I'd had a gun, I would have shot myself that night.

I don't mean to be melodramatic. I would have.

I heard, after I'd graduated and moved to New York, that Baker had left his young hippie wife for Ivy. They were together a few years, I think. The revelation gave me immense but temporary relief. Everything Baker had said about my story could, I decided, be explained away by the fact that *he* had been the one fucking Ivy, or was soon about to be. "I guess chivalry's not dead," I remarked to Fred, who had moved to Brooklyn too.

But this was around the time Fred stopped humoring me, around the time our friendship thinned to nothing. "Baker's a good guy," he said.

Ivy and Baker split after her first novel was published, a slender volume that was celebrated with some hysteria for its precociousness and whimsical lyricism. I heard through the grapevine that Baker was less than supportive. Her follow-up story collection was tolerated as a minor disappointment, and I'm sure you know about her second novel—you've probably read it. Everyone has.

Ivy Ocampo, this book would never have been written without you.

She had laughed, Miss Giles, when I gave her my autograph. It was in the nicest possible way, but she laughed before she thanked me and took the paper I'd offered her.

Souterrain

PIERRE MAILLARD LAY DYING of a stroke in his creaky old canopy bed at the age of seventy-six. Above him drooped a swag of faded blue, patterned with tiny silver stars, but he did not see it. Born blind, he saw nothing, not even darkness. In the cool and quiet predawn, sheets and plumes of numbness and electricity traveled through his body in silent auroras. As his mind crackled and clouded, it returned him to his earliest memory:

He is emerging from an afternoon nap. Piano music drifts up the stairs. His noisy dreams fall away, and the solitary, bittersweet melody draws him back into the world. Sunlight warms his face; his wandering fingers sleepily strum the bars of his crib. He doesn't question who is playing. The sound of the piano is as essentially his mother as the warm, lavender-smelling body that embraces him. Pulsing with low, slow chords, the comfort of her flows around him, moves through him like breath.

———

SIX MONTHS AFTER Pierre's death, early on a June morning, a man named Lili Harmou, age thirty, steps in front of the Métro between Saint-Paul and Bastille and is killed. The train is of the automated, driverless variety, and so no one sees his last moments, his dark figure separating itself from the tunnel wall.

The authorities politely label Lili's death an accident, which it is not, though it is a terrible mistake, a dark blossom sprouted from tangled roots of other mistakes and accidents. To list only a few: In 1983, a girl was sent to buy tea in Algiers. In 1942, a woman craved butter. In 1927, a man bought a piano for his wife. There is also this: Lili believed Pierre Maillard was his father.

PIERRE'S GRANDDAUGHTER, Iris, inherited his tall, narrow house on a narrow street in the fifth arrondissement. To acknowledge that her grandfather's death and bequest were well-timed felt disloyal—her grief was honest—but Iris *had* been thinking she needed a change from New York. Another lighthearted romance had turned sour and dull. Best to pack up and leave.

She flew to Paris in early December. White lights garlanded the city so densely it seemed to have been caught in a luminous net. Pear (she had always called her grandfather Pear) had been dead for three weeks. His body had been discovered by Madame Harmou, his housekeeper, and kept by the undertaker until Iris could arrive and see to his wishes. Iris was thirty-one and blessed with a portable career as a makeup artist. At photo shoots and fashion shows she lacquered the mouths and contoured the cheeks of South American bombshells, bewildered Siberian teenagers, daughters of rock stars. Her French was fluent, almost native, learned from her mother, Hélène.

Hélène, Pear's only child, had run away at nineteen, following a man to San Francisco after her own mother, Pear's wife, died of breast cancer. She or the man lost interest before long (though not before she became pregnant with Iris), but Hélène never returned to France, never saw her father again. When Iris asked why she would not go, Hélène sometimes said that she preferred America and sometimes that she could not leave her latest boyfriend to fend for himself and sometimes that she hated airplanes. When Iris suggested she take a ship, Hélène said, darkly, that she and her father were happier apart. In any event, she was not surprised to be passed over as heir. "Why do you think I was always sending you to visit?" she said to Iris on the phone from Tallahassee, where she was living with a man who raised epiphytes, plants that grew on other plants and did not need to root anywhere. "I wanted to remind him you were his next of kin, not all those refugees he collects."

"I thought you just wanted to get me out of your hair," Iris said mildly, remembering the eagerness with which her mother had waved her down a jet bridge every summer.

"Darling, don't be so dramatic," Hélène said and hung up.

Pear had requested there be no funeral of any kind, and his coffin was squeezed into the family tomb at Père Lachaise without ceremony, the little limestone Maillard chapel that stood slightly askew, its cast-iron gate fastened with a medieval-looking padlock.

Paris cemeteries, Iris learned, were always being dug up to cram in more people or evict those who were behind on rent. A million people were buried in Père Lachaise, in seventy thousand graves. *C'est normal,* the lawyer told her. He also said Pear had paid up another fifty years on the lease.

And after that?

Ah! *Bien sûr,* madam, if nobody renews in a timely fashion, you will all be exhumed and your bones moved to an ossuary and the plot sold again to someone else.

Pear's will contained a handful of small legacies to friends and to some of the people he had helped over the years—the refugees Iris's mother so disdained. A larger sum was left to Lili Harmou, the son of his longtime housekeeper, and another, still larger amount was set aside for the continued employment of Madame Harmou. The arrangement pleased Iris, who had known Madame Harmou since the summer she first arrived at Charles de Gaulle airport, six years old, her small hand passing from the manicured grasp of an Air France stewardess to the warm, dry fingers of a solemn dark-haired young woman who smelled of mint and explained she'd come on Pear's behalf to collect her. They rode in a taxi in silence, Iris struggling to stay awake. Madame Harmou, she quickly learned, was not given to superfluous conversation. Her care was gentle but impersonal, never playful, and Iris's summers passed as long, quiet reveries, broken only when Lili was around—poor Lili, an irresistible target for all her pent-up cantankerous energy.

Madame Harmou had only seemed to talk to Pear. Iris would hear their voices sometimes, behind the closed doors of his study, though they fell silent if she so much as creaked a floorboard.

The week before Christmas, on Pear's street, as Iris was returning from a walk, a dark-haired man in a dark suit and burgundy scarf brushed by. "Lili!" she called.

He turned, at first quizzical in an ordinary way, and then, when he recognized her—the strangest thing. At first he stared at her with alarm, as though she were some ranting lunatic accosting him. His body tilted as though he might simply ignore her and hurry away. But, no, he smiled tightly and came to brush her cheeks with *bisous,* wafting her in expensive cologne. Some time ago, Pear, a reliable email correspondent, had mentioned that Lili ran a night-club. *As his mother says,* Pear wrote, *he has always had a gift for the nocturnal.* Iris had not seen Lili in years. For a long stretch of their twenties he was away, working in, maybe, Marseille.

"It's been so long," she said. "How are you?"

"I'm well. And you?"

"Settling in. Missing Pear."

She expected him to say something about Pear, who had always been good to him and his mother and had left him that not insignificant bequest, but he only nodded. His gaze drifted. His blue eyes had always been so striking, so unexpected against his skin, which was goldish, ocherish, like unpolished brass. When she was a child and didn't recognize attraction as such, she had thought he irritated her. When they were teenagers, she had been intimidated by his long hair and clothes full of safety pins, his jeering friends, his silence. He went into the Métro with spray paint, she knew, and into the catacombs, not the tourist part but the miles of tunnels that clung to the city's underside like a shadow, officially forbidden but accessible to those in the know.

"You look very dapper." She made a little flourish, half flirtatious. "Pear said something about a nightclub? I mean, as far as your work?"

"Yes."

"You manage one?"

"Three." Nothing more. Stony, looking away.

"Well," she said. "I don't want to make you late. It was nice running into you."

She turned and walked quickly toward the house, twisting with humiliation. He had seemed almost repulsed by her, but she had been more attracted to him than ever. What did that say about her? Nothing she didn't already know. When she paused to fish her keys from her bag, though, he was still standing where she had left him, watching her.

After the new year, Iris bought a ticket to the catacombs. She had not been since she was a teenager, when she had gone a few times to mope and commune with the dead and roll her eyes at the tourists. The tunnels were as she remembered: dim and chilly, with skulls and femurs stacked high, neatly arranged, nothing to stop you from running a finger over them, though touching was against the rules. But who could resist?

She glanced at a brochure. In the decades before and after the revolution, when the cemeteries became overcrowded, the dead were dug up and their bones poured down chutes into the tunnels, which were old limestone quarries, the source of Paris.

A group of British teenagers clowned around taking pictures, bones in the background. What had Lili done down here as a teenager? Just painted his initials? Sometimes on the Métro she watched out the window, wondering if any of the brash, illegible tags were still Lili's, or if his had all vanished under more recent layers. "He could get in trouble burrowing around down there," Madame Harmou had said while Iris listened at the door of Pear's study. "And for what? I don't understand. The police have caught him before. He crumples up the tickets and throws them away. You can't do that forever."

At the exit of the catacombs, Iris opened her bag for a man who looked inside with a flashlight for stolen bones, then waved her up the stairs. During the daytime in this leafless season, the city sometimes reminded her of an enormous mudflat: resolutely beige, cracked through with a web of streets, the khaki river matching its embankments. But now, in the pale, wintry evening, the buildings looked bluish and chalky. The streetlamps and yellow apartment windows had not yet asserted themselves, and all that limestone, all those ancient sea creatures, dead and compacted and dug out of the mirror-image city below, glowed with a delicate, lunar light.

BUT, BEFORE, back in the canopied deathbed, in the cool and quiet predawn, as the walls of Pierre's inner labyrinth continued to disintegrate, another memory opened off the first like a cavern:

He is a young man in Paris, a student. At a party, a friend puts on a record: Beethoven, Piano Sonata No. 8 in C Minor, *Pathétique*. When the adagio begins, a glass of red wine slips from Pierre's fingers and breaks on the parquet. He barely notices. Slashing haphazardly with his cane, he crosses the room and crouches beside the stereo.

"Again," he says when the movement ends. "Please."

A hand on his shoulder. A zip and a crackle as the needle is reset. He listens with his forehead against the rough fabric of the speaker. This is the music. It has been lost for years, lost like his mother, lost like her piano, which was no longer in the house when he returned after the war. Had it been chopped up and burned? Had an enterprising soul somehow carted it off to sell? Had it gone to reside in a country château to be pounded away at by a circle of singing Nazis? His mother will never return, but as he listens, he believes she might be just in the next room, lavishing her caresses on a mass of smooth wood and ivory, taut steel strings, sheet music easily sent cascading, pedals smooth and cold as cobblestones that, when he was small and would lie on his back beneath the instrument, hissed faintly as she depressed them with her small feet, her narrow leather pumps.

A sparkling tightness in his head. He is lying on his back, idly touching the varnished wood of the piano leg. Or is it a bedpost?

Perhaps he is in his crib, his fingers passing over the smooth bars. Music floats up the stairs.

AS A CHILD, Lili often came to Monsieur's house after school to wait for his mother. While she finished in the kitchen, she might give him a cloth and set him to dusting bookshelves or the long banister that coiled up five floors to the attic, or she might allow him to sit on one of Monsieur's hard sofas and do his schoolwork. He had not liked Iris, who was a bored, waspish child, vigilant for any opportunity to disconcert. Sometimes she would make a show of examining Lili in silence before bursting into peals of laughter. "Nothing," she would say when he asked what was so funny. "You wouldn't understand." It had always been a relief when she went back to America.

For Lili, the belief that Monsieur Maillard was his father took shape slowly, forming in his young consciousness from wisps of instinct and conjecture: stray phrases, certain silences, the lack of other candidates, the way his mother talked to Monsieur when she thought no one was around. His mother had told Lili that his father had married her in Algiers, brought her to France, and, when she was pregnant, had been hit by a car and killed. Lili did not believe her.

What was his name? Was he Algerian, too? Didn't he have any family who would want to meet me?

Please don't trouble me about the past, Lili.

By the time he was nine, Lili had become certain.

Monsieur asked after Lili's marks in school and patted his shoulder and sometimes offered him coins or candies, which was all very nice, but sometimes Lili would stare at the closed doors of the study where Monsieur sat all day dictating into a tape recorder or running his fingers over papers goosefleshed with braille and wish for Monsieur to burst out, arms open, cane aloft. *My son,* he would say. *Come here to your papa.*

Thanks to the boy who lived in the apartment next door to Lili and his mother and whose father had a collection of dirty videos, Lili had a clear idea of what Monsieur must have done to his mother. His mother was slender and very young, with glossy black hair. Men often looked at her. Had Monsieur, still in his forties and newly widowed when Lili's mother arrived, been intrigued by her scent, her voice? Had he simply been unable to resist his curiosity? Had he reached out and found a curved hip, a small breast? Lili could not ask his mother. If he forced her to admit such a thing, her humiliation would always linger between them.

I am your uncle, Lili thought when he looked at Iris, when she sassed by on the stairs, bumping him out of the way. He decided he must be patient with her, in what he understood to be the way of uncles, even though she was a year older, even though she laughed at him.

Then suddenly she was a busty American adolescent in plaid shirts and Chuck Taylors and elaborate makeup, as witchy and sharp-eyed as a fortune-teller and rarely glimpsed by Lili, who only came to Monsieur's house when his mother insisted. The sight of Monsieur infuriated him in his teens: the injustice of being unacknowledged, the indignity of watching his mother meekly cook and clean for the man who had fathered her child. So he busied himself with getting messed up and chasing girls and exploring the Métro with his spray paint, leaving his mark wherever he could, even in the hard-to-find stations abandoned and sealed off since the war, ads for 1940s shoe polish and face powder still plastered to their tiles. Pascal, an older Tunisian kid with facial piercings, showed him how to cross from the Métro into the catacombs. Some tunnels and chambers were flooded; some were full of jumbled bones. Six million Parisians, Pascal said. Robespierre and Marat down there somewhere, in pieces like the rest. Disarticulated.

There was privacy underground. Being unknown and unacknowledged was a natural state. So was silence. Sometimes he turned off his headlamp and simply walked, running his fingers along the stone, trusting he would be able to find his way back out.

Monsieur was a kind man, a good man, Lili's mother was always reminding him. Monsieur spent his days droning out letters and articles and motions on behalf of the persecuted and displaced, dictating endlessly into his tape recorder or to one of a string of assistants. When the doorbell rang at the tall narrow house, usually strangers were waiting on the steps: people from Asia and Africa and the Middle East, men from what had been Yugoslavia, Polish laborers with concrete dust in their hair, sometimes veiled women or men in priests' collars or dour government suits. Monsieur opened his door to all these strangers, and yet he remained closed to his only son, pretended Lili was just a kid he knew.

Once Lili saw Iris with an unknown man on a bench in the Jardin du Luxembourg. It was broad daylight and children were playing nearby, but the man had his mouth on her neck and his hand under her plaid shirt. Her eyes were closed, her lips parted. Without meaning to, Lili stopped and stared. Iris opened her eyes and looked directly at him, heat lingering in her gaze.

He asked his mother later what she thought of Iris, and she had considered the question (which Lili told himself he was asking out of avuncular concern and not because he couldn't stop imagining *his* mouth on Iris's neck, *his* hand under her shirt) before saying she did not think Iris was a nice girl.

As Lili grew older, he might have relinquished his belief about Monsieur if his mother had not seemed to confirm it when he was eleven. His class had studied genetics, and Lili had, in turn, studied Monsieur. Monsieur was left-handed, like Lili. His earlobes were attached to his head, like Lili's. His eyes were blue, like Lili's—so unusual, everyone said, Lili's eyes with his complexion. Surreptitiously, Lili examined Monsieur's thumbs to see if they were straight or curved, his fingers to see if hair sprouted on the middle segments, his forehead for a widow's peak. He had wished to see Monsieur's toes, to ascertain if the second toe or the big toe was longer, but, alas, Monsieur always wore polished black shoes. Evidence was mixed, but: the left hand, the earlobes, the blue eyes that wandered their sockets like creatures in an aquarium.

One day his mother found him weeping in the attic. He liked the attic partly because no one else seemed to. It was accessed by a normal door at the top of the stairs and was quiet and dim, its big windows battened behind wooden shutters. Disused furniture made an alpine landscape under white sheets. His mother knew to look for him there.

"Little one," she said, "what is it?"

"I don't want to go blind," Lili said.

She bent down and took his chin in her hand, lifting his head to look in his eyes. "You can see fine, can't you? Why would you be blind?"

"Monsieur is blind."

"Monsieur was unlucky. What does that have to do with you?"

In his fury, Lili reached up and pushed at her shoulders. "Don't lie! It insults me."

She stared down at him. "What are you talking about?"

"I know Monsieur is my father. I know it." Lili lowered his face to his knees and cried. When he could catch his breath, he said, "At least, if I go blind like him, then someone will have to admit the truth."

His mother was silent. She stood with her arms folded, gazing at nothing, light from the shutters striping her body. Finally, she said, "You won't go blind, Lili. Monsieur was born without sight. You are already eleven. And eleven is old enough to keep a secret." She pulled him to his feet, wrapped her arms around him. "You are lucky," she murmured, "to have such a good man for a father, to have his blood in your veins. You must try to become a man like Monsieur one day. But, Lili, you must also never breathe a word."

"HAS HE EVER mentioned the Gliks?"

Monsieur's cousin Rosalie was in the kitchen, whispering over a cup of tea. Madame Harmou had been working for Monsieur for a year or so. Lili was only a baby.

Madame Harmou, forming little pastry boats to be filled with apricot jam, shook her head.

"I suppose he wouldn't. I shouldn't say anything, but really it sheds so much light, and I expect you must be wondering why he was so eager to help you—why he helps all these people. I would hate for you to think he expects anything improper." Rosalie, bracelets rattling, waved her hands to cut off any potential protest from Madame Harmou. "Listen. Here it is. In the war, Pierre's parents sheltered a family. Jews, you know. In the attic. A couple and their four daughters. Pierre was only a small child. The man, Monsieur Glik, had been his mother's piano teacher for years. Anyway, someone betrayed them. We didn't know who. They were taken away. All of them. Pierre bribed someone in the archives after the war—turns out it was a neighbor who turned them in. In exchange for butter."

Rosalie cast an accusatory glance at the yellow brick lying in its dish on the counter. She went on: "They all died. All six Gliks. In

Auschwitz. Pierre's father was shot. His mother died of typhus in prison."

Madame Harmou knew she was supposed to voice her horror and disbelief, to shake her head. But she also knew Rosalie was perfectly capable of carrying on both sides of a conversation herself and so continued to work in silence.

"Horrible, no?" said Rosalie. "My parents raised Pierre. I think of him as my brother. These charitable impulses of his—he inherited his parents' wish to do good. By doing good, he's trying to honor them. Their misfortune was your salvation, Madame Harmou. And that is my little bit of insight for you today." She leaned forward to catch Madame Harmou's eye, patted her hand, and was gone.

Madame Harmou raised a wrist to wipe at her tears, streaking her face with flour. The story was awful, but she had heard many awful war stories. Her own grandfather and all three of his brothers had been conscripted during World War I, taken from their orchard and sent to Europe, where they had never been, only to die immediately in the mud. No, it was the thought of Monsieur, his goodness, which was so profound, that moved her.

"LILI!"

He stopped and turned, and there was Iris after so long, short and sturdy in black jeans. A blunt bob of hair, red lipstick. Her coat and scarf only somewhat disguised the swell of large, alert, carefully buttressed breasts. His desire for her stunned him, the violence and immediacy of it. It did not dissipate even after he was rude to her, nor after he walked away and went about his nightly work like an automaton, gazing over a blue velvet room of sparkling people, sparkling bottles and glasses. Even after a week, the fever raged, did not disperse even when he was in the middle of fucking some other girl. After two weeks, he asked to be sent to Cannes to oversee an underperforming club.

Beside the sea, he thought less about Iris, but still she was there. Iris Maillard. If Lili believed in God and could ask him one question, it would be: Why Iris? Of all women, why was Iris the one to inhabit and abrade him, to take over his thoughts, to make him strange to himself? The more he tried to squelch his desire, the more it thrived. Maybe he was simply a degenerate, an incestuous pervert. Maybe he was being punished for something.

You must try to become like Monsieur one day, his mother had said, years ago. *But, Lili, you must also never breathe a word. Monsieur made me promise never to tell you, and everything we have we owe to Monsieur. Monsieur helped me when I had nothing. Monsieur has provided for us.*

It was my fault, she said. *I tricked him. I exploited his weakness as a man, his loneliness, his grief for his wife.*

Lili, she said, *it would kill me if you said anything to him. I would die of shame.*

In Cannes, he found himself thinking sometimes that if his mother were dead, he could have Iris and no one would know anything was amiss. Then he regarded himself with horror, wondered if he was losing his mind.

IN THE COLLAPSING COSMOS of Pierre Maillard, wisps of memory drifted and dissipated, more and more of them, leaving long, feathery, vanishing trails.

Madame Harmou flits through, her nearly silent footsteps like those of the cat he'd had as a newlywed, the whisper of a dustcloth, the heat of an oven, the smell of mint. Mint tea, mint soap. Her son,

Lili, is a polite voice, eager, some unmet need in it that inexplicably saddens him.

He remembers his daughter, Hélène, as a child: small and compact and tart, an unripe fruit of a girl, not yet the unruly creature she would become, musky and furtive, brushing by.

Then he is lying beside his wife, Martine, in the canopy bed as she drifts between life and death, his fingers tracing the bones of her hands and arms. She smells of morphine. She is so young, only forty-two, but her skin is papery and fragile under his fingers, as though the cancer were trying to justify itself by making her old. His lips find her ear. The small cavern seems, at that moment, like a portal into the beyond, but he can't think what to whisper into it, what message to send to his parents, to the Gliks.

After she dies, he lets grief get the better of him. He is cruel to Hélène. He is very drunk and will never remember exactly what he says, but, in a rage, he implies she was to blame for her mother's death, that her sluttish, selfish behavior brought calamity upon them. The man from San Francisco is the rope on which Hélène swings away, off into the void.

The cat—he remembers the cat, presented to him by his cousin Rosalie as a wedding gift, a warm, liquid, unexpected thing curling around his ankles. Martine describes the cat as pumpkin-colored, and the glossy feel of the animal's coat becomes forever linked to the taste of squash.

He is even younger, still a student. He has asked around and found a clerk in the archives who will help. He tells her what he is looking for and slips her some cash, which she refuses, then accepts. He does not tell her about the fear that has nagged him from childhood, his hope she might exonerate him. No, said his aunt and uncle who had taken him in during the war, no, it was not his fault that his parents and the Gliks died. But he does not feel innocent. He feels, always, a nagging, amorphous fear. The clerk finds for him the document describing the betrayal and arrests and brings it to a café in the evening. Briskly, she reads aloud the few sentences. *Butter,* she says. Then a rustle of papers, her voice again, warmer, worried: "Monsieur, are you all right?"

He is eleven, returning to Paris for the first time after the war. His uncle guides him carefully through the tall, narrow house, steering him around ruined furniture, warning him where the banister is not to be trusted. He feels stray papers sliding under his feet, bits of plaster, grit. The house had been occupied by the Gestapo and then the Americans and then six displaced families crowded together, his uncle says. His uncle, a lawyer, has wrested the property back from the government and begun the most essential restorations (paid for out of Pierre's large inheritance). "Where is the piano?" he asks. His uncle doesn't know.

The house is rented out until Pierre is older and returns for university, studying law and also learning, with his long, tapping cane, the curbs and cobblestones of his birth city. His aunt buys the canopy bed, the bed where he will die, in a flea market. All the markets are still glutted with a war's worth of orphaned furniture. For the bed's drapes, she finds fabric she tells him is blue, patterned with tiny silver stars.

BY MAY, Lili believed he had rehabilitated himself and could safely return to Paris. In June, despite his best efforts to avoid her, he ran into Iris on the rue de Rivoli, far from Monsieur's house. She was so burdened with shopping bags, so pleased to see him, so flushed and pretty that he had no choice but to accompany her home, carrying the bags. He tried to deposit her things and flee, but she insisted he stay for a glass of wine. "Drink one small token of my gratitude," she said. "That's all I ask."

She sat on a sofa. He perched on the edge of a chair and gazed at his hands or up at a chandelier where spiders were making lace, anywhere but at her. Iris said she had gone to the catacombs after they ran into each other the last time, and hadn't he gone into them a lot as a kid? Not the public tunnels but the other ones? There were more than the ones open to tourists, weren't there?

Miles more, he said.

Did he still ever go? Would he take her?

As a matter of fact, he said (reluctant, thrilled, bargaining with himself), a DJ he knew, his old friend Pascal, was spinning at a catacomb party that very night. A secret party. It would be in one of the Nazi bunkers. He could take her, if she wanted. "But first," he said, pointing up at the chandelier, "I need to clean that."

Iris said not to be silly. It would have to be done specially. But Lili, fetching a ladder from the attic and taking a soft cloth up among the gently chiming prisms and beads, felt that the neglected chandelier said something embarrassing about his mother, about small advantages taken of a blind employer.

And so he found himself underground with Iris. Techno ricocheted off walls still painted with RUHE (or QUIET) in a Teutonic font. Iris danced, arms overhead, wrists turning. He had told her to wear rubber boots, and, grooving in her yellow Wellies, she looked cheerfully apocalyptic, a disaster worker getting down.

Lili went to shake Pascal's hand in the glow of his laptops. "Like old times down here," Pascal said, slipping him a tablet of Ecstasy. "Feel fantastic, yeah?"

The drug had always seemed aptly named to Lili. Fireflies floated through him, multiplying. He pressed his cheek against the bunker's cool wall. The Nazis could never have imagined. Everything would be fine. There had been no need to be so worried. Love is love. Love is good. Iris pulled him into the crowd. He could tell she wanted him too. The music was more than music. The music was love. He told Iris this, and she looked at him askance but laughed. He clasped her wrist. Blood was moving through her veins in time with his blood in his veins, in time with Pascal's beat, in time with the clenching of his jaw.

He led her away, down one tunnel, then another. He took her through a passage where the bones were piled almost to the ceiling, so high they had to wriggle over them on their bellies. The rattling clacking sound pleased him. In another tunnel, beige water lapped against their shins. He paused to dip his hands, to feel the drops run off his fingertips. "Hence the boots," Iris said, splashing after him. The music faded to a distant beat and then nothing. He stopped in an open chamber where multiple tunnels fanned off into blackness. He turned off his headlamp and took her flashlight from her hand and turned it off, too. When he inhaled, the darkness entered his lungs, cool and inky. They were not touching, but he sensed her warmth. The Métro rumbled somewhere overhead.

"We might as well be in outer space," he said, "or dead and buried. Maybe there isn't so much of a difference, you know. They're both things I'll never see."

"You know," she said, "you could have gotten some of whatever you're on for me, too." Before he could apologize, she laughed. "It doesn't matter. Just don't get us lost."

He didn't know if he reached for her or her for him, but the feel of her overwhelmed him, the way her body took shape out of nothing. After a moment—more than a moment?—he unlocked himself, staggered away, his fingers trailing along the wall, every seam in the stone loud through his nerves. He didn't go far.

Around a corner. Far enough to regain control. She called after him, frightened. He crouched for a minute. The sensation of his own fingers raking through his hair soothed him. Her face in his flashlight when he came back was determinedly proud, a woman who believed she had been the victim of a childish prank.

"I'm sorry," he told her. "Please believe me that this is a bad idea. You should slap me, please. It would make me feel better."

"But the only thing that would make *me* feel better," she said, "would be for you to kiss me again so I don't feel like such an idiot."

They made love in the catacombs, partly dressed, against the wall. He felt as though he were inhaling and inhaling without ever reaching the capacity of his lungs, as though he had become an infinite vessel. When he led her back aboveground, the warm, humid air and the bright night filled him with awe. The Eiffel Tower fizzed with electricity. From its apex, searchlights rolled and tumbled across the sky.

But in the ultramarine quiet just before dawn, while Iris slept beside him beneath the starry, bellied-out blue of the canopy over Monsieur's bed, a chasm of irrevocability swallowed him up. The drug's buoyancy, its iridescence, had gone and left behind a terrible vacuum.

Quietly, he slid out from under the covers, picked his clothes up off the floor. He dressed in the dark hallway, crept down the stairs.

He eased open the servants' door and there was his mother, head bent, one hand groping in her large cloth purse. At first she looked at him in blank surprise. Then he saw her understand. He fled. The street cleaners had already been through, and the cobblestones were slick and gleaming. He could not bear to be underground and so walked the three miles to his apartment rather than take the Métro. He paced. Sat down, stood up again, drank warm vodka from a bottle, chewed some pills without being sure what they were. Whenever he was not guarding against it, whenever the slightest slack came into his mind, there it was. More than a thought, almost a wish: *If she were dead, then no one would know.*

THE BACK DOOR OPENED as Madame Harmou was searching for her keys, and Lili appeared, hair tousled, eyes bloodshot, clothes streaked with pale mud and dust, a vision of his teenage self—sleepless, bearing traces of the *souterrain*—but older, horribly so, blue shadows in his face. For a moment she experienced only bafflement, then a brief, vertiginous notion that it was evening and he had come looking for her, even though he had not been to the house since Iris arrived. Ah, no, there it was. As soon as her mind alit on Iris, Madame Harmou knew why she was encountering her son, why he looked so anguished at the sight of her.

"Lili," she said, reaching to restrain him, knowing he would—as he did—twist past her and be gone. She stood on the threshold, looking after him. A moped sped by, vibrating on the cobblestones. She turned and went inside, lugged her bags up the stairs. She had come early to bake bread. She liked being in the house, made excuses to be there. In the kitchen, she filled a bowl with warm water and added a spoonful of yeast, a pinch of sugar. She would not allow herself to think yet. Outside, yellow light seeped through the early haze.

"Good morning." Iris was in the doorway in her robe. Madame Harmou knew she herself had never looked (would never look) the way Iris did: as pink and tenderized as veal, dreamy from sex, only half in the world. Nor could Madame Harmou fathom how much Lili must have wanted this particular woman, who looked like quite an ordinary woman without her makeup. The realization of what Lili had done revolted her, even though, in reality, he hadn't done anything wrong. That wishful lie, told so long ago, intended to spare them both from shame, had rusted into place. She almost believed it herself.

After Monsieur was dead, she had considered telling her son the truth. But what would Lili think of her, his mother, for allowing him to be angry at Monsieur for so many years? To feel so much righteous indignation at an innocent man? This business with Iris . . . Madame Harmou had not predicted it. The lie aside, Iris was not a good girl for Lili. She ran around with men, like Hélène had. She must have tempted Lili. Madame Harmou decided she would wait a day, let Lili settle down, and then she would tell him.

Iris said, "Is there coffee?"

"I'm sorry," said Madame Harmou. "Not yet."

"It doesn't matter. I'm going back to bed."

Madame Harmou made coffee in the American machine Iris had brought with her, sifted flour, turned on the oven. Buying bread was simpler, but she liked the alchemy of kneading and baking. Sometimes she made Algerian flatbread from semolina, but usually she made simple, sturdy, dense wheat loaves.

Not long after Lili's birth, Monsieur had taken her aside. "I don't think you have anyone to talk to, Madame Harmou. Do you want me to introduce you to some nice women, good women, also from Algeria? Women with babies?"

No, she had not wanted that. She wanted no connection to home.

"Then I hope you will talk to me sometimes. Especially about the boy. It would be a terrible hardship, not to speak about your child to anyone, and you would be keeping a lonely widower company."

She had found him lying dead in bed, flat on his back, mouth agape, eyes open, sunlight blazing into the milky irises. She had reached to close his eyes but could not, in the end, touch him. She was not sure she had ever touched him. Lili had cried like a child when she told him the news, his face in his hands. She had not seen him cry since the day in the attic.

Even before she knew about the Gliks, even before it became the site of her terrible lie, she had not liked the attic. She did not like the white-shrouded furniture, the rustlings of mice, the small corpses of moths scattered beneath the shuttered windows. She did not like the ṣlanted bars of light that fell onto sheets and floorboards the way they had fallen on tablecloths and tiles in the empty café in Algiers, its shutters closed against the midday heat, as she had ventured inside, calling out an uncertain *bonjour,* feeling the presence of an unseen person. Persons. Her father had sent her to buy some tea. When she returned without it but refused to give an explanation, he had pinched her arm and accused her of stealing his money, even though she'd fished the coins from her pocket and held them—all of them—out in one trembling hand. Her assailants had only been blurry shapes through the cotton dish towel they stretched over her eyes.

Sometimes she caught herself examining Lili's face, trying to subtract her own features, searching for the face of a man she had never seen. He must have had blue eyes. When she discovered she was pregnant, her favorite uncle, a magistrate who had studied law with Monsieur in Paris, wrote Monsieur a letter on her behalf. Monsieur's wife had just died. He wrote back that he would give her a job; he would help with her papers. Madame Harmou was only sixteen then. Her uncle, embracing her before she boarded her ship, promised never to tell her father where she had gone or why. Better to break his heart with the unknown than with the truth.

Near the end of Monsieur's life, when she was sitting with him in his study, he had said, "I will tell you this, which I have never told another soul. I think it will be a relief to tell someone."

The room had grown dark around them as he told her about the Gliks, the piano teacher and his wife and daughters, how they were taken and his parents arrested. He thought he remembered the policemen's voices and heavy footsteps, but he suspected the memory was counterfeit. His parents had not come to the nursery to say goodbye. Maybe they had no opportunity, or maybe they did not wish to draw attention to him. His nanny took him to her own apartment, and in a few days his uncle came from Lyon to collect him.

During the long and difficult journey to Lyon, his uncle in his distraction nearly lost Monsieur several times in crowded rail stations when he walked off without him, forgetting he could not see to follow. The abandonment was accidental, but Monsieur had believed he was being punished for what had happened to the Gliks and his parents. He wept and apologized, and his uncle had gathered him into his lap on a train station bench and wept and apologized, too.

When bombs fell on Lyon in 1944, Monsieur was hiding in the cellar with his uncle and aunt and cousins Rosalie and Marcel and their dogs, down in the cool earth like so many potatoes, dust showering onto their heads after each detonation. When the liberating army came, he heard their jeeps and tanks, their motorcycles and boots. His uncle, joyful, lifted him onto his shoulders, above the crowd, where Monsieur swayed in the open air and called, in confused excitement, for his mother.

Some months later, at the movies with his cousins, he did not see the concentration camps on the newsreel, the emaciated people, the piles of corpses, but the narrator explained enough. He had to be carried out. A doctor was summoned.

"Who are the Gliks?" the doctor asked Rosalie and Marcel, squatting on the cinema lobby's tiled floor as he replaced his stethoscope in his bag.

From then on, Monsieur could not abide the mildewed cool and plush seats of movie theaters, the booming voices.

"My parents," Monsieur said to Madame Harmou, "must have decided it would be safer to keep me in ignorance of the Gliks upstairs. They must have thought it would not be difficult to conceal their presence from me. I was already, as it were, in the dark. I admit, I'm offended by this still. Maybe it's childish, and certainly irrelevant, but I am. I believe I could have been trusted, even though I was so small. The Gliks must have crossed the city in the night and come in while I was asleep, just before one of the deportations. They were extremely quiet, only moving around the house late at night when I was asleep, but still sometimes I heard sounds. My parents did not consider how sharp my hearing was, how much I depended on it." He paused. His eyes swiveled unevenly up to the ceiling.

"All six of the Gliks died in Auschwitz, Madame Harmou. And my father was shot in Paris, and my mother died of typhus in prison."

"I know," said Madame Harmou. "Rosalie told me years ago."

"Ah." He was silent for a moment. "I should not be surprised." Then he said, "There is one more thing."

Monsieur had played sometimes with a neighborhood boy, Luc, the rare child who did not seem bothered by his blindness. In retrospect, Monsieur wondered if Luc might have been a little simple. Luc's mother was an entrepreneurial collaborator, it turned out, and it was she who traded a tip about the Maillards' attic for butter.

He learned this from the archive clerk he bribed, from the papers she brought to the café. Luc's mother had gone to a Vichy policeman and told him she wanted butter. She wanted to cook with it; she wanted to rub a bit on her cracked feet; she had a piece of information to trade for it. Dutifully, the policeman noted this all down. Being unusually thorough, he also recorded her reason for suspecting the Maillards.

Poor Monsieur, only five years old, had decided, in his innocence, that the sounds from the attic were the murmurs and shufflings of ghosts. Ghosts, he whispered to his friend Luc, who, wide-eyed, repeated the story to his father and to his mother. The Maillards have ghosts in their attic.

Madame Harmou will tell the story to no one—why should she?—and when she dies, it will join the dark matter that surrounds the living: the memories of the dead, undetectable but still exerting force.

IN 1927, Monsieur Maillard, Pierre's father, buys his wife a piano, a parlor grand with rosewood veneer and mother-of-pearl inlay. She needs, he says, something to pass the time, at least until she becomes pregnant. She asks around about teachers, and a friend recommends Hermann Glik, newly arrived from Austria with his wife and baby daughter. "He's a Jew," the friend says, "but he's an excellent musician and really very polite."

A week later, Madame Maillard positions her hands over the keys the way Herr Glik has shown her.

"Like this?"

"Very good."

It is her first lesson. She does not expect she will have much time for piano once she is pregnant, which she expects will be soon.

She does not foresee it will take, as it does, ten years and five mis-carriages before she holds Pierre in her arms, perfect except for something odd about his eyes. She does not expect to give up hope of ever having a child, to seek comfort in her power to bring down tiny hammers on the sonorous strings, to learn from Herr Glik how to expel music from her body and send her sorrow with it. She does not expect another war to come, that she will play for hours so the Gliks, in the attic, can listen.

"C major scale, please," he says. "Like we discussed."

Feeling foolish, peering nearsightedly at the black dots arrayed on the pages in front of her, she presses the keys.

"Yes," he says, "but don't worry about looking at the paper now. It's very simple. Only white keys. One note follows another, follows another, follows another. So."

He demonstrates, leaning over her shoulder to reach the keys, singing the names of the notes in his soft voice and clipped accent as he goes. "Now two octaves," he says.

As he reaches the high C and begins to descend, she interrupts. "Herr Glik, you play so much more beautifully than I ever could. What if you came every week and played while I listened? I would pay the same rate, and it would be so much nicer, don't you think? I will be a mother soon anyway, so there's really no point in you taking the trouble to teach me. It would be a waste of your time."

He sits in the spindly dining chair she placed for him beside her piano stool and regards her from above his long, unfashionable mustache. "Madame Maillard," he says, "I'm sure you will be a wonderful mother and very soon, but we can't know the future. If you wish to study the piano only to while away the hours, then we will part now as friends. But if you respect the instrument, you will not waste anyone's time. Those hours will pass, and you will put music into them, which, in my opinion, is a good."

She doesn't know quite what he means, but she is beguiled by the intensity of his gaze, the seriousness with which he is treating her intentions. "I'm not sure what to do," she says. She laughs a little.

Herr Glik has a new baby and is worried about money, about making a life in a new city. He says, "Think, too, how nice it will be for the baby to grow up with music in the house, to learn to play himself one day. Or herself."

She likes the thought. She imagines herself giving concerts for her friends, playing lullabies to soothe her baby. "Very well," she says. "Let us proceed."

Angel Lust

SIMON ORFF WAS on his third wife. He lived with her in a glassy beach house in Malibu. His second wife had returned to New York after their divorce, and his first, Holly, the mother of his two daughters, his only children, lived with them and Simon's successor in the hills just below the Hollywood sign. Vanessa, or Van, was seventeen, and Monterey, called Monty, was thirteen.

On a Friday afternoon in October, a clear day with little surf, Simon stood on his balcony smoking a cigar and scrolling through his phone while he waited for Holly to drop off the girls.

"Dolphins," Natalie, his current wife, called from inside.

Simon glanced at the ocean. Dorsal fins rolled up through the water. "Yeah," he said, but apparently not loudly enough because she appeared in the sliding door, leaning against its edge, one bare foot flexed against the other's top.

"Did you see?"

"I saw," he said. "Beautiful."

She came to press against his back, her forehead between his shoulder blades. "Very convincing," she said into his shirt.

Simon suspected she was using him as a windbreak, as she was underdressed even for the warm day, in tiny shorts and a thin T-shirt. Whenever Holly came to the house, Natalie, who was twenty-six and as compact as a gymnast, showed skin and bounced around and chirped in a higher, more cheerful voice than usual. No one could say Natalie didn't make an effort. After two years of marriage, she still acted like she was trying to charm Simon into a second date.

"Doorbell," Simon said, stubbing out his cigar and taking her hand as he went to answer. He was not above flaunting Natalie to Holly, though he'd never gotten a perceptible rise out of her with any of his women, not even the TV actresses or the movie star. Holly had the self-control of a Zen master. When he had allowed her to discover his cheating, she had not made a scene, had simply spent a few weeks closing herself to him and then left. He had not cheated because he stopped wanting her—he *still* wanted her, years later—but, even so, he had succumbed to anticipatory horror of her aging, of losing his desire. Lasting satisfaction seemed impossible when more women were always springing up, when there were so many points of comparison walking around, so many what-ifs.

Before he gave up on shrinks, one had suggested he might be a sex addict, but he thought of himself as more of an idiot savant, terrible at love but almost mystically in touch with the grand biological suction that pulled people together.

Vanessa and Monty were standing well back from the door when he opened it, slumped in identical, defeated postures against the waist-high Buddhas that decorated his walkway, arms folded across their chests. An abundance of suitcases were strewn around their feet. Both had long yellow falls of bleached and curled hair and wore interchangeable Bohemian getups: flimsy dresses, bare legs, and loose boots drooping with straps and buckles. Their faces were dwarfed by huge sunglasses, and Van cradled her Chihuahua, Scarlett, in the crook of her arm. Holly, perceptible through the tinted windows of her SUV only as more sunglasses and pale hair, waved and drove off. Simon watched his gate close slowly after her bumper. According to Van, she had taken to describing their marriage as a *misunderstanding*.

"Ladies!" said Natalie. "Looking fly, as always."

The girls stared her down. "Thanks," Monty said finally, flinching slightly, torn between an instinct toward politeness and fealty to her sister, who hated everything chipper, especially Natalie.

By the time Simon had grabbed his bag and kissed Natalie goodbye, Van had already opened the back of his Range Rover and was heaving in the first of her suitcases. Monty dropped the dog through the open window of the backseat.

"Are you sure you don't want me to come?" Natalie said, trailing after him. "I'd be *happy* to."

"No," he said. "You stay here." Natalie's presence would complicate things beyond usefulness. He assumed she understood in some way that he was bringing the girls along as a distraction, a talisman against the grimness of his task. If he had to referee their squabbles and navigate their quicksilver emotions while sifting through his dead father's possessions, he hoped the house would not seem so empty, or he hoped at least the emptiness would feel more neutral.

"I would say—again—that we don't want to go," Van said when they were all in the car, "but you don't care."

"Not even a little," he said. "You overpacked. It's only one night."

"We like having our things," Monty said with the breezy air she adopted when quoting Vanessa.

He steered south along the Pacific Coast Highway, past fish restaurants, past the secretive gates and garages of other beach houses and blinding stretches of ocean, then cut east, headed north, eventually merging onto the 5, the state's jugular. The girls sat together in back, looking at their phones, their ears plugged with little white buds and their eyes concealed by their sunglasses. Van jiggled Scarlett as though she were a colicky baby. The dog emitted a constant high-frequency whine that was almost, but not quite, out of Simon's hearing.

"Monty, what did you learn in school today?" he said.

The girls each plucked out one earbud. "What?" said Monty.

"I asked what you learned in school today."

"You're such a cliché," said Van. In a dumb-guy voice, she mimicked, "What did you learn in school today, little lady?"

"I wasn't talking to you," he told Van. "You don't go to school." Van was studying for her GED with a tutor. Pursing her lips, she sealed off her exposed ear and turned to the window, tucking Scarlett's skull under her chin.

"When can *I* stop going to school?" Monty asked.

"When you have a PhD," Simon said. He'd never gone to college but had put a degree from UC Santa Barbara on his résumé. No one had ever found him out, not even his wives. He was both proud and ashamed of all of it. "Come on. What did you learn?"

"Lots of stuff."

"What stuff?"

"I don't know. Like some stuff about the gold rush. And! Oh my God, did you know a corpse can have a boner?"

Loudly, over music only she could hear, Van said, "I knew that."

"They taught you that in school?" Simon asked Monty.

Monty waved a hand. "It's what I learned. I think it's gross."

"I think it's cool," said Van, still too loud. "One last hurrah."

"It'd be so embarrassing," said Monty.

"You're dead anyway. You can't be embarrassed."

"But what if I'm hovering above myself watching myself be dead?"

"Actually," Simon interjected, "they call it angel lust."

"Call what angel lust?" Monty said.

"When a corpse"— he stopped himself from saying *gets excited*— "has an erection."

"Why do you even know that?" Van demanded.

"It's a term. People who deal with dead bodies use it. A friend of mine—"

"What friend?" Van always wanted to know the players.

"Mitch Kettlebaum. He was at Universal with me. When he was a kid, he was home sick from school, and his mom was out of town for some reason. So his dad brought him along to work, which would have been fine except his dad was a coroner. He sat Mitch at a desk piled with folders and told him to do his homework or whatever, keep himself busy. But Mitch started opening the folders, which had all these grisly photos, and in one was a full-size glossy photo of a guy in a dress hanging from a banister with a belt around his neck and his, ah, equipment out."

In the mirror, Van nodded sagely. "Autoerotic asphyxiation," she said.

"The twist was that the guy was wearing his mother's dress, Mitch said, and she was the one who found him."

"How old was he?" Monty asked.

"I don't know. Middle-aged."

"No," she said, "your friend."

"Oh. Ten or eleven, maybe." Simon had always thought there was the seed of a movie in Mitch's anecdote. At least a great scene.

"That's horrible," Monty said. "His dad sounds really irresponsible."

"Dad let us see all those horror movies when we were little," Van said.

"Movies aren't real," said Simon.

Two years previously, without consulting Simon, Holly had yielded to Vanessa's begging, found her an agent, and taken her around on auditions, and when Van was still sixteen Simon had found himself sitting in a movie theater watching her get her throat slit in a low-budget horror flick. Then, right after the film came out, Holly informed him that she had walked in on Van having sex with her boyfriend in Holly's bed. ("But we put a towel down," Vanessa explained.) The boyfriend in question was a television actor, a player of bit parts on crime, law, and medical shows: a teenage murder suspect here, a cancer patient there. Simon knew, even if the boy didn't, that his looks and talent would not age well, and he would vanish from the scene soon enough.

Vanessa, on the other hand, had the potential to be a star, at least for a little while—her golden beauty compensated for her mediocre acting—but now Simon could not look at her without seeing her either being murdered or having sex. That Van so strongly resembled her mother didn't help, nor did the fact that he had first bedded Holly when she was Vanessa's age. Seventeen and a star high jumper, an L.A. girl with parents too committed to being cool to disapprove of their daughter running around with an older man. Simon had been twenty-five, still a studio lackey, a dusty country mouse disguised in suits bought at Saks from a sympathetic saleswoman who gave him discounts in exchange for his going as her date to events where her ex-husband would be. He had slept with the saleswoman a few times, all the while thinking of Holly, of Holly's legs, long and tan and perfectly relaxed as she sailed backward over the bar. If he could have chosen a moment to freeze time, he would have stopped her just before her dangling ponytail touched the fat, blue cushion, the toes of her white track shoes pointing at the sky.

The freeway drew the Range Rover out of the city and up over the Santa Monica Mountains, down and then up again toward Tejon Pass. The dry grass was a perfect golden yellow, the color some Beverly Hills stylist had tried to make his daughters' hair. Grazing black cattle were so dark against this luminosity that they appeared as voids, four-legged holes to starless space. The gray pipes and open chutes of the aqueduct climbed up and slid down among the dams and artificial lakes. On the other side, as Simon descended the winding Grapevine into the San Joaquin Valley, a dusty haze hung over the fields and orchards, muting the green of the leaves and making the whole place, a fertile place, seem barren.

They passed a feedlot of shit-crusted Holstein cows milling around towers of hay bales. Monty said, "Those are just milk cows, right?"

Simon nodded. "Right."

"They still get slaughtered," said Van. "Dairy cows aren't retired to a petting zoo somewhere."

"Why would you tell me that?" Monty said. She had always been a softhearted child, outraged by the mistreatment of innocents. "I didn't need to know that."

"You're not even a vegetarian," said Van.

"Yes, I am," Monty said. "Right now, anyway."

"Monty's doing the Master Cleanse," Vanessa told Simon, holding Scarlett up to her face and pursing her lips.

"Which one is that?"

Monty waved a metal water bottle at him in the mirror. "Water, cayenne pepper, maple syrup, lemon juice."

"That's all you're eating?"

"Plus the laxative teas," Vanessa said. "You wouldn't believe what comes out of you."

"I don't like this," Simon said.

Monty shook her head fervently. "No, it's good. It gets all these toxins out of your system. Mom does it sometimes."

"Toxins," Simon repeated.

"I read that Delia does it," Van said.

Delia Fairbanks was the star of a film Simon was producing, a teen comedy called *Curfew*. "Delia does lots of things I wouldn't want you to do," he said.

Vanessa leaned forward between the seats, radiating anger. He had refused to cast her, and she had not forgiven him. "Like what? Be in movies?"

Delia, who was twenty-one, was trying to sleep with Simon. Delia was a cokehead. Delia was bulimic. Delia had an enema once a week—she had told him herself. Delia cried when she accidentally ate cheese. "She spends all her free time reading books," he said, "and she goes to bed by nine every night. She's taken a vow of celibacy, and she's sworn off shopping."

"Shut up," Vanessa said. "That's not true."

THE HOUSE WHERE Simon grew up was plain, square, small, and stucco, lonely in an infinite flatness of farmland. Simon had not been inside for five years. He had driven out every Christmas to collect his father, but Alfred was always waiting at the end of the gravel driveway, standing beside the green duffel bag he'd had since his army days. Once Simon was an hour late on purpose to see if the old man would give up and go back inside or at least sit down, but there he'd been, standing on the road's dusty shoulder, patient as a mailbox. Alfred hadn't said anything when he got in the car, just turned on Rush Limbaugh and folded his arms. Simon had felt bad enough to wait half an hour before wordlessly switching off the radio. The old man had died without fanfare and rotted in his armchair for at least two weeks before the guy checking the gas meter spotted him through the window.

Bell peppers grew in the fields around the house, land that had once belonged to Alfred, but the old man had sold it off to a conglomerate except for a few acres where he kept a row of orange trees, some dust and gravel, and bits of farming equipment too rusted to sell. As far as Simon knew, his father hadn't been with a woman since his mother. Difficult to believe that in thirty years, Alfred hadn't found a lonely neighbor, a weathered floozy in a bar, a hooker, someone. Simon's mother had died young: an aneurysm at forty-eight, when Simon was still in high school. Simon would be forty-eight in a month, an age that had once seemed impossibly distant, too young to die but old enough to be fully formed, and would have seemed insignificant, just another year, if his mother's death had not turned forty-eight years into its own unit of measurement, a lifespan.

As he turned into the drive, dust rose up and settled on the Range Rover's shiny black hood. The house looked as it always had except for a swathe of tiles the wind had pulled off the roof and deposited near the front door in a heap of red shards. Alfred's beater truck was parked off to the side. In the far distance, mountaintops hovered against the newsprint sky, their bulk obscured by haze. A key used to be hidden under a rock, although Simon couldn't be positive it still was. He stooped, pawing around while the girls loitered in the car, unwilling to concede they had nowhere else to go.

"Found it!" He held up the key but elicited no response from the Range Rover. He went and tapped on the window. Inside, Scarlett yipped faintly. He tapped until they opened up.

When they were all finally in the house, standing on the gritty tiles of the dark entryway and peering into the afternoon murk, Monty said, "I think I smell something bad."

"No," said Simon, though he, too, was straining for any lingering, morbid whiff of his father. "The cleaners have been here. The chair was the problem, anyway, and that's gone."

Vanessa set Scarlett down on the tiles. The dog lowered herself to sit, found the tiles too cold for her bald little ass, and assumed a bow-legged crouch instead, shivering and pop-eyed. The girls, floating in their pale, diaphanous dresses and surrounded by their excess of luggage, looked like storybook figures, a fantasy of orphans. "Why can't we stay in a hotel?" Vanessa asked.

"There isn't one for forty miles," Simon said, flipping a light switch without effect. "We're going to go through everything and take what we want. Then we can go home."

"I feel bad looting Alfred's stuff," said Vanessa. The girls had always referred to their grandfather by his first name.

"Why? You loot your mother's things all the time." For emphasis, he nudged a monogrammed suitcase with his loafer. "Say goodbye to the house while you're at it. The people who bought the land are going to tear it down." He hit another switch, and a lamp fluttered to life.

Monty's eyes filled with tears. "You sold it?"

"To the pepper farm."

"You didn't tell us that," she said passionately. "Why can't we keep it?"

"It's not a puppy," Van said.

"You always say you hate it here," said Simon. "I could never get either of you to come see Alfred."

Vanessa scooped up Scarlett and started jiggling her again. "It's not like you came here either. That's why Alfred was dead in his chair for so long."

"He was dead in his chair because he was a hermit with no friends. It wasn't my fault."

"Just admit it. You didn't care about him." Van had Holly's way of pushing out her jaw and raising her eyebrows, and Simon's temper was goosed as if by his ex-wife.

"The day I was finally going to leave here," he said, keeping his voice low, "Alfred slashed the tires of the car I'd bought with my own money. He pretended he didn't know anything about it. He said some local kids must have done it—Mexican kids, he said—but I know it was him." Simon had been twenty and had been forced to spend another summer at home, working, saving up to buy new tires before he went to L.A. It wasn't as though Alfred liked having him around. He was just afraid that if Simon left, he'd surpass him. To the girls, Simon said, "I had to hitchhike to college. Alfred sold off his land for nothing just to spite me. He ruined himself to make me feel guilty."

"How do you know it was Alfred who slashed the tires?" Monty was still near tears. Simon wondered how she survived such an emotional life. She was like Scarlett, exhausting herself in a tizzy of muddled feelings and then collapsing into extravagant periods of sleep.

"I just do."

Vanessa looked distressed, but her voice still reached for

haughty. "How was I supposed to know anything about your relationship with Alfred?" she said. "If you told me anything ever, then I wouldn't think the wrong thing all the time."

Simon stared at her. He had long since given up on having any influence over Vanessa's thoughts. "*Everyone* thinks the wrong thing all the time," he said. "It's not a big deal."

SIMON BYPASSED his own room. He knew what was in there: nothing. A bed with a naked mattress. A desk with empty drawers, an empty closet.

He went to his father's bedroom and started going through the bureau. He felt a twinge of sadness for the socks and graying T-shirts he dropped in a trash bag, some stingy echo of Monty's grief for the doomed house. Tired old suspenders, red paisley hankies, belts. He remembered sorting through his mother's things. The clothing of the dead emanated a melancholy as pungent as mothballs.

"There's nothing here," Vanessa said from the doorway. "Seriously, I've never seen someone with so little stuff. All I'm taking is this." She held up a record, *Hymns by Johnny Cash*.

"Do you have a record player?"

"Fine," she said. "I won't take it."

"I only meant that you could take Alfred's record player, too."

"I don't want a whole *record player*. Just . . . never mind."

Irritated, Simon pulled open the last drawer, extracted a pile of frayed BVDs, and added them to the trash. In the back of the drawer was a tin of dried-out black Kiwi shoe polish and a postcard from Mexico City. He turned the postcard over. Nothing. Not even an address or stamp. The surface of the dresser, too, was bare.

Cynthia, Simon and Natalie's decorator, was always complaining about how he cluttered up her tranquil, minimalist designs with impulsively purchased objets d'art, like the four-foot-tall electric-green vase acquired while filming a rom-com in Paris. "Nothing should even try to compete with this spectacular view," she had said, opening her arms to encompass his enormous windows, the distant horizon, Natalie on the couch. But Simon didn't like expanses, flatness. The Malibu house made him uneasy. He preferred Holly's neighborhood with the winding streets, high walls, and cascades of bougainvillea that conjured, for Simon, the secluded, beguiling atmosphere of a harem.

Van gave a big sarcastic wave. "Hello. Dad. This is terrible. It's boring. There's no cell service here."

Simon looked at his phone. "*I* have service." One little bar.

"That's great for you. I don't. And there's no Wi-Fi. It's not okay you didn't tell us we'd be, like, cut off from the world. My friends will be worried."

"It's one day, probably. They'll survive. You'll survive. Can't you find something to do?"

"We're bored," Monty said by way of rebuttal, sidling around Vanessa and flopping on her back on the bed with her feet hanging off the edge. Her legs looked twiggy in her clunky boots. "This is sad and boring," she said to the ceiling.

"Why don't you two play outside?"

"I don't *play*," Vanessa said in disgust. "I'm not a *child*."

"Neither am I," said Monty.

But they went out anyway. From the bedroom window, Simon saw them sitting on plastic crates under the orange trees. When had childhood become such an embarrassment? He had not wanted to be young either, back when he was, but only because he had recognized that age and work and money would be his means of escape. His daughters wanted the allure of youth but not the simplicity.

Monty was combing Vanessa's hair with her fingers, and Vanessa was staring at her phone, probably willing a tendril of 5G to find it. Simon tried to fight off the usual images and failed: Van fucking, Van being murdered. Since when was boredom a humanitarian issue? Simon was bored, too, bored with his work, his children, his father's bleak possessions, his eager, nubile wife. Where was the person whose job it was to make him un-bored?

Delia Fairbanks had, at first, herded him into a sort of avuncular familiarity when he was on the set of *Curfew*, punching him in the belly, telling him odd lies and calling him gullible when he pretended to believe her, stealing his cigars. Then, while popping her small fists against the slight softness at his waist, she had said, "Should I be offended you haven't tried anything with me?"

"No," he said. "You should be relieved."

He was old and wise enough to avoid a mess as toxic as Delia. But then one day he had sat with her in craft services, and while she nattered at him, he watched her pick fat black olives out of her salad and eat them absentmindedly off her fingertips like a child. As she popped one black-capped finger into her mouth after another, he felt the beginnings of temptation. That seed of purity buried in so much counterfeit smut intrigued him. During his early career he had wanted to make gritty, uncompromising dramas, but he'd been destined for candy-colored high-school flicks and films that ended with a couple kissing, the camera pulling back to reveal a charming, sunny street, a skyline, back and back to suggest that the whole planet was merely an elaborate backdrop for this one kiss.

From the top shelf of his father's closet, Simon pulled down a red leather valise, a woman's bag, cracked with use and age, empty except for an ancient packet of marigold seeds and another postcard of Mexico City, also blank. Had his parents even been to Mexico

City? He had no idea. Probably his father had forgotten about the valise years ago. Probably there was nothing for Simon to decode, no secret message having to do with Mexico City. The paltriness of his father's possessions made them seem like clues to something, some larger mystery. In Simon's memory, his mother and father had been quiet in each other's company, placid, not affectionate, which he supposed for some people might be happiness and for others could be misery. In the bathroom, he found a threadbare towel and a dreary collection of old creams and ointments. Toenail clippers. A stray tube of lipstick turned pale and waxy. A straight razor. Simon was holding that murderous instrument up to the light, marveling at his father's technological stubbornness, when Vanessa said, "Dad."

He jumped and spun around. "What? What is it?"

Confronted with the razor, she looked surprised but not afraid. In the horror film, she had come into her pink-and-white bedroom, humming to herself, while the killer was hiding under her bed. From that angle, through the killer's eyes, the audience watched her strip off her cheerleading uniform. Then her ankles danced up to the bed, and the killer reached out and grabbed one. Van's thirty-foot-tall face had opened in a scream, showing the fleshy darkness at the back of her throat and her perfect white teeth. "I really need to check my phone," she said. "We're going out to get some food."

"I thought we'd all go to Louie's later."

"We're hungry now, and we hate that place."

"You don't hate Louie's. I thought Monty was only eating syrup anyway."

"I'm just riding along," Monty called from the bedroom. "Hey, whose bag is this?"

"Grandma's," said Simon, realizing he couldn't know for sure that the red valise and the lipstick had indeed belonged to his mother and not some other woman.

"I can't get it open," Monty said.

Simon craned around the doorway. Monty was not talking about the valise, which sat unnoticed on the dresser, but was lying on her stomach on the bed and fussing with something on the floor. He could see straight up her dress. The sight of her thong shocked him, a ruched purple *V* that disappeared between her shadowy, childish buttocks. He retreated back into the bathroom. "Where were you going to go?" he asked Vanessa.

"The truck stop back by the 5. They have a Subway. And Wi-Fi."

"You won't eat at Louie's, but you'll drive twenty miles to get a sandwich? We can go to the Chinese place instead."

"We hate all the places around here. People look at us too much."

"But of course you're not *trying* to attract attention." He made a sweeping gesture at her bare legs and clavicle, her eyeliner, her hair. "You're the one who wants to be in movies. Think of all the people who'll look at you then."

"I get *paid* to be in movies."

"In *a* movie."

She pushed her jaw out, just like Holly. "I wouldn't be getting paid to eat a hamburger at Louie's while a bunch of Mexicans stare at me."

"Don't be racist," Monty said in the other room, her voice muffled.

"People are Mexican here!" Van shouted back. "I'm just stating a fact."

"No," said Simon. "We're eating as a family."

"Oh my God!" Monty squealed.

"Is it so horrible that we'd eat together? Jesus!"

"Oh my God, oh my God!"

"What?" Simon said, going back to the bedroom. "What is it?" Monty had dropped from the bed onto the floor. She was pawing through an open briefcase he'd never seen before, full of photographs, hundreds of them, all of naked women.

"Get away from there," he said.

Monty leapt up onto the bed and rolled around, squeaking with shocked excitement.

"Let me see!" Van demanded.

"No." Simon scooped up the briefcase and set it on the dresser, his back to the girls. Van grabbed his arm. He shook her off. "Get away, Van!" He opened the case.

"Who are they of?" Van asked Monty. "Did Alfred take them?"

"Oh, my God," Monty said, breathless. "I think they're of Grandma."

Simon pushed the photos around. They were all of his mother, in a variety of poses, naked or wearing pushed-up nightgowns or big, plain bras but no panties, her skin canary yellow from the fading of the prints and the lamplight that had illuminated her on the same bed where Monty was currently burying her face in the pillows.

"It's true!" Van yelled in Simon's ear. She had snuck up behind him. "Oh, my God! She looks like a banana! A hairy banana!"

"Grandma and Grandpa were such freaks!" shouted Monty.

Vanessa threw herself onto the bed next to her sister. "What's so freaky about taking naked pictures? What do you know?"

"I know tons!" Monty shrieked. "I know more than you think!"

Simon looked from the mess of jaundiced skin and rampant bush that was his mother to the flailing legs and disheveled blond hair of his daughters. They were yelping and laughing, verging on hysteria, tussling the way dogs will when seeking release. He felt the early swelling of a nervous erection, the kind he used to get when he was around Monty's age.

"Stop!" he cried. "Enough!"

The girls went quiet and still, watching him. Monty lay on her side, crowded up against the headboard, her dress flipped up high on one thigh. Vanessa, lower on the bed and curled around her sister's legs, reached up and tugged Monty's hem down into place.

IN THE FIELD that abutted Alfred's property, hunched workers picked bell peppers and carried them in tall buckets on their shoulders to a truck parked between the rows. Simon stood on the front step and watched, fingering his cigar case in his pocket. Usually he loved the ritual of cutting and lighting, but now the prospect seemed tiresome and overwhelming. He wished he had some cigarettes, the Camels he'd smoked in his teens and twenties. He had tossed Van the keys to the Range Rover, told the girls they could go and eat wherever they wanted because that had seemed easiest, an efficient retreat from chaos. In the dusty gloaming, the peppers had the muddy color and dull shine of organs, hearts or livers. When it was nearly dark, another truck came for the workers, drove slowly away with them all crowded in the back. The truck with the peppers followed. He checked the time. Van and Monty had been gone more than an hour, and he had done nothing but stand and watch the harvest. Already he was turning into his father, becoming someone who stood and stared at nothing.

He went inside, sat on the sagging couch in weak lamplight, put *Hymns by Johnny Cash* on the record player, and considered what to do with the photos. Burning them seemed melodramatic, but he had no wish to take them home and begin decades of custodianship. He wondered where his father had gotten them printed and if he had been embarrassed to pick them up. Whenever Simon was single, he used an old nude Polaroid of Holly to bookmark whatever script or novel galley was on his bedside table. When he wasn't reading anything, he kept the photo under the pen tray in his desk and checked on it occasionally, wanting to make sure she was still there, only eighteen or nineteen, on her back in the rumpled sheets of an afternoon bed, legs crossed, face averted in giddy embarrassment. He would have to destroy that before he died; he should have destroyed it already.

He couldn't know what Vanessa had seen in his face or, heaven forbid, the contours of his pants that had made her cover up her sister. Sometimes he tried to imagine what life would be like if sex did not exist, if humans divided mitotically and there was no cause for the mess of desires that had led Simon to have had many, many lovers, more than he could remember. He had kept track for some years but eventually stopped counting, thinking it was better to forget, simpler. After all that, he could still be surprised by the real grief he could cause even the most casual partners. He took the necessary precautions, unspooled airtight, preemptively exculpatory talks about just having fun, keeping things light, but two people in the same bed, almost in the same body, could still operate according to radically different systems. During the act, he went away somewhere alone, somewhere internal but as empty as space, and then, while he came back unchanged, relieved of a simple pressure, sometimes—often—the woman underwent a mysterious shift, became euphoric but fragile, melancholy in anticipation of being discarded or flippant in an effort to conceal a new, hard edge of possession.

He always tried to do what was easy. He philandered when it was easy, married when it was easy. Decades on the path of least resistance and yet nothing was easier. Had it been easiest for his father to hole up in his house and wait for death? The photos revealed too much and also nothing. He didn't trust himself to discern healthy marital lust from compulsion or unwelcome obsession. Few of the photos showed his mother's face, and those that did captured a neutral, detached expression. He had seen, in harrowing close-up, the flesh from which he had emerged, but the meaning of those ruddy folds eluded him.

Johnny was singing "Snow in His Hair." Out the window, headlights appeared down the road, moving slowly. He went outside, thinking it must be the girls. Sure enough, the Range Rover turned and crept up the driveway, but the face behind the wheel was Monty's, stricken and staring. She rested her forehead against the steering wheel. He went around and opened her door. A strange smell struck him: perfume and teenagers, something sour underneath.

"Where's your sister? What are you doing driving?" he demanded. "*Why* are you driving?"

Monty shook with huge, infantile sobs. She lifted her hands imploringly and let them fall. He wondered how long it had been since she'd eaten.

"You don't have a license." He felt a twinge of vertigo. Did she have a license? It seemed possible he had lost track of his place in time, dropped through a few years without noticing. No, she was thirteen. He was sure. "Monterey?"

"There was a dog," she gasped. "Van hit it, and then she wouldn't stop."

"A dog?"

"It ran into the road. She didn't even try to miss it. I said to stop, to see if we could help it, but she wouldn't. She drove *faster*, Dad. She tried to tell me it was a coyote and not a dog—but it was a *dog*, I saw it, a gray *dog*—and then she said there was nothing we could do, but she didn't *know* that. And I called her a murderer, because she is. We could at least have tried. She's such a *bitch*. She thinks she's a movie star, but she's just a *fucking bitch*. She's a stupid cunt!"

How could Monty have this much passion even when she was half starved? Where did it come from? "Where is she?"

"At the truck stop. At Subway. I took the car when she was in the bathroom."

Her face, full of grief, was a child's face. Strands of hair clung to her damp jaw. Her mascara, streaking her smooth, downy cheeks, made her look like a tragic urchin, a child whore, Brooke Shields in *Pretty Baby*, Jodie Foster in *Taxi Driver*. He saw Van's face, thirty feet high and full of light, retreating from him, her lips parting as the knife rose into the foreground. His mother on all fours. Van wandering through a maze of parked semis while men leered and honked their horns. An animal tide washed through him. He wanted to strike Monty and to embrace her.

"All I wanted was to get through my life without running over a dog," she said.

"Monty," he said, "you can't worry about all the dogs in the world. It's too much."

"I'm sorry," she said, and he thought she meant about the dogs until he saw she was pointing at the passenger seat. Watery vomit had collected in the seams of the leather, an afternoon's worth of lemon juice, maple syrup, and cayenne pepper. She started to cry harder. "I'm really sorry."

"Okay," he said, patting her shoulder. "All right." He pulled his phone from his pocket. Still that stalwart little bar. "I'm going to call your sister. Do me a favor, and go get something to clean that up."

She slipped past him, then turned back, her face a mask of sadness. "Why did you bring us here?" she asked.

"I just wanted some company," Simon said, but she was walking away. He remembered how, when she was a child and had thrown a tantrum in the car, he had pulled over, dragged her by the arm to the road's grassy verge, tugged down her shorts, and whacked her twice on the ass. Monty had watched him over her shoulder with the same tragic expression he'd just seen, her small face coated again with tears.

A whimper came from the car. He opened the back door and found Scarlett on the floor, staring up at him with mournful, buggy eyes. He lifted the dog and held her quivering body against his chest with one arm, jouncing her the way Van did, like she was an infant. She felt fragile, as breakable as a bird. Van had been a small baby but not a fragile one, and he had never worried much about her getting hurt. He worried about her running away, being lost or taken. And now she was lost, and he was doing nothing. He was too afraid, too daunted by the scene that must ensue—the scolding, the mediating, the reconciling—even to call her, to retrieve, at least, her voice.

His phone buzzed against his palm, startling him. It was Holly.

"I'm in the car," Holly explained, her voice cutting in and out. "On my way to pick her up."

"She called *you*?" Simon said. "You're driving all the way out here? That's crazy. I'll get her. I'll be there in half an hour."

"No, I'm already on my way, and she specifically wanted me to come."

"So now I need to be finessed."

"It's not like that," she said. "We all know women aren't your strong suit. I mean, they are but they aren't. We're trying to make this easier for everyone. It will be better if I'm there."

She was manipulating him—*easier*—but, in spite of himself, he relaxed. "You should have called me. It would have been helpful to know my thirteen-year-old was driving around by herself at night."

"What would you have done? Chased her down on foot? Called the cops?"

"Why wouldn't Van just stop and see if they could help the damn dog?"

"She says she couldn't deal."

"What does that mean?"

"She didn't want to know if it was dead. She didn't want to see it up close. She was afraid."

"That's no excuse," Simon said, knowing he would have been afraid, too.

MONTY WAS MILLING around the kitchen with her wretched water bottle, and Simon sent her outside to work on his passenger seat with towels and some saddle soap he'd found in a cupboard. After she sopped up the mess and cleaned the leather, a mania seemed to take possession of her, driving her to soap and polish all the other seats and to clean every crevice of the dashboard. Then she uncoiled Alfred's ancient garden hose and washed the car in the dark. "You don't have to do any of this," he told her. "I only wanted you to clean up your puke."

"I just want to, okay?" she said. "I need to keep busy." She crouched down, sponging a hubcap. The bottom of her dress had gotten soaked, and the hem dragged in the dust and gravel. "I need to *do* something."

"You should eat."

"No!" She looked up at him, fierce but supplicating. "I have one more day. I won't quit."

"Okay," he said, backing off. "One more day. Then you eat."

When they came up the drive, Simon was standing in the front door watching Monty buff the Range Rover with a towel. Holly's SUV stopped, humming a low note. The engine died, but the headlights stayed on. Van and Holly were getting the lay of the land, exchanging a few final strategic words. Simon, caught in the glare, shielded his eyes. Monty stood in the headlights, letting the towel drip, backlit in her filmy dress so that her body was a shadow in a glowing cocoon. Vanessa got out, arms folded over her chest, and came toward her sister. At first it looked like they would embrace, but then, with remarkable speed, Monty whipped Van across the face with the wet towel. Simon heard the slap but reacted slowly, almost dreamily. Van had dropped to the gravel, and Monty, shocking in her savageness, was already kicking her with one of her complicated, fashionable boots before he managed to move from the doorway. Vanessa rolled away, arms over her head, as Simon lifted Monty, still kicking, into the air and hauled her away. "She's not a person!" Monty was screaming. "She has no soul!"

His daughter's body was light but wild with anger, surprisingly strong. Van stood up, took a step in his direction. Blood dripped from her nose. Monty strained, wanting to be set loose, her boots scraping at the gravel. "Holly!" Simon shouted at the car. "Holly!"

Vanessa was a slapper and a clawer, and she went for her sister's face with messy swipes, catching Simon as often as not. Monty's boot heels scraped his shins as she kicked. Then Holly was there, too, behind Van, grabbing her arms and pulling her back until they'd opened a few feet between the girls. Monty stomped hard on Simon's foot. The pain was so sharp and so surprising that he let her go, or pushed her away, really, and she charged at Van and Holly, knocking them over and going down with them in a heap onto the gravel. "Quit it, you psycho!" Van yelled. "What is *wrong* with you?" Holly wriggled out from under Van and got to her knees, trying to separate them.

Simon limped for the hose, cranked it on. He pushed out a strong, cold spray with his thumb, aiming it at Monty, then Van, following them as they scrambled away, catching Holly accidentally at first and then coming back to her on purpose, as methodical as a hit man, spraying one then the other then the other, filling in any dry areas left on their clothes, riding a malicious high that he would never quite understand and that would still trouble him years later. He had always perceived a chaos in women about to break loose. Now he was driving it back into them, putting shattered pieces back together like film run in reverse.

When he still lived in this house, he had seen his father break up a dogfight this way, driving the snarling animals apart, filling their snouts with water so they grimaced and sneezed.

"Simon," Holly shouted. "Stop! Enough!" He kept spraying. Holly picked herself up, ran back to the house, and turned the water off. The hose drooped in Simon's hand.

"What are we doing?" Holly said. "What kind of family is this?"

Simon and the girls looked at one another in guilty solidarity, codefendants. The word *family* took him aback. He did not think of himself as having a family, only wives and children.

"This is bad," Holly said. "This is really bad. What the fuck? All of you."

In the headlights, the thin jersey of her long-sleeved shirt, now drenched, showed the elastic edges of her bra, the line of her ribs, the shallow dimple of her navel. Holly was not so different from how she'd been—the lithe high jumper, the young body in his faded Polaroid. He had been young, too, on the other side of the camera, just being a little kinky, taking a picture of his girl, wanting to preserve that afternoon and the vision of her body on the bed and the way he'd felt. He had been unaware of how time would flow through the photo like water through a grate. Van and Monty sat crying on the gravel, ghosts of their mother. The man and woman who had conspired to make that Polaroid had made them, too. Simon might have fanned them into being as he waved the snapshot in the air, waiting for the image to appear. When he went back to L.A., he would destroy it. Like his father's photos, it was a memento of a loss that had already been endured.

La Moretta

When we came back, the people were gone.

Gone?

Well, they were watching from the windows. I could see their faces. And an old lady was praying in the road.

And then what happened?

I got out of the car.

And then?

I don't remember.

Let's go back to the beginning.

Again?

Yes.

Where's the beginning?

Start with the dog.

THE DOG WAS a black-and-white thing, patchy and shaggy as though stitched together from pelts of smaller animals. Bill had been certain it was menacing them, stalking toward Lyla with its head down and its weird, pale eyes fixed on her, and when it came close, he jabbed with his boot and caught it on the haunch, sending it skittering sideways. Once out of range, it hesitated for a moment—tail tucked, milky gaze moving mutinously between Bill's feet and the pavement—before it turned and trotted away across the square, disappearing down an alley.

"I hope that made you feel big," said Lyla.

"I was protecting you," Bill said.

"What a hero," she said. "He was only looking for food. He came close because I held out my hand. And then you kicked him. You kicked a hungry dog."

"A *feral* dog. He looked like he was about to attack. He could have given you rabies."

Lyla took a floppy Romanian cigarette from her purse and lit it, squinting. She had announced she would quit smoking after they got back, after she took her RN exam, and she seemed to be trying to cram a lifetime's worth of cigarettes into these weeks of connubial bliss. "You're the one who wanted an adventure," she said.

Since the beginning of their honeymoon, whenever something went wrong she had been eager to remind him of that, asking, *Is this enough of an adventure for you? Aren't adventures fun?* But here they were, in Bucharest, sitting on the edge of a fountain and looking at an elegant, dormered building that could have been in Paris except for the soldiers standing guard in ill-fitting green uniforms. Even the flag flying from the mansard roof looked almost French, except for its yellow middle and its coat of arms: wheat and a red star and an oil drill. They would reach Paris eventually, near the end of the trip, but the thought of the time and travel separating them from the City of Light exhausted Bill. In the near distance, an enormous cement-slab apartment block was going up, nursed by three wobbly cranes.

It was July 1974. They had graduated from Boston University, gotten married, and departed directly for Europe. For Christmas, Lyla's parents had given them a thousand dollars for a honeymoon, sowing the seeds of months of argument. Bill wanted an adventure, but Lyla, who had already had too many adventures, wanted to relax. She wanted sun and wine. They should rent a house in Italy, she said, and just stay put.

"But where's the thrill?" Bill had asked.

"We could take a side trip," Lyla said, "and drive over the Alps into Switzerland. That's fun."

"So you've already done it," he accused her, and, reluctantly, she admitted she had. When she was sixteen, she and some friends had driven from Paris to Genoa and taken a ferry to Tangiers.

"Was Froggy there?" he demanded.

"Guillaume was the one with the car."

Tell me about Guillaume.
He was some French kid. She gave it up to him.
You resented that he took her virginity.
I don't think that's so unreasonable.
You resented her for not being a virgin.
No. If I did, it was only a little.
There were others besides Guillaume.
Yes.
Were you a virgin before Lyla?
No.
Don't lie.

If you already know the answers, then why all the questions?
If I already know the answers, then why lie?

LYLA'S FATHER WAS an army colonel, recently and bitterly retired, and she had grown up all over the world. Bill was from Worcester. He had been outside the country only twice: once as a teenager to visit his uncle in Toronto, and once when he was seven, right after his father left, when his mother had taken him to Bermuda. Of Bermuda, he remembered cars on the wrong side of the road, pink buildings, and his mother losing her temper when he ordered shrimp cocktail and then refused to eat it.

As a compromise, Bill and Lyla spent the first week of their honeymoon in Venice, and then they had rented a car, a stubby white Simca, and driven into Yugoslavia, all the way down to Dubrovnik and back up to Sarajevo and over to Belgrade and into Romania. After Romania, they would carry on to Hungary and Czechoslovakia, skirt East Germany, pass through Munich to France and Switzerland, and fly home from Italy, their marriage tempered by almost two months of very thrifty travel. Driving in Europe made Bill nervous, but even though Lyla was always mentioning that she wouldn't mind taking a turn, he insisted she be the passenger and enjoy the view. She rode curled into a ball, thin arms folded across her chest and bare feet on the dashboard, her toes leaving little smudges on the windshield and her dress falling back to expose a curve of haunch. From time to time he reached over and sent an investigative finger under the elastic of her underwear, seeking the familiar sticky mysteries, puzzling over his legal possession of them.

The week in Venice seemed to revive Lyla, making her cheerful at dinner and more playful in bed than since before their engagement. She had also admired Dubrovnik with its blue harbor and red-roofed Old Town, but Bill had not cared for the city. The blank stone faces of the medieval walls and the hulking forts with their suspicious-seeming slit windows gave him the creeps.

Why else didn't you like Dubrovnik?
  I didn't like the food.
  Why else?
  We had a fight.
  About what?
  Nothing. I'd had too much to drink.
  The truth has already been recorded.
  All right, I was upset.
  About what?
  Her past.
  You hounded her. You wouldn't let her sleep.
  I guess that's true.
  How did she respond?
  She said she was different now, that there was no point in bringing all that up. But eventually she told me everything. I think she wanted to—she didn't seem too bothered. I already knew some of it, the stuff that wasn't so seedy. But the rest was worse than I thought. Drugs and men, stupid risks. She had run wild. I wasn't sure whether to believe her.
  How did you respond?
  I told her she didn't seem fresh to me anymore. I told her she seemed used up.
  Then what?
  She laughed. She said if she was used up it was because of me.

Then what?

In the morning, we tried to be sweet with each other again.

Then what?

EAST OF BELGRADE, the Simca's ignition locked up, and the only solution was for a blacksmith to cut through the steering column with a hacksaw so Bill could hot-wire the car every time he needed to start the engine. At the Romanian border, a long line of cars waiting behind them, a guard inspected their passports and then stood and watched, puzzled, fiddling with his rifle, while Bill smiled out the window and tried to seem casual as he reached under the steering wheel and twisted two wires together to spark the starter. Lyla had taken a grim satisfaction from his sweaty anxiety.

Bill liked Bucharest less than Dubrovnik. He had been curious about the city since high school, when Nixon visited. On TV he'd seen rows of soldiers in white gloves, crowds lining a grand boulevard, a triumphal arch, Nixon standing in his limo and waving with both arms while Ceauşescu, weak-chinned and beaming, patted him on the back. But the people seemed dour and grudging. Few spoke English. He did not like the roving dogs or the food or the dark, fusty beer or the looks of the Stalinist apartments that were sprouting up everywhere. Density in general unnerved him, which was why he had spent only one semester in a dorm at Boston University before moving to the boardinghouse in Brookline where he had met Lyla.

She lived in the room directly above his and kept a nursing student's odd hours, and he had gotten to know her first from the French jazz that seeped through his ceiling and her footsteps in the dark hours of the morning. She asked him up for coffee, a thick, Turkish variety, and he had become intoxicated by the story of her peripatetic military upbringing—the years in Berlin and Bangkok and Paris—and by the exotic trinkets that decorated her room and the rich bitterness of the coffee. He was not surprised at her interest, her first invitation (he was very good-looking, and girls had invited him for coffee before), but he was surprised when she asked him to stay and took him to bed. Something about him had seemed to disappoint the other girls, snuffing out their flirtatious lights and making them distant and distracted before they could consummate anything, but Lyla's sharp attention never faltered. She pressed him for details about Worcester: the heavy snows, the thuggish Howard family that had shared a clapboard duplex with Bill and his mother, his brick high school, his failure to make the hockey team. She had a stern, dark, compact beauty that was undiminished by the old peacock-blue robe she favored when at home, the silk tattered under the arms to a loose mesh of threads. She smoked brown cigarettes with gold tips. She drank wine with lunch, but he never saw her drunk.

You fell in love with her.
 I thought I did.
 What do you mean?
 It was all poses, and I fell in love with the poses.
 She tricked you?
 More like I caught her when she was in the middle of shedding a skin.
 Let's get back to the dog.
 What about it?
 What happened after you kicked it?

LYLA STOOD and walked quickly away, taking short, angry drags on her cigarette. Bill could see the soldiers watching her, studying the twitch of her ass under her paisley shirtdress. She was wearing red Dr. Scholl's sandals, and the clip-clop of the wooden heels startled some pigeons into flight. Bare toes in a foreign city seemed decadent to Bill, even dangerous, but she had brushed off his concern, remarking that his hiking boots must be sweltering. She disappeared down the alley where the dog had gone, and he went after her, ignoring the soldiers' smirks. The alley was narrow and sooty and turned several corners before spitting him out onto the edge of a traffic roundabout. Lyla was standing nearby, watching the cars and buses.

"I don't see him," she said.

"Don't worry about him," Bill said. "Street dogs are wily. Anyway, there's no shortage." He pointed to a grass medallion at the center of the roundabout where one dog was humping another and a third lay sleeping on its side. He took Lyla's hand. "Why do you love me?" he asked. It was a game they had.

"Because you're kind to animals." She fell silent, gazing through the traffic at the island of dogs. In his boots, his ankles prickled with heat. He squeezed her hand, prompting, and she said, "Why do you love me?"

"Because you are always realistic about danger. Why do you love me?"

"Because you're fearless. Why do you love me?"

She turned to face him. The end of the game was signaled by telling a truth. "Because you agree that we should leave here and go out into the country tomorrow," she said.

They left in the morning, Bill driving and Lyla with the map open across her lap. There wasn't much traffic, and they passed quickly out of the city and into a countryside of startling colors:

electric-green pastures, fields of sunflowers, yellow houses with blue roofs, lakes thatched with reflected reeds. By noon, they were in the Carpathian foothills, where fir trees and stands of birch edged the fields and villages were smaller and farther apart. They stopped in one and found gas for the Simca and stuffed peppers for lunch, and then they drove on, up the steepening slopes, occasionally passing gray factories with sinister black smokestacks and spindly water towers, the land inside their barbed-wire boundaries littered with rubble and corrugated pipes.

In Venice, Lyla had bought two carnival masks, one for each of them. The masks were made of thin, flexible leather, smooth on the outside and rough against the face. Bill's was white with a high forehead, two eyeholes, and a long, tapering beak, like that of a hornbill. It was called *medico della peste*, Lyla told him: the plague doctor. Lyla's mask was a simple black oval with round eyes, a straight nose, and no mouth. *Moretta*, she said the shopkeeper had called it, meaning dark. It was a ladies' mask, worn on convent visits. Bill's mask had two wide green ribbons to tie around the back of the head, but Lyla's had, on its underside, a black button. The button was held in the wearer's teeth, necessitating silence.

The Simca passed through a short, unlit tunnel. Lyla crumpled the map against the windshield, turned around in her seat, and, after some rummaging, came up with the plague doctor mask. She tied the ribbons behind her head.

"What are you doing?"

She swung her long white beak toward him. "Don't you like it?"

He looked at the familiar brown irises staring out of the two lifeless eyeholes. "It gives me the heebie-jeebies," he said.

"What will the locals make of it?" The leather snout turned her voice hollow. "Can you imagine some shepherd seeing us go whizzing by, a bird-monster riding shotgun?"

"You should take it off," Bill said. "We don't want to call attention to ourselves."

"Are you afraid? Is it the communists or the vampires?"

"Neither," he said. "We just shouldn't take unnecessary chances."

"We're not spies. They let us over the border even though we looked like Simca thieves. We're not going to get hauled off to the gulag because I'm wearing a mask. Don't be so timid."

"I'm not timid."

The mask blinked at him defiantly. Then she turned to look out the window and bumped her beak on the glass. Bill snorted. Her mouth, just visible under the mask's bottom edge, turned up. He put one hand on her knee. "Why do you love me?" he asked.

"I love your devil-may-care attitude. Why do you love me?"

"I love you because you know how to blend in. Why do you love me?"

The beak swung around. The eyes blinked. "I love you because you're nothing like my father."

"And I love you because you're going to take off that mask."

"No," she said.

She wouldn't take it off?
No.
Why?
I don't know. I guess she wanted to push my buttons.
Your buttons?
Listen, I already knew the marriage was a mistake.
When did you know?
Before we got married.
When?

LYLA'S FATHER, Colonel McHenry, had retired in a scandal around the time Lyla entered college and retreated to a house on an island in Maine that he bought cheap off his younger brother. Lyla's mother spent the winter and most of the spring and fall in Florida, where her sisters lived. "Gordon thinks winterizing a house means buying mittens," she told Bill. "He thinks fun is being blasted to bits by nor'easters. He thinks companionship is rabbits."

The rabbits lived in a row of hutches on the leeward side of the house and ate pellets and grasses and made more rabbits until the day came for each to have its neck snapped over a wooden dowel by the Colonel. Bill, on his first visit to the house, had mistaken the creatures for pets until the Colonel corrected him with stern impatience, saying, "I respect these animals, but I have no affection for them. They are a practical measure."

That visit took place the summer after junior year. Bill had met Lyla's mother once before, on a spring break trip to Florida, but never the Colonel. In Rockland, before they caught the car ferry, an old man ran a stop sign and hit the side of Bill's already beat-up Ford, crumpling Lyla's door so it would not open, and when they finally arrived at the house, she had to crawl over the shift and follow Bill out his side under the Colonel's unimpressed gaze. With his beard and curly hair, the Colonel looked more like a lobsterman than an officer, but he had the upright posture and shrewd eyes of someone who considered himself an authority. He barely looked at Bill when he shook his hand, and Bill understood that already he had been found wanting.

Over cocktails and dinner on the ramshackle deck, the Colonel said little, and afterward he stayed inside to listen to a discussion of the Watergate hearings on the radio while Bill and Lyla and Lyla's mother went for a walk. For most of that first night, Bill lay awake, alone on a mattress in a loft over the kitchen, his fingers worrying one of the rabbit-fur blankets that seemed to be everywhere, the leavings of the Colonel's winter dinners, fulminating about how the Colonel had no right to disapprove of him. After all, it was the Colonel who had allowed Lyla to acquire the pet monkey in Bangkok that would eventually bite her and give her a mysterious fever; the Colonel had looked the other way while Lyla and her Paris friends debauched themselves; it was on the Colonel's watch that Lyla had been defiled by Guillaume.

Lyla had been cagey about the reasons for her father's early retirement, so Bill had gone to the library and scrolled through reams of microfilm. The Colonel was known to be fearless but also eccentric and unforgiving. In France, Korea, and Vietnam, he had earned a Distinguished Service Cross, two Silver Stars, and two Purple Hearts. He had installed a brothel on his base near Nha Trang, claiming he was curbing the spread of VD. He allowed his soldiers to give the black power fist instead of saluting. There were rumors he had personally executed a grunt for raping a young girl, but the investigation went nowhere. Then, in a kamikaze act of defiance, he had gone on CBS and criticized an operation overseen by a superior officer in which the official body count of Viet Cong approached two thousand but only a hundred and forty-two weapons had been captured. If not for his exceptional record, he would have been court-martialed instead of being allowed to retire.

When the Colonel clanked a kettle onto the stove shortly after dawn, Bill woke with a sense of having been wronged. "Good morning," he said, looking down at the top of the Colonel's head.

"Morning," the Colonel said. "How would you like a swim?"

They walked down to the dock, bringing a thermos of coffee and two more rabbit blankets. A cold, thick fog lay over the water, which looked black and unfriendly. "We'll swim to the buoy," the Colonel said, stripping off his sweatshirt and walking out on the dock, throwing his arms around in circles to stretch his shoulders. The muscles on his back flattened and bunched.

"What buoy?" Bill called.

"Just keep up."

The water was colder than Bill had anticipated, frigid enough to make his chest constrict. He swam a panicky crawl, trying to avoid putting his face in. The Colonel vanished into the mist, and when Bill paused to get his bearings, he discovered that the dock, too, had disappeared. He listened for the Colonel's splashes, but the fog and water played tricks. Following his best guess, he struck off again, trying not to think about the darkness under him.

You thought he'd set you up.
I thought he was making a point.
He baited you into humiliating yourself.
It was some kind of macho thing.

WHEN HE NEXT PAUSED, Bill heard the Colonel calling, but he didn't respond. He listened and then swam on until his legs became too cold to keep up a strong kick, and his feet started drifting downward, tugged toward the bottom. He cried out, but his voice was barely a croak. He tried again. "Colonel! Colonel McHenry!" No answer. Bill kept jerking his feet up, away from the darkness. He wondered how far he had swum, if he had managed to go past the buoy or if he was still stupidly close to the dock. He thought about the man the Colonel had executed and about the long winters alone on the island, all that time to brood, to weave new, tangled notions of justice. Perhaps the Colonel had brought him out here to fake an accident, to keep him from Lyla.

Then came the Colonel's voice, and Bill answered, and the Colonel stroked out of the fog. "Keep your panties on," he said. "You're fine. Just float on your back." He grabbed Bill under the armpits and began propelling them backward. In a minute, a red buoy loomed out of the gray. "Let's take a break," the Colonel said. "Grab on." Bill clutched at a steel cleat. His feet, drifting forward with the current, touched the cold, slimy chain that held the buoy to its cement anchor down below, and he recoiled, bumping his knee on a sharp metal edge. He wondered if he was bleeding, if there were sharks. The Colonel, holding to a cleat of his own and studying him with dispassion, said, "Have you been watching the hearings?"

"I've b-been reading the n-newspaper," Bill said, teeth chattering, incredulous that the Colonel wanted to talk politics. "Lyla and I read that stuff all year, t-together. It was one of our h-habits."

"But you haven't been watching on TV."

"Not much."

"For God's sake, why not?"

"We've been . . . b-busy." Bill did not want to say the scandal terrified him: the naked pettiness, the accelerating doubts, the way the system seemed to be rocking on its foundation. He had been so pleased to vote for Nixon's reelection—the first time he'd been old enough to vote for a president.

"That's the one thing I wish I had up here: a TV. Just for now. I'd like to see their faces." The Colonel leaned his head back, dipping his hair, as relaxed as though he were enjoying a soak in a hot tub. Beads of salt water crept through his beard. "It's interesting," he said to the fog, "how you can tell yourself all kinds of horseshit and believe it."

"Denial," Bill said, trying to be agreeable.

"Not that telling the truth is always an unmitigated good."

"L-like when you went on the news."

The Colonel regarded him without expression. "Lyla told you."

"I looked it up."

"Since you went to all that trouble, I'll tell you I thought I was being courageous, but now I suspect I needed a means of escape." He seemed to mull his own words over for a minute, then, perhaps distracted by the uneven whistling of Bill's breath through his teeth, said, "You should have told me you weren't a strong swimmer."

"I can s-swim. This water is really cold."

"The temperature's over fifty. You should have half an hour no problem. It's fear that's getting you." He dangled casually from the buoy. "Lyla is very difficult," he said.

"I don't think so."

"She's still a child."

"I d-disagree."

"I can't stand to watch you shiver anymore. Roll over and I'll drag you in."

That was the day Butterfield told the Senate committee about the tape recorders. Bill, whose chill took hours to dissipate, was sitting under two rabbit blankets and drinking a cup of tea beside the radio when the fateful question was asked and answered. *Mr. Butterfield, are you aware of the installation of any listening devices in the Oval Office of the President?*

I was aware of listening devices; yes, sir.

The Colonel had slammed a hand down on the kitchen table and roared with laughter.

That night Bill and Lyla played the game for the first time, although Bill didn't mean it to be a game. They were walking along a rutted road with a flashlight while the Colonel stayed by the radio and Lyla's mother carried the remains of their lobster dinner down to the shore for the tide to take.

"Why do you love me?" Bill asked.

"Because you're such a good swimmer," Lyla said. "Why do you love me?"

"I'm serious."

"I'm serious, too. Why do you love me?"

Bill took a deep breath and looked up at the stars. He had never seen them so bright, sinking specks of light marking the depths overhead. "Because you make me feel like I'm part of a larger world. But, really, why do you love me?"

She laughed. "Because you don't secretly tape our conversations. Why do *you* love *me*?"

"I already told you. Why won't you be serious?"

"Tell me another reason."

"Lyla."

"I'm only playing. Just one more."

"All right." Bill thought for a minute. Then he said, "I love you because you are almost as useful as a dead rabbit."

"And I love you because you ate lobster shit."

"What lobster shit?"

"The green stuff."

"You aren't supposed to eat that?"

"Some people spread it on toast."

"Now your dad thinks I'm an even bigger imbecile."

"He probably thinks you just have a taste for it."

"Did Guillaume swim to the buoy?"

"Guillaume never came here." She was striding more quickly, and Bill hurried to keep up. "Once he and Dad raced up a volcano in Sardinia."

"Who won?"

"I'm not sure they ever said." The flashlight veered over the knotty trunks of windblown pines. "You know what I've always thought is weird about Nixon?"

"Nixon?"

"How happy he can look, even with that face. When people are applauding, he's positively radiant. He's a sunflower."

He tugged on her hand to stop her and took the flashlight and turned it off. The sky became even deeper. "Lyla, why do you really love me?"

She was a patch of darkness, faintly contoured. "I love you because you make the world seem smaller," she said.

That's when you knew?
   Well, that's when we got engaged.

LYLA REFUSED to take off the mask, and for two hours she and Bill did not speak. Bill held tightly to the wheel and concentrated on the road, trying to ignore the long-nosed white shape in the corner of his vision. By midafternoon the road had deteriorated, often shrinking to one narrow lane, and half a dozen times Bill came around a hairpin turn and was confronted by a rattletrap truck or startled cart horse and had to reverse back down the bend while the Romanian driver followed, gaping at Lyla in her mask. Potholes were a constant threat, and in places there was no pavement but only dusty, rocky gray clay. Rounding yet another corner, they saw a stone castle nestled between ridges, the sharp peaks of its red tile roof rising above the trees.

"I believe the Count is expecting us," Lyla said.

Bill ignored her. She reached up and untied the mask's ribbon, and her face, freed from its pale shell, was as stern and well-formed as always but also somehow novel, as unexpected as a pearl exposed by a shucking knife. The sight of her was such a relief that optimism crept through him. "There's my girl," he said. She was beautiful, after all, and he had loved her. He *did* love her, he thought. Maybe he just had cold feet. There was no reason you couldn't have cold feet even after marrying.

They had come to several junctions during the time when they weren't speaking, and Lyla had said "Right" or "Left," and he had followed without question. But now, as the castle disappeared behind them, Bill realized he had no idea where they were. The plan had been to drive through Brasov and then find a village in which to spend the night, but they had never come to Brasov. "So," he said, reaching over to twine his fingers in her hair, "where are we?"

"I don't know."

"What do you mean? You're the one with the map."

She pulled her head away from his touch. "I thought we would have an adventure."

"Are you saying you got us lost on purpose? Tell me you're not saying that."

"It's not such a big deal, Bill. We haven't been swallowed by a black hole. We're still on this earth. We're not in a hurry. There are roads that will take us from here to anywhere. We'll just find a village and spend the night, and then we'll ask which way to Hungary, and then we'll ask which way to Budapest, and so on."

"What village? We haven't seen one in an hour. We're on the edge of a cliff."

"We won't be forever. Just keep driving."

He stopped in the middle of the road.

"What are you doing?"

"I'm not driving until you look at that map and figure out where we are."

"We are precisely two miles from East Nowhere, Transylvania."

"Lyla, I am telling you to look at that map."

Lyla stared at him. Without breaking eye contact, she balled up the map and opened her door.

"Don't do it," he warned. But she got out of the car, walked to the rocky edge of the road, looked down at the narrow river far below, and chucked the map out into space. "You irresponsible bitch!" he shouted, wrenching open his door. "You stupid little girl!" He rushed at her, crossing the road in a few long strides, and she tensed and twisted away, dropping to a crouch.

She was afraid of you.

Only in that moment. Not in general.

You accused her of being insensitive to danger, and yet she thought you might push her over the cliff.

She was just reacting on instinct.

You hated her.

No. I was angry with her. I wanted her to be safe. I wanted us to be safe.

Then what?

We got back in the car.

AS LYLA HAD PREDICTED, the road soon became less precipitous, and within an hour they came to a village in a high valley. Bill, dismayed and relieved to see all the little peaked roofs, did not apologize. Lyla said nothing. They bumped down a muddy lane lined with small houses, mostly wood or plastered brick. They saw no evidence of an inn, and the people standing and gaping in doorways did not seem welcoming. They looked so much like something out of the Brothers Grimm that Bill wanted to laugh: the men in belted tunics, the women in head scarves and dresses with aprons. Both sexes wore leather boots or else woolly wraps around their shins, tied in place with leather thongs. A few children of indeterminate sex threw pebbles at their tires. On the outskirts, past a wooden church with a steeple pointed like a witch's hat, they came to a large house, separated from the road by a long dirt track and surrounded by fields. "Stop," Lyla said. Clutching her phrase book, she got out of the car and went jogging up the track and disappeared over a rise. Bill waited. A hay wagon passed, so tall and piled so high that when it was gone, wisps of hay dangled from the branches of the trees that overhung the road. When Lyla returned, she was flushed.

"We'll stay here," she told him. "It looks like some big old house that's been collectivized. I talked to the guy who seems to be in charge, and we figured out a price. It's cheap."

"Did you see the room?"

"I'm sure it's fine."

"Did they seem friendly?"

"Who?"

"The people in the house!"

"We don't have to be friends with them."

Bill steered up the track. An old man in a sheepskin jacket and straw hat was waiting. Beckoning for them to follow in the car, he tramped ahead, around the house, and down another track to a small outbuilding—a former barn or sheep shed, it looked like— with a crumbling tile roof and two Dutch doors. They parked and got out, and the old man, muttering, opened one of the doors and ushered them in. A faint stable smell persisted, but the room was empty except for a lumpy mattress on the floor, a low table with an unlit lantern on it, and a tusked, grimacing boar's head mounted on the opposite wall. Light came through the thick glass of a single high window, revealing a delicate tangle of cobwebs in the boar's open mouth. Still muttering, the old man took a green bottle and a small loaf of bread from the woolly interior of his jacket and set them on the table with a little bow. Then, like some ludicrous bellhop, he took Bill and Lyla back outside and gestured across a hayfield at a distant outhouse.

When he was gone, they sat on the mattress and gazed up at the boar. Its glass eyes were tiny and scratched, and its bristly hair, full of dust, stood up at odd angles as though caught in a breeze. The skin on its furrowed snout had begun to peel away.

"What is this room?" Bill said. "Does someone live in here?"

"Maybe they died," Lyla said. "Maybe it's haunted. Maybe it's a sex room."

Bill said he would take a walk. He set out across the hayfield. On its far side, men were mowing with scythes. They swung the curved blades into the tall grass and fat green swathes toppled over. Women followed behind with rakes, spreading the hay out to dry in the sun. Bill and Lyla had passed hundreds of haystacks on the drive, cylindrical at the base and pointed at the top with a pole sticking out the apex, and Bill thought they looked like primitive huts, their doors always turned secretively to the horizon. He paused to watch, soothed by the swish of cutting and the hum of the evening insects. The man nearest to him was young, around his age. His baggy trousers and boots were the same as the others', but instead of a tunic he wore a blue soccer jersey. Bill wondered if the man was married, and, as he wondered, the other noticed him and returned his stare. Bill didn't know if he should wave or speak or walk away, but finally the young man frowned and upended his scythe. Pulling a stone from a water-filled holster at his waist, he shook the drops off and began striking the stone against the blade, clanking and scraping. Bill walked on, through more fields, until he came to a long, narrow pond, green with algae. By then it was dusk, and before he made it back to the barn, the sky had bruised to purple-black. In the gloom, he hooked a foot in an animal's unseen tunnel and fell to his knees, his hands stung by the prickly aftermath of the reaping.

Lyla had lit the lantern. She was sitting on the mattress with the green bottle. He sat down beside her and took a swig. It was a sweet, strong wine, almost like a cordial. "Did you think I was going to push you off that cliff today?"

"I think I did."

He passed back the bottle. "I would never do that."

"The perfect crime," she said. "No witnesses. You could make up some story about me deciding to frolic on the edge of the road—everyone would believe you. Crazy Lyla makes her last bad decision."

"Why do you love me?" he asked, knowing what the answer would be.

"I don't think I do," she said. "I wanted to. I thought a nice American boy would be good for me." She took a drink. "Why do you love me?"

"I did—at first—but I haven't for a while." As he walked, he had thought about that question, playing a solitaire version of their game, but he had not anticipated the relief that poured through him like an elixir. The unexpected truth came to him that everything would be all right. They had no children, no assets. They could simply part ways like duelers taking an infinite number of paces.

Just like that.

We agreed we would finish out the honeymoon, enjoy the time together, and then we'd go home and get divorced.

And neither of you was offended not to be loved.

I don't think so. It made things so much easier.

You hated her.

I didn't.

You wished she didn't exist.

I just had everything wrong.

What did you have wrong?

I was trying to catch up with her past, but I couldn't even run in the right direction.

Then what happened?

You know what happened.

Tell me.

I went out to take a piss.

HE WENT INTO the hayfield and the chilly, sweet-smelling air and stood and peed where he was. The stars, as on the night he proposed to Lyla in Maine, were shockingly numerous. The Milky Way bloomed across the sky at an angle, and he realized he had always foolishly assumed he was traveling upright through space, as though the galaxy were a wheel and he the axis around which it revolved. But his body was not plumb to the universe; there was no up or down. He might be dangling headfirst over the sky or rocketing through it sideways—there was no difference. Shaking off the last drops, he felt full of the grandeur of the cosmos, and his penis, as though answering or mocking him, began to stiffen. Some similar spirit must have moved Lyla, because when he went back inside he found her lying naked in the lantern light, her face obscured by the somber black oval of the *moretta*. The plague doctor mask was beside her on the bed, and she picked it up and held it out to him.

Her eyes were steady as he tied on the mask. Looking at her face, he saw a concentric system of nested rings: the pale border of skin between the dark of her hair and the dark of the mask, then the black eyeholes encircling narrow rings of glossy white around narrower bands of brown around inky pupils. Her nipples, too, were circles within circles, and he wanted to bite them but his long white beak bumped her if he came too close. His eyeholes narrowed his field of vision, reducing her to an oblong picture, something seen through a periscope: the translucent, looming shape of his beak, her immobile forbidding face, the enticing soft body. The leather caught his eyelashes, dragging on his lids when he blinked. His hands crept into the picture, squeezing her arms and pinching her nipples. If he hurt her, she didn't let on. He thought about the button between her teeth and wondered if she would be able to hang on to it while she came. Perhaps she would bite it off.

Her hand approached, caressed his crooked proboscis, and he was surprised not to feel her touch, as though his nerves might have spread through the leather like mold. He pushed her legs apart, maneuvering his head between them like a camera. When his beak bumped against her, finding a vague cleft, some soft resistance, he realized again that he had been expecting to feel with it, even to smell with it. This charade of anonymity was what she had wanted, he decided, possibly from the moment she bought the masks, and only now that they had deconsecrated their relationship could he give her what she wanted. For once he was confident he was cutting a path untraveled by others.

She did not bite off the button, but her eyes rolled back, giving the *moretta* a blind, white stare. The plague doctor had slipped down, and Bill's orgasm was half suffocated in the snout, half blinded by the displaced eyeholes. They lay on their backs under the musty blankets, already full of nostalgia for each other. "Why is it called the plague doctor?" Bill wondered aloud.

"I asked the shopkeeper," Lyla said, "and it's something about what the doctors used to wear when they went around to see people with the plague. They'd stuff the nose with spices and dried fruit to purify the air. Of course they were actually just spreading the plague around. The guy tried to sell me the whole costume. There's a top hat and a long cloak, and a heavy stick to fight off the infected when they mob you in the street. That's what he called them: *infetti*."

"Morbid."

"Macabre," she said sleepily, rolling onto her side and facing away from him.

On the opposite wall, the half light flattened the boar's peeling snout and cast a sheen on its dusty, rumpled bristles. Its eyes caught the movements of the flame, creating the illusion that it, too, was peering out of a mask. Bill waited until Lyla's breathing had settled before he snuffed the lantern.

In the morning, they were sweet again. Lyla found the old man and got him to point her down the road in the general direction of Hungary, which turned out to be back the way they had come. Finally Bill felt the way he had hoped he would on his honeymoon, giddy and horny, racing toward a bright future as he accelerated down the road between the village houses, the Simca squeaking on its chassis as it popped over ruts and holes. But then a boy ran into the road, and Bill hit him. The boy rolled up the hood, striking the windshield hard enough to crack it. Lyla was still screaming after Bill had stopped and the boy had rolled back down the hood and fallen off its end.

He lay in the road, his mouth working slowly, a rivulet of blood dribbling from his nose. He looked about ten. People began to creep out from their doors, tentatively, silently, like deer coming into a clearing, but then a woman in a kerchief burst wailing from a house and billowed across its garden, struggling with the gate latch before she could run to fall on the boy, clutching him.

Lyla knelt beside her and tried to get her to release the child. "I'm a nurse," she said. "You have to leave him be. You might hurt him. Don't shake him. He might have a neck injury. Just leave him!"

The woman's cries had broken the spell, and now other people gathered closely around, staring down at the boy, shouting and moaning, shaking their fists, menacing Bill, crowding close and buzzing their language into his face.

Go on.

    I'd rather not.

    Go on.

    Lyla found her phrase book, and managed to get them to calm down. Eventually we figured out that the nearest ambulance was in the next village, twenty miles away. There was a doctor there, too. A man said he would go with me, to show the way. Lyla said she would stay and try to help the boy.

    Then what?

———

TWENTY MILES TOOK an eternity on the winding, rutted roads. At one point the car was engulfed by a huge herd of sheep, all marked with slashes of red paint on their backs, and Bill had to sit and wait, inching forward, thinking about the suffering boy and fretting about Lyla, until an ambling shepherd in a nubbly gray fez came and cleared an alley through the woolly, bleating bodies with his crook, walking ahead of the Simca's bumper like an escort at the front of a motorcade. The villager who had come along was silent. Except when he pointed the way, he kept his hands folded in his lap, the thick fingers interlaced. In the other village, they found the ambulance—they had to wake up the driver, who seemed drunk— and they fetched the doctor and started back.

We were gone for almost two hours.

And when you returned?

We came into the village, and the people were gone.

Gone?

They were watching from the windows. An old lady was praying in the road.

And then what happened?

I got out of the car.

And then?

I saw.

What did you see?

THE BOY WAS DEAD. He had been moved to the side of the road and covered with a black cloth. The shape of his small body showed through the cloth but was indistinct, like something pulled from an imperfect mold. An old woman knelt beside him, all in black, clutching a rosary and talking to the sky. Bill looked for Lyla but did not see her. He thought she must be in one of the houses, helping to comfort the boy's mother. The ambulance pulled up behind the Simca and stopped, and the doctor got out with his bag and, wiping his brow, went to the boy's body. He lifted up the black cloth to look underneath and blew a breath out through his lips, making a put-put-put sound like a faulty engine.

There were faces in the windows of the houses. Bill wanted Lyla to run out from wherever she was so they could jump in the car and race away. He walked down the road looking for her, too nervous to call out, giving the doctor and the shrouded boy and the praying woman a wide berth. The praying woman's eyes flicked down from the sky, passing over him. He turned, following her gaze, and there in the deep shadow in a narrow space between two houses he could see something on the ground, some heap of something. Glancing around, aware of being watched, he approached the opening, peered inside. The thing was on its stomach, facedown in clammy gray mud scored with cloven sheep tracks. He could see it was wearing Lyla's clothes, but he thought it must be the dead boy, somehow moved or multiplied. The passage was too cramped for him to roll it all the way over, so he tugged at its feet, sliding it out, dimly absorbing the long hair matted with blood. He rolled it over. Lyla's lips were bloody and torn; her front teeth were broken; her eyes were tiny slits in fat, purple pouches, bulging domes like the eyes of a chameleon. He recoiled. Pale circles watched him from the windows of some houses. Other windows were blank with lace curtains. The woman in black was still praying.

The scene tilted on its axis. The houses and the faces and the stretch of rutted road and the newly mown fields humming with insects all swung up, away from Bill. The village was coming in line with the Milky Way, and the galaxy, spinning like a circular saw. The ground fell out from under his feet. The day accelerated around him, the sun falling toward the horizon. He was somewhere infinitely spacious but also as tight as a straitjacket. He drifted down into the darkening sky, pulling himself along the links of a cold and slimy chain, down to where the oysters grew.

And then what happened?
   There's nothing else.
   The truth.
   I wasn't there anymore. I was here.
   Where's here?
   You know better than I do.
   I only know what you know.
   Then that's the end of it.
   Let's go back to the beginning.
   Where's the beginning?
   The shrimp cocktail.
   The shrimp cocktail?
   In Bermuda. With your mother.
   That's not the beginning.
   The dog.
   Not the dog.
   The Simca.
   No.
   The rabbits.
   No.

The buoy.
Stop it.
Guillaume.
Who are you?
Here. Bite on this button.

In the Olympic Village

THE GYMNAST LIES beside the hurdler. The gymnast, a man, is short and white and, toes to shoulders, an isosceles triangle. The hurdler, a woman, is tall and lean and brown. Her hairdresser back in Miami bleached orangy streaks into her hair that are meant to be gold. They were to match her gold-painted acrylic fingernails and the gold track shoes she wore even though she was never expected to medal and did not get past the quarterfinals, in which she'd fallen over the second hurdle. She and the gymnast are in a narrow twin bed, his. His roommate had agreed to sleep across the hall, on the floor between a rings specialist and the gymnastics team's old warhorse, age twenty-eight, who is at his third Games and spends most of his time icing his knees.

Through the wall, they hear the individual all-around silver medalist having furious sex with a Frenchman who throws the discus. The gymnast, though well-satisfied by the hurdler, listens and feels wistful for that kind of exultant, lusty celebration. He had hoped to bring home a medal. In the team competition, they finished fourth. Of the American men, he was predicted to have the best chance at the all-around—he was second at Worlds—but he fell off the pommel horse and stepped out of bounds on the floor exercise. "Get your head in the game," his coach had said, holding him by the face. "Focus up." His teammate, the new silver medalist, had been brilliant on the high bar, better than ever before in his life, and excellent on the floor and solid through the other rotations. He was on all the late-night talk shows, cool in front of the cameras, making little jokes. In the event finals, he picked up another silver and a bronze. He is only twenty.

"Did you know he was gay?" the hurdler asks, curling one long arm up over her head and tapping a gold fingernail against the wall. Her bicep stands up, so distinct he can see exactly where the muscle attaches to the bone.

"Yeah, but he's not public about it."

"Maybe now he can be more out."

The gymnast considers. "I think he might like his limelight to be no-hassle."

A prolonged groan vibrates through the wall, and the hurdler makes a round-mouthed face of astonishment. "Faster," she says. "Higher. Stronger." They giggle and look at the ceiling to avoid each other's eyes. If they could only lie quietly and make small talk like most first-time lovers, everything would be fine, but the other couple's sounds remind them of their recent sex and embarrass them.

They have left the lights on because why not? They have nothing to show but perfection. She is utterly hairless, long-limbed, flat and tight in the belly, pale across her breasts and pelvis with stark tan lines from her speed suit. Her toenails are ten chips of gold. He is less elegant but just as functional: powerful bulldog legs, a wide pale chest, abs like the bumps on a turtle's shell. The hair on his legs and in his groin is sparse and blond, and tufts of it, trimmed short, sprout from his armpits. Their bodies have been trained to sweat; they gleam with it. The smell in the room is clean but animal.

They had met during the opening ceremonies, when the whole U.S. team marched into the stadium together and around the track. On television, shot from high above, they were five hundred dots rattling around, a casual army out for a stroll. The gymnast and the hurdler found themselves walking side by side, waving and smiling up at no one, everyone, God himself, both wearing the white berets and blue blazers and white pants and shoes issued by the team. They looked like yachtsmen. "We look like yachtsmen," she remarked (not for the first time—she had tried it out on an NBA player while they were still waiting in the staging area).

"Ahoy!" the gymnast said and then felt stupid. Her face, joyous, looking down on him, was framed by the astral popping of camera flashes and the open, undulating roof of the stadium. Above her beret the night sky was pale with firework smoke. Later, the torch was lit.

SHE HAD EXPECTED the sex to be more *gymnastic* somehow. She had imagined a cauldron of chalk beside his bed, him dipping his hands and then brushing them together, white palms emerging from a cloud of dust. Then he would raise his arms overhead and leap onto the bed and . . . Her imagination failed to come up with what, exactly, he would do, but she thought there would be something, some special move, some impossible position, some defiance of gravity. "You'll only be happy," her mother would say, "with a man who's exempt from the laws of physics." But he is a farm boy, when you get down to it, and only twenty-two. She is twenty-five and has styled herself as the street-smart kind of track star (scowling on the blocks, wearing dark shades, talking tough) even though her parents live in a big-housed, green-lawned, palm-treed suburb and have a (white) cast-iron jockey to hold up their mailbox. She is not disappointed exactly—the gymnast was very attentive, unlike the last man she slept with, a middle-distance runner who lay motionless on the bed like one of those ancient figurines with the huge phalluses—but she is somewhere short of contentment. She had not anticipated how calloused his hands would be: yellow and rough where the skin has torn and healed a thousand times.

"Does everyone make a joke about sticking the dismount?" she asks.

"That's funny," he says. "And what do you mean everyone?"

"What are you going to do after this?"

He rolls onto his side to face her. "I thought we'd go to sleep," he says, "but if you want to go out, I can rally."

"No, I mean after the Olympics."

"Oh." He has a mole on one cheek, and it vanishes into a crevice of his smile. "I'm going back to Wichita to coach gymnastics."

"Like at a college?"

The mole reappears. Its presence on his face is the one asymmetrical thing about him, but, taken alone, it is brown and perfectly circular. "No, at a gym. For kids. I really like kids. Someday I want to have my own gym."

"You know," she says, "it's nice to hear a man say he likes kids without worrying about sounding creepy."

His eyes, pale blue with short blond lashes, move over her face. He is not sure if she is kidding and, if she is, what she means exactly. "I have five little brothers and sisters," he says.

She is an only child and feels an only child's shock at the notion of a family that is not just three points connected by three lines, but a polyhedron. "Five?" she says. "Jesus."

He nods. His buzz cut rasps on the pillowcase. "Matthew, Mark, Luke, Mary, Rachel, and me."

She starts to say *Jesus* again but stops herself. Her mother is Catholic, but the hurdler herself does not believe. At track meets, her mother pulls a rosary through her trembling fingers; she was holding it today when God let the hurdler fall in the quarterfinals. Now she is asleep in her hotel on the other side of this foreign city. She believes her daughter is a virgin. The cries of the silver medalist and his Frenchman rise to what the hurdler hopes is a final crescendo. *"Sacré bleu!"* she says.

The gymnast's mole vanishes again. In a deep, discus-throwing voice, he says, *"Ah, oui. Baise₂-moi, homoncule!"*

TWELVE DAYS PASSED between the opening ceremonies and this night when the hurdler and the gymnast are in bed. During those days, they crossed paths often enough that destiny and not just coincidence seemed to be in play. They bumped into each other at meals and passing through the Village gates and in the lounges where athletes gathered to watch other sports and scout possible flings. While the gymnast and the hurdler stood chatting and waiting for their chicken sandwiches or for their IDs to be checked, they remembered flashbulbs and firework smoke, plumes of flame dancing up from the torch. Sex during competition was frowned upon: Passion drains the body's resources and wilds the mind. The swimmers were among the first to be done, and they swept through the Village like a chlorinous band of pillagers, their tan faces marked with white bandit masks from their goggles.

The gymnast and the hurdler bumped into each other at the event finals for women's gymnastics. She had requested tickets partly because she was hoping to see him and partly because she has always loved gymnastics. As a child, she wanted to be a gymnast until it became obvious she would be too tall. "But she's very, very fast," her coach told her mother, watching her barrel down the long blue runway and leapfrog the vault. "Very fast."

The hurdler and the gymnast sat together. They had chosen each other. They were waiting to be liberated from their sports.

"How was your day?" she asked him.

"Good," he said, watching his teammate on the balance beam. "Did some practice. Did some PT. Looked at tapes. You?"

"Pretty much the same."

The girl on the beam was tiny and precisely wrought. She bent backward into a handstand. Her legs opened parallel to the beam, and there was something pagan and offertory about the flatness of her crotch, her right angles, the *T* she made, like an altar. Then a foot came down and she was right side up and upside down again and right side up. "Let's go, Katie!" shouted the gymnast as the girl paused with her arms raised, back arched, facing the crowd, her ribs showing through her leotard.

"Do you know her?" the hurdler asked.

"Sure," he said. Staring down at the beam, he rested his chin on his fists. He must have understood what the hurdler was asking, because he said, "She's a good kid. Only sixteen. Really handles the pressure."

The hurdler envied the attention the girl commanded. There weren't seven other girls alongside her on seven other beams, the way the hurdler always shared the track. This girl could stand there all alone, like a bird on a narrow branch above a sea of blue mats, her dainty sternum betraying the flutter of her miniature heart, her hair full of gel and glitter and barrettes. Everyone would watch. She went flip-flopping the length of the beam and flew into the air.

On landing, she teetered sideways, crossing one leg over the other, and the hurdler was glad.

"HOMUNCULUS," the hurdler says. "I learned that word in Latin. I didn't know it existed in French."

"My mom called me that when I was little," he says. "You took Latin?"

"I went to Catholic school."

"Are you Catholic?"

"My mother is. Cuban-style."

He leaves it at that. His mother, picking him up from gymnastics: "*Allons-y, homoncule.* In the car." In the gym, from the first, he had loved the different apparatuses, unforgiving steel and graphite, not alive and helpful like they looked on TV. A dust, probably toxic, rose from a pit full of foam blocks and floated in the light that angled through the high windows.

Stroking the orange streaks in the hurdler's hair, the gymnast thinks about the moment when he fell off the pommel horse. He remembers being up on the handles, his legs rotating around him, feet drawing circles in space, rocking on his hands one-two one-two to let his thighs swing under, and he remembers turning and reaching and closing his fingers around the shocking nothingness, emptier than air, that exists where something solid is expected. The world had dropped out from under him so quickly and with such finality: the tipping crowd, the side of the horse, the lights in the raftered ceiling, and then the mat smacking him on the hip. On the sidelines, his coach flung his fist at the floor like someone skipping a stone. The gymnast had stood, walked to the chalk bucket and back, saluted the judges, and sprang up to finish his routine.

Through the wall, the discus thrower and the silver medalist have gone quiet. The gymnast wants them to be smoking cigarettes, but there is no smoking in the Village. He could tell the hurdler had been surprised when he spoke French. His mother is French, a long-ago exchange student who fell in love with his father and Jesus and came to accept the astonishing flatness of Kansas.

"What are you going to do after this?" he asks the hurdler.

"Probably rally and go to a bar," she says.

"Cool," he says. "Just what I was thinking. Let's go."

She is the little spoon, though she is taller, and she frowns back over her shoulder at him. "I was kidding."

"So was I."

"Oh."

"So," he tries again, "what are you going to do?"

He feels tension come into her body. "I don't know," she says. "Anything but motivational speaking." Her shoulder, contoured with muscle, lifts toward her ear, less a shrug than a hunch. She rolls away, onto her stomach, and he puts his hand on the small of her back. Even there she is hard with muscle. Before he went to bed with the hurdler he would have expected to be thinking of his girlfriend in the wake of an infidelity. Realizing he is not thinking of her, he thinks of her. What time is it in Kansas? He doesn't know. Daytime. She is at work. She is small, a former gymnast, now a preschool teacher. He loves her; he will probably marry her. He had not planned to be unfaithful, but he doesn't feel particularly bad about what has happened. He had heard the stories about the Village—thousands of perfect bodies crammed together and hopped up on pride, ambition, euphoria, pain, relief, disappointment, everything else—and he has found they are true but also insufficient.

"Banging is like an intramural sport there," the twenty-eight-year-old warhorse said during training camp, taping a bag of ice to his knee. "You feel like you're going against the Olympic spirit *not* to get some."

But opportunity is not an explanation; he has passed up plenty of opportunities before. Something is in the air here. As a child he had liked to imagine himself leaving glowing trails in the air when he practiced his routine, like bioluminescence, so that his movements would not be lost but would be recorded in space. Now he imagines what it would be like if everyone left such trails, if glowing circles spooled the track, if a mist rose from the pool and hung over the city, if a bumpy line followed behind the hurdler, if light shot from the gymnast's own whirling feet on the pommel horse as though from a Rain Bird sprinkler. He imagines all that energy, all those lingering vectors, mixing in the air and binding everyone together. Sex, he thinks, is both an extension of and a relief from the pointlessness of sport. They swim back and forth, run around and around, paddle from one buoy to another, bicycle to nowhere. Nothing is created but speed, momentum, heat, disturbances in air and water. However far someone can throw a javelin, it will still not be very far, all things considered, and it will not hit anything except turf. They mate in their twin beds, miming creation.

THE GYMNAST AND the hurdler did not watch each other compete. Their schedules conflicted. But she saw him on TV when she was stretching on the floor of one of the lounges. They aired a little segment about him in the first week, before his events had begun, with stylized shots of him wearing a determined expression in front of the parallel bars, the pommel horse, the vault. "These shoulders," the narrator said over a close-up of the gymnast's knotted back crucified between the rings, "carry the hopes of a nation." His hands rotated in slow motion around the high bar, then released, and the bar bounced in empty space, shedding chalk dust.

The hurdler wonders about this naked stranger, this triangle of muscle, this *homoncule*. Why shouldn't he know a word she doesn't? Just because he's into Jesus and is from Kansas and loves children is no reason for him not to speak French. She also saw a replay on TV of when he fell off the pommel horse. He had looked so bewildered, sitting on the blue mat, and then something had crossed his face that she didn't understand. Relief? At the end of the suspense? The pressure? She can't imagine having been a favorite. Even if she hadn't fallen, her body simply couldn't have run fast enough to get her onto the podium. Her desire, desperation even, to win is no match for the limitations of fast-twitch muscles and lung capacity, the dark alchemy of glucose and lactic acid, the length of a femur in relation to a tibia. The woman who won gold is a fearsome machine, over six feet tall, perfectly engineered to run. After the closing ceremonies, the hurdler plans to sit by her parents' pool for a few months and think things through. She will allow herself to gain five or ten pounds. Then she will face the strange fact that she has many decades left to live.

After gymnastics, she had tried dance (too tall again), and tennis (weak backhand), and cross-country (miserable), then track, and then hurdles, and this is what all those years of agony, the runs, the weights, the pop-eyed, screaming, tyrannical coaches, the ankle surgeries were for: a tryst with a gymnast before she goes back to Florida. She thinks about her foot catching on that hurdle. It was only this morning. She had come off the blocks all wrong and barely made it over the first hurdle; her stride was too short; her rhythm was choppy; the second hurdle was too far away when she made her leap, and she went down, the length of her spilling onto the track with her gold-tipped hands splayed out in front, her golden shoes at the end of her long, long legs. The rubber smell of the track, the sound of the crowd—she could have lain there forever if only to avoid getting up.

He rolls her over and climbs on top, and she is conscious of how short he is, his feet between her calves. They kiss until they are startled by a loud *pop!* from next door. "Champagne," he says.

She makes a face. "I was afraid Black September was here."

"Who?"

She regrets having mentioned it. Her pillow talk is rusty. "You know. Munich. When terrorists killed those Israeli athletes."

"Oh." He rolls off her again and frowns, elongating his mole. "Oh, right. That picture. The guy in the ski mask on the balcony."

"Yeah."

"Security seems pretty tight here."

"Yeah. It was a dumb joke. Not in good taste."

"It's okay." He waits a minute, and then with the air of changing the subject, he says, "My teammate said that sex in the Village is like an intramural sport. He said they should give out medals for it."

"Do you think you should get a medal?" She is irritated without knowing why.

"No." He looks hurt. "No, I just thought it was funny."

"I've noticed that, for men, medals are like this incredibly powerful pheromone. Any guy with a medal has a harem full of groupies the second he gets off the stand. But it's not the same for girls who medal. Have you noticed that?"

He thinks. "No."

"It's true," she insists. "It's like there's something off-putting and unladylike about trying hard enough to win. Or about being that strong."

She feels stupid for letting her hairdresser put the streaks in. They are so garish, so expressive of hopeless aspiration, and the bleach has made her hair brittle and rough. Poor girl, people must have said: She thought she was going to win and then she fell in the quarterfinals. But the hurdler never thought she was going to win. She just wanted to participate in the hope. A miracle would have been needed for her even to make the finals. Most years, she wouldn't have qualified for the team, but a couple of girls were out with injuries, and she ran a personal best at Trials. At the Games, she is part of the general population of athletes, the middle fifty percent, which hardly seems fair, given how fast she is—she was NCAA champion two years in a row. But here she is one insignificant inch of the dark, anonymous curtain against which the stars take their bows. The Olympic Village, cross-sectioned like a dollhouse, would be gloomy with disappointment, she thinks, and pinpricked with spots of triumph too bright to look at. How many of its rooms, she wonders, are occupied by couples like them?

He is playing with her hair again. "I would like you even if you'd won a medal."

She realizes she is about to cry and that she doesn't want to do it in front of him. He would be kind and consoling, but this cry must be solitary. She had thought being with him might stave it off. "Remember the opening ceremonies?" she says.

"Sure."

"I wish that could be the only thing I remember from this."

She has stung him, she sees, and she feels remorse but also grim satisfaction.

"You don't mean that," he says. "You'll want to remember everything."

"Maybe you're right," she says. "But I should go."

"I was hoping you'd stay."

She sits up, and he gazes placidly at her breasts. "Why?" she asks.

He indents her left nipple with the tip of his index finger, like somebody pressing an elevator button. "This was fun."

"But now it's over." She hears how dramatic she sounds and, to cover her embarrassment, drops her voice even lower and gives him a wry smile. "Everything," she intones, "is over."

"I wish you'd stay."

She shrugs and gets out of bed.

WHEN SHE IS GONE, he finds he doesn't miss her. The bed is small enough already. He had thought, a few hours ago when he met her for dinner, that they would have more time together, a real affair, but now he decides that the difference between one night and three doesn't matter. Their encounter is probably the only one-night stand he'll ever have. She had decided he wasn't very smart—he knows this and is not offended. Her opinion won't make him smarter or dumber, and he has never thought of himself as being particularly smart, anyway. He remembers chalking the high bar during team warm-ups, dangling from it like an orangutan and shuffling sideways, sidestepping his chalky hands from one end to the other to leave behind an even layer of white dust. He had been terrified then, looking up at the blank scoreboard, but now he has failed and survived and fear seems like something he will never have to experience again.

The silver medalist and the Frenchman start back up, and the gymnast puts a pillow over his head.

The hurdler, walking down the hallway and thinking about the gymnast, decides it's probably for the best that he didn't win a medal because she doesn't think he would have known what to do with all those choices. Now he will marry a nice woman and someday own a gym with bars and vaults and a pit full of foam blocks. He will have the infinite Kansas horizon, the perfect white disk of the sun. She sees herself swimming through the shadows of palm trees in her parents' turquoise pool. She sees the gymnast's unborn children flying through the air, twisting and flipping, never needing to land.

You Have a Friend in 10A

I'M TOLD I WENT catrastic for the first time in 1984, when Jerome Shin (yes, the director) took me up to my bathroom—my gaudy childhood bathroom with the big pink Jacuzzi and mirrors on all four walls—and cut me my first line and asked me to hold his balls while he jerked off. The request was casual, like my stepmother telling me to hold her purse while she fixed her lipstick. "Just hold them?" I said.

"Yeah," he said, pulling down the top of my dress and looking skeptically at my half-grown tits. "Just hold them."

The pouch sat on my palm like rotten fruit while he worked his sad, skinny dick. It was a year or so after his young wife drowned. He must have been in his early forties then. I was fourteen.

"Now tug them!" he barked, scrunching up his face.

Startled, I tugged until he came onto my thigh and the hem of my dress. (My stepmother's dress. I returned it to her closet without cleaning it.) My father's party murmured through the floor and the pipes. All those people milling around, trying to out-fabulous each other, talking about green lights and opening grosses and sex.

Probably every bathroom in the house was hosting some variation on our theme. Jerome cast me in his next movie.

My agent said we had to change my name. "No one uses their real name," he said, "and yours is terrible." We were at the Polo Lounge; he was eating a Cobb salad. He reached over with his fork and knocked my hand away from my fries. "Actors' names are just labels you stick on a fantasy," he said. "You know, like Armani or something. But it'd be nice to keep some reference to your father." So I went from being Allison Lowenstein-Karr to being Karr Alison. No one could ever explain why we dropped the second *l*. "It's a no-brainer," my agent told me. "Go with it."

In retrospect, I don't think I *felt* catrastic in the bathroom with Jerome. I remember feeling flattered and grossed out and high and sophisticated. Still, my Helpers identified that night as when my system first became seriously susceptible to degradons, when I started to lose track of my Esteem. Jerome, they told me, was a Usurper—which I've never quite been able to sort out because Jerome's movie is what made me famous, and the Church only ever liked me because I was famous. Jefferson Morris himself told me that the Founder says the important moments in life aren't just points along a single straight line but are moving, swiveling hubs within a three-dimensional web and belong to multiple trajectories, both ascending and descending. When I held Jerome's balls, I was beginning my descent into fucked-up druggie despectum, but I'd also hooked into that steep skyward line that would bring me to Billy and Jefferson and the teachings of the Founder. But then there was everything else, too. Like I said, I can't sort it out.

BUSINESSMAN, computer businessman, Steelers fan, Asian grandmother, clean-cut guy who's probably a pervert, sullen punk kid, guy with big gold jewelry, retired couple with too much luggage, harried couple with too many children, Texan. They file past my seat, departing souls taking slow zombie steps down a fluorescent tunnel. "Well, I guess it's hurry up and wait," an older blond lady says to no one in particular. We're all in this together, she is saying. A flight attendant squeezes past to get to the harried couple, who seems defeated by the overhead compartment, by their bags and diaper bags and children's suitcases bursting with pointless junk. "Don't mind us," says the blond lady. But I like the flight attendants, their big hair and sexy blue vests and shiny red nails. The guy in the middle seat doesn't seem to recognize me, which is just as well. I look out the window at the odd vehicles racing around the tarmac, the shadowy people behind the terminal windows, the transparent flutter of jet exhaust.

I am going to my mother's house. An act of desperation. The last time I saw her, three years ago, we got in a fight before I could even get through the door—

Where's Helena?

With Billy.

You left her with that loon?

Don't even talk to me about leaving. And he's not a loon.

He's a loon. Him and that Jefferson Starship guy and their Looney Tunes religion.

It's my religion, too.

It's not a religion. It's a roach motel for idiots.

You don't know. You don't know anything about the Founder. You're just a blip.

What's a blip?

Someone who doesn't know anything about the Founder.

You're brainwashed.

You're a Nazi.

—and then she slammed the door in my face, and I lifted up the metal flap of the mail slot and hollered through it that she was a cunt and a Usurper and I hoped she and her degradons had a very nice life together. But now I've left the Church, or the Church has left me, or we left each other, and Billy of course left me, and Quentin is dead, and I spent all my money trying to get Helena back and failed, and I tried to be in a play, and my friends finally, nicely, suggested I should look for my own place to live.

I'm in coach but near the front, and I see a tall man in a white uniform take a seat in first class. My heart flies up like a flushed dove but gets caught and tangled in a net. If I were hooked up to an Aurograph, it would be going crazy. I remind myself that Quentin is dead. Most everyone's settled down and buckled up now, except for a paunchy guy who's going to break the plane apart trying to stuff his huge suitcase into the overhead, his round belly assaulting the face of the woman in the aisle seat, sweat stains in his armpits. A flight attendant comes and splays her red nails across the suitcase as though calming a frightened animal. She lifts it down and takes it away. The pilot comes out of the plane's little locked brain and shakes the hand of the man in white, bending down, nodding and somber as they exchange a few words.

THERE ARE all kinds of stories about me and Billy. The Church bought me for him; he's gay; I'm gay; I was impregnated with the Founder's frozen sperm; I was impregnated by Jefferson Morris; I was impregnated by Quentin; I was never pregnant at all.

I'd only been out of Cloudvista a couple of months when my agent called, all excited. "Billy Bjorn wants a meeting. Wear something classy. Don't swear. Be sugar sweet, and try not to act like a junkie."

"What's the script?" I asked.

"Who the fuck cares?"

"Aren't you coming?"

"He wants to meet you alone. They specified."

Billy is not tall, but he wasn't as short as I expected. He moved around his office with the same gymnastic energy as the commando squirrels I watched out the window at Cloudvista while they leapt and dangled and corkscrewed, raiding the bird feeders. He has strong, active hands, and I imagined an invisible tail whirling behind him as he poured me a glass of mineral water, then darted to the window to point out a jet taking off from Santa Monica ("I've been thinking about getting one like that myself—what do you think? Do you like it?"), then fiddled with papers on his desk, then flopped down beside me on a long white couch and unleashed his grin. Everyone knows Billy's smile, but you can't really understand its effect until you're confronted by it in person. You lean toward those teeth, swim upstream, struggle closer to the origin of all that dazzle, that gush of stardust. Suddenly I was Suzanne in *Tin Can Palace*. I was that bitchy lawyer in *Pleadings* who doesn't want to be charmed by him but is. I wasn't a washed-up twenty-year-old with a pill problem. I was inside a glorious sphere of light. I *was* a glorious sphere of light.

"You," he said. "You are special. I can tell. I've always liked you on-screen, but now, talking to you in person, just sitting here looking at you"—he broke off and gave his famous trill of incredulous laughter. "Just look at you," he said, taking my hand. "You just—you—you have so much to give. There's something about you. I didn't expect to react this way—I mean, I wasn't planning—but—just look at you!"

I echoed his laugh and tried to amp up my smile. My smile is not my strong suit, though, and remembering that, I faltered and looked away. He put a finger under my chin and turned my face back. "And you've still got a sweet shyness," he said. "Great. Really great."

"I'm just so happy to meet you."

"Yeah?" He shook his head and laughed again, staring at me, giddy. "Yeah. Am I crazy here? Are you feeling this, Karr? Because I'm feeling something—whew—something big."

I had to turn away again. On a side table stood a framed picture of a young man in a white uniform with gold braid and colorful rows of ribbons. "Is that your son?" I asked, knowing it was. Quentin was the product of Billy's first marriage, to his high-school sweetheart. After her, he married an ethereal movie star, and after her, he married a model from Ecuador, and after her, he married me.

"Quentin, yeah. My boy." He sprang off the couch and picked up the photo, staring at it for a moment before he dropped back beside me, closer now, our thighs touching. I felt thrilled and twisted. I felt something big. I felt like I was a shred of myself caught on a sharp hook. I felt like a gust of wind. I felt desperate to get high and certain I would never want to be high again.

"I didn't know he was in the navy," I said, looking at Quentin's face, which was a distorted version of Billy's square bullet of masculinity, narrower and softer.

"He's not." Billy took my hand. "Listen, Karr. Do you ever feel like you need help?"

"What do you mean?" *Don't act like a junkie, don't act like a junkie.*

"Do you ever have doubts? Do you ever worry about rejection? Do you feel like there are people trying to bring you down?"

I thought about the men in suits who had greeted me in the lobby and ridden with me in the elevator to Billy's office. They had asked

after my father and stepmother by name. I said they'd moved to
Hawaii and opened a Zen center, but the men already knew. With
a pair of synchronized winks they mentioned an interview I gave
when I was seventeen in which I had said I wanted to marry Billy.

"I just got out of rehab," I said to Billy. "So. Yeah."

His eyebrows squeezed his forehead into a rift of concern. His
gaze fried me like light through a magnifying glass. Just when the
tension was about to break me, he said, softly, "I can help you."

"LADIES AND GENTLEMEN," the pilot says in that twangy, folksy
pilot voice, "today we have the honor of transporting the remains
of Petty Officer First Class Reginald J. Roberts, who was killed in
action in Afghanistan and is being escorted home to his family by
Lieutenant Commander Howard Stanton. Out of respect to our
fallen warrior, I ask that you remain seated upon arrival until Lieutenant Commander Stanton has deplaned."

Everyone's attention goes to the windows. We are curious for a
glimpse of the casket being loaded. I can't see anything. The officer has taken off his white hat, and his bald spot peeks over the
back of his seat.

"Do you know anyone who's died in the war?" the blip next to
me says. He looks like he's in his late twenties but might as well be
older. Central casting has printed "Middle Management" on the
back of his head shot. A book on how to be an effective leader is
stuffed in his seat pocket.

"No."

"I do. A high-school friend of mine. He went into a house and
shot a guy who was wired to blow up. Bits of the other guy's tis-
sue got embedded in him and caused all kinds of infections. That's
what killed him eventually. Imagine having pieces of a dead person

rotting inside you, someone you killed, someone who didn't even speak your language and who's going to take you with him. Makes me sick. It's like a horror movie."

He's basically describing degradons—invisible little pellets of bad feelings from Usurpers that stick to your body and make their way into your Esteem—but I remind myself that I don't believe in degradons anymore. I probably never did, not really, but the language of the Church has rooted in me like a fake accent I can't shake. "Awful," I say. "I'm sorry."

"It's weird to think of that poor guy down in the cargo hold with our bags and everything." He looks at me, and I can see he wants something but I don't know what. "It's weird to think of flying after you're dead."

Holding his gaze, I uncoil the cord of my earphones from around my phone and put them in my ears.

A WORD ABOUT the Aurograph. People say it's nothing more than goofy science-fiction wishful thinking, but I can tell you there's magic in it. You focus on your life, and energy flows out of your brain and through the electrode bonnet into the monitor. Green waves appear on the black screen, spiking when you hit a catrastic moment, showing where your spirit has gotten all gunked up, and when that happens, you get excited; your Helper gets excited; you feel like undersea explorers who've just found a wreck. To maximize your Esteem, you have to isolate all those moments and let yourself be helped through them. "You are a hot air balloon," Billy told me on one of our first nights, his hand on my belly, his breath in my ear, "and all around you are invisible tethers held by people on the ground, people who are trying to hold you down, usurp your Esteem. They don't want to let go, Karr. They won't. But you have to snip those tethers. You have to cut yourself loose so you can fly. You can do it—I know you can. You just need a little help."

"Think about something that has troubled you recently," my Helper said after my wedding.

I had planned to think about the helicopters that hovered above the château day and night and the paparazzi who clamored at the gates like angry peasants, but instead, Quentin welled up in my mind, standing at the window where I first saw him. A green line climbed the monitor.

"Okay," said my Helper, "the Aurograph has registered your distress. What were you thinking about?"

"The night before the wedding," I said.

"What in particular?"

"We had a big dinner for everyone. I was getting ready to come down to the ballroom, and I was alone in my room after I got my hair done, and I thought I heard someone calling my name. So I went and opened the door, and there was Billy's son."

"He was calling your name?"

"No. He was at the other end of the hall, looking out the window. I'd never met him before, actually. He'd been away on the *Esteem*."

"Who was calling your name?"

"No one."

"Why does this memory trouble you?"

("Quentin?" I said, and he turned. He was wearing his white FounderCorps dress uniform, the one he wore in the picture in Billy's office. Even from the other end of a long hallway, I could tell Quentin was different from Billy. Everything flows out from Billy, whooshing and blasting you back, and you fight to get closer.

But everything pulls toward Quentin, and I felt queasy, like I should brace away.

"Should I call you Mom?" he said, not sarcastically but sadly. I was twenty-one. He was twenty-six.)

"I just wish," I told my Helper, "I'd had the chance to meet him earlier so we could have felt like more of a family at the wedding."

Already I had begun to understand that the infallibility of Billy was a cornerstone of the Church, and my Helper looked uncomfortable. "Quentin has very important work to do on the *Esteem*. He helps people reach the highest levels of study."

The *Esteem* is the last of the Founder's ships. According to Jefferson Morris, the Founder says the ocean is the place where we are most open and compassionate. Anyone who wishes to be really and truly free of degradons must spend time studying on the *Esteem*. I said, "I know. I don't mean to be critical. It was just a little awkward."

"Do you resent Quentin's obligations to the Church?"

"No."

"Do you wish your husband paid less attention to the Church and more attention to you?"

"Sometimes."

"I'm going to recommend a class for you—it's called Overcoming Selfishness for the Sake of the Self. There's an intensive version available at the Ranch."

"Okay."

"Can you think of another moment in your past that troubled you in the same way?"

I reached, as I often did during Helping sessions, for the years between Jerome Shin and Billy.

You've seen my first movie, the one Jerome put me in. I think it holds up pretty well. Kind of gritty but still kind of a caper. Not as good as Jerome's last movie, but Jerome was one of those people who knew he'd do his best work while he was dying.

When we started filming, I didn't want anything from him—certainly I had no pressing urge to be reunited with his scrotum—but I was still offended he didn't try anything with me. He was soft-spoken and professional. He made sure I put in my hours with the set tutors. "Allie, are you comfortable with this?" he asked before we filmed my scene in the bath.

Eventually I figured out he was boinking Genevieve Henry. Her beauty didn't register with me back then. I thought my knobby knees and flat ass were what every man wanted, not Genny's mouth like a fat berry and her weary eyes. I ditched my chaperone and went to her trailer and asked if we could talk. She was sprawled on a love seat in a black silk bathrobe patterned with white orchids, reading a paperback spy novel. "Sure, baby," she said, tenting the book on her chest.

A bottle of white wine stood open in an ice bucket on her table. "Can I have some of that?"

"Sure, baby."

I poured a glass and took a dramatic swig. As I told her what had happened with Jerome, she kept smiling as though I were some pleasant scene she had paused to admire: a children's playground, a pretty sunset, a string quartet playing Vivaldi.

When I was done, she said, "That's all?"

"Well," I said, "I guess so." I had never told the story before, and out loud it sounded flimsy and quick. "I just thought you should know Jerome's a child molester."

She swung her small mouth off to one side and studied me. Finally, she said, "You're not a child. You're already a bad little chick." She twisted her lips around some more and looked at her book for a minute. Then she turned a page and said, "Baby, if you want to be in the business, you should think about how much you're willing to put up with, because if you think you've been creamed on for the last time, you're wrong."

What did she see when she looked at me? When I rewatch the film, I see a gangly, eager girl pretending to be jaded. I see a little circus pony, a raw nugget of pure ego. Those movie people snorted me and smoked me; they cooked me in a spoon. Now they say I'm weak. They say I'm unfeeling to abandon my child to a cult. But you try getting out of that prenup, the one where you agreed to forfeit any claim to your husband's tens of millions in case of infidelity, where you certified that any and all of your children would be raised in accordance with the Founder's teachings, regardless of your own status within the Church. And you wanted your child to grow up happy and secure, sheltered from doubt, able to fly above our despectulated world, and you signed it, not knowing you would be labeled a Usurper, and since your child must be raised in accordance with the teachings of the Founder, and the Founder said children must be shielded from Usurpers at any cost . . . Well, you try getting out of that one. Especially if Helena won't even talk to you. She knows better than to talk to Usurpers.

IT WAS TRUE I hadn't been creamed on for the last time. People put me in more movies. My father was getting into drugs, so I did too, the way other fathers and daughters joined Indian Princesses or went out to brunch after church. At first it wasn't anything major. We'd sit by the pool and share a joint when my stepmother wasn't around. "Kiddo," he'd say, "tell Daddy how it feels to be a star." And I'd say something random like, "Daddy, it feels like biting into a dead mouse" or "Daddy, it feels like really bad gas," and he'd *howl*, he'd nearly fall off his chaise. But then my stepmother was around less and less—she couldn't quite bring herself to leave him, not that she had such a high horse anyway, Our Lady of Dexedrine—and we took our show on the road, driving out to house parties in Bel Air or Malibu, Dad looking like Don Johnson in his blazer and T-shirt behind the wheel of his Corvette (ice blue with a caramel interior, speedometer flickering like a flame as he accelerated). We'd cross the threshold together and part like strangers, wading through shadow worlds where the air was thick with bodies and ash and stardust, neither wanting to witness the other's search for relief. "Catch you on the flip side," he'd murmur.

Those were times I was catrastic—no question. I had a trick where I could squeeze the insides of my knees against my ears so hard I created suction. I would do it in cars, bent forward, trying not to puke, and I would do it on my back when I got bored with getting fucked. I could see but not hear the guy say, *You're so flexible.* I was walking around covered with a thick fur of degradons, and I didn't even know it. But I also remember the way the night sky looked from the quiet bottom of a glowing blue swimming pool, the shifting membrane of light that separated me from the darkness, the drunks who drifted and murmured like ghosts around the edges.

In the mornings, my father and I would drink coffee in pained silence until our shame burned off like early fog. Soon we'd be back out by the pool, riding the fizz of my stepmother's speed back to civility, sharing a copy of *Variety* and a pitcher of mimosas and gossiping about the night before, pretending I hadn't been a limp and addled baby bimbo and he hadn't spilled a baggie of coke and morphed into a crawling, snuffling thing, an anteater with a plastic straw proboscis, hoovering up white dust from the grout of someone's Spanish tiles.

I remember a party at the Chateau Marmont after I got fired from what would have been my fifth film and someone pulling me down from a balcony railing when I pretended I was going to jump, and then the Corvette's speedometer was flickering and Dad was saying I was a star and fuck 'em, just fuck 'em, and I yelled at him to go faster because faster was hilarious until the spinning began, a real spinning and not just the world running around trying to catch up with me. They found me sitting on the crumpled hood and smoking a cigarette, barefoot, loopy, apparently unmoved by the moans coming from the driver's seat. His left leg had to be amputated above the knee.

Just try keeping that out of the papers.

A MOVIE STAR, especially when he has divorced you and stolen your child with his lawyers and his prenup and his riches, is like God. Omnipotent, omnipresent. His huge grinning face looks down over the road to the airport. He waves his invisible squirrel tail on the little TV in the taxi, talking to Regis, pumping his fist in the air about something while the driver dubs him with whatever guttural language he's chortling into his phone. At the airport, he walks across the newsstands, holding his new girlfriend by one hand and your daughter by the other. He flickers across seatback screens. His voice whispers out of a hundred cheap headsets. The man beside you has recognized you after all; he gives a quick sideways glance when the guy in the aisle seat chooses Billy's latest. A buddy comedy. It lost money. Billy can be funny, but self-seriousness clings to his humor like mildew. His career is suffering, not catastrophically but noticeably. People think his zeal for the Church is off-putting. They think he is controlling, a megalomaniac, but they don't feel sorry for me. They only think I am even more of a fool.

The naval officer stands and walks to the lavatory at the front of the plane. I am relieved to see he is not watching Billy's movie. Maybe he's not supposed to partake of the in-flight entertainment. Maybe he's supposed to sit and think about the guy in the box who's soaring on his back over the Great Plains. For three years I've felt like I should be sitting and thinking about Quentin. I wasn't allowed to go when they scattered his ashes off the *Esteem*. Jefferson Morris made an official announcement that the Founder had asked Quentin to cast off his body and move into a new dimension, embarking on a fact-finding mission into the afterlife. He is expected to report back as soon as he is able.

Most gossip within the Church centers around whether the Founder is alive or dead. Jefferson Morris says he is in exile, that he wishes to communicate only through Jefferson so as not to interrupt his state of perfect Esteem. Dozens of blip reporters and disgruntled ex-Church members have tried to track down the Founder, to prove he is dead, but the trail goes cold in 1970, after he sailed away on a solo round-the-world trip. His first communication reached Jefferson Morris five months later, announcing he had found perfect Esteem and declaring his intention to remain in exile. No wreckage was ever found; no SOS call was ever received. There is a photo from an Italian newspaper (June 20, 1973) in which a man sitting at a café in the background is either the Founder or his long-lost Florentine twin. The FounderCorps keeps an office waiting for him at every Church center and a house for him at the Ranch, dusted every day and made up with clean sheets and towels just in case he decides to return. I have nothing I can keep ready for Quentin except myself.

On our honeymoon, Billy woke me up in the middle of the night. "Karr," he whispered. "Karr. I know the secret."

"What secret?" I asked, woozy, disoriented by the gilded ceiling of our hotel suite.

"About the Founder."

I rolled onto my side, facing him. His cheek, jaw, and shoulder were blue; the rest of him was dark. "What about him?"

"Whether he's alive or dead. I know."

The room was silent except for his breathing and, in the distance, one of those warbling European police sirens that always make me think of World War II. "Well?" I said.

Billy put his hand on my naked side. "He's both." I waited. He rolled me lightly back and forth as though trying to shake a response from me.

"I don't think I understand."

"He's found a way to be both. That's the miracle. That's perfect Esteem. None of the burden of life, none of the finality of death. He did it, Karr. He's the only one in the world, in the *history* of the world."

"Wow," I said.

"Yeah," he said. Then with true wonder: *"Yeah."*

I unbuckle, and Middle Management and the guy on the aisle get up so I can go pee. On my way back, I lift two little bottles of vodka from the drinks cart. Tacky, I know, but I am going to see my mother.

MY MOTHER HAS a talent for disgust and finality, and I've always had the impression she left me with my father to prove we deserve each other. But we needed someone who was disgusted with us, someone solid and human who smelled like office supplies. She lives in a small city full of fast-food chains and big-box stores and is a secretary for a personal injury lawyer. After we wrecked the Corvette, she came and checked Dad and his new steel shin and acrylic foot into Cloudvista and took me back with her, driving for fourteen hours straight while I slumped against the door of her Honda, watching the mesas and mountains go by. "No more movies," she said. "I'm not even going to say 'not for a while' or 'not until you're old enough to handle it.' Not ever. Someday you'll thank me."

"They won't forget me," I told her. "They'll come find me."

"Who's they?" she said. "There's no one who cares about you in that whole godforsaken city. Maybe they cared about the money you made them, but they didn't care enough to stop you from flaming out, did they? Your father spent all your money, by the way. Every cent. It's all gone."

"No, it isn't. It can't be."

"Gone, Allison."

I screamed, gripping the dashboard with my fingers. She glanced at me, then back at the road.

She was living with an amiable boyfriend named Tom, who surprised me by not wanting to fuck me. He just wanted to build birdhouses and play the mandolin and bake quiches for my mother. I went to a small school where the other kids were impressed by my celebrity for about a week but then changed their minds when they realized I didn't have anything to say. After a year, I got called out of history class, and there was Dad waiting in the office to take me away.

"Did you buy this with my money?" I asked about his new black Corvette.

"I've got a slam-dunk project," he said, gunning us away from my school, the speedometer licking up like a green flame, "with a part in it for you. We're going to get everything back—you'll see. Daddy just needs your help. Daddy can't do it without you."

That was true, and we both knew it. On the other hand, my mother didn't need us. She didn't even need us to need her. When we were back in L.A., she called and asked if I had gone with him willingly. When I said yes, she hung up, and I didn't see her again until I was nineteen and it was my turn to go to Cloud-vista. After I got out, she was the one who set me up with the shrink who told me to imagine the tiger. "Imagine a tiger," he said in his hypnotic voice, "and imagine yourself taming him by feeding him all your doubts, all your worries, all your pain, all your fear. The more he eats, the more he glows. When you find yourself in situations where you're doubting yourself, just imagine the tiger beside you, radiating light, and imagine everything and everyone else covered with a thick layer of dust." He had a lot of show-business clients. He said he understood the stresses we were under. He told me about an actress who won an Oscar after one year of imagining the tiger.

I WANT TO NAP, but as soon as I close my eyes, I have a funny feeling and pop them open. Sure enough, the sullen punk kid in front of me has his phone between the seats and is taking a picture of me. I put my hand over the phone, and it goes away.

"That must be annoying," Middle Management says.

"Yeah." People often hit me with a big dose of chummy compassion as an opening gambit, like I'll be so grateful someone finally understands my plight. Wistfully, I think of Billy's jet.

"You were amazing in that Jerome Shin movie. We watched it in a film class I took in college."

"Thanks." I unscrew the top of one of the little vodka bottles and pour its contents into a paper Starbucks cup I saved. The liquid turns faintly tea-colored from the coffee dregs. I raise the window shade a few inches and look down at a dazzling river, gleaming gold and shaped like a wild jungle vine.

"Is it true they brainwashed you?" the guy asks in a serious tone meant to assure me that my answer would be kept confidential.

I think of a television interview of Jefferson Morris I'd once watched in which he'd said, *How do you wash brains? Seriously. I've had it on my to-do list to find out, since supposedly it's all I do all day. Do you put them in a big bucket with some dish soap and scrub? Do you clip them to a line to dry?*

"Pretty much," I say.

"Wow."

I salute him with my Starbucks cup and empty it. Then I pour in the other bottle.

"Did you believe in Neptunius and all that?"

The sullen punk kid in the next row is watching Billy's movie too. Billy, his skin slightly orange on the shitty airplane screen, drives a red convertible. He grins and wears sunglasses. He pumps his fist. A man comes down the aisle wearing big headphones and a neck pillow, moving slowly, buoyantly, like he is walking on the bottom of the ocean. The headphones' cord trails behind him. I crane to see the naval officer, but all I can see is his bald spot. He is the only person on this plane I want to talk to, and so it is to him more than the blip next to me that I say, "The Founder said truth is in the heart of the believer."

"Who? Oh, right, you mean—right, that guy. X. Genesis Wilderness, or whatever."

"F. Genesis Inverness. But people in the Church consider it impolite to say his earth name."

"Isn't he the one where nobody knows if he's alive or dead?"

Billy kisses a blond starlet on-screen, and I lean closer to Middle Management and tell him the biggest secret I know. "Actually," I say, "he's both."

He laughs, a high-pitched trill like Billy's. "He's *both*? He's like a vampire or something? Wait, so, you *did* believe." Suddenly, he gets serious, concerned for me. "Do you still?"

"I'm just saying belief isn't necessarily something you either have or don't have, like a car or something. You can't just think 'Do I believe X, Y, and Z?' and then go look in the driveway and find out. I mean, do you really believe that book will make you a leader?"

I can see he wants to push his book farther down into the seat pocket. He presses his lips together. He is getting disgruntled, the way people do when our conversations don't line up with their fantasies. "No offense," he says, "but it all seems so silly."

LAST YEAR I did a play Off-Broadway, and during previews someone in the crowd shouted when I made my entrance, "Hail, Neptunius!"

I tried to cover the moment by briskly dusting my fake coffee table. My costar's jaw tightened as he read his fake newspaper. Our plywood living room had been perfectly real a second before, but suddenly its falseness mortified me. What was I doing, a grown woman, a mother separated from her child, dressing up like a fifties housewife and reciting words typed out by a notorious drunk and wife-beater who's been dead for thirty years? Those people filling up the dark with their glinting eyes—did they pay money to see the play or just to gawk at me? Out in the world, people stare as I go about my business, like I'm a traffic-stopping freak for buying coffee or having lunch in a restaurant. I gaze back at them through the lopsided hole in the Elephant Man's sack.

What I want to say to the man on the plane is that I've spent my whole life believing in silliness.

WHEN WE FIRST MET, Billy took me on his motorcycle from his office to the Santa Monica airport, and then a helicopter whisked us to Palm Springs, where a big house with a swimming pool was waiting, stocked with foie gras and cold lobster salad and strawberries but no booze. No one heard from me for two weeks, but no one seemed to miss me. After Palm Springs we came back to L.A. and allowed ourselves to be photographed together, the cameras snapping like piranhas, and then Billy drove me in his Aston Martin to the Ranch to meet Jefferson Morris.

"Jefferson," Billy said over dinner, "I've got to tell you, Karr is the most compassionate woman I've ever met. She has a real gift for giving and receiving help. It blows my mind. Truly. She's exactly what I've been waiting for. The moment she walked into my office—I don't know, it was like I reached a new understanding of Esteem right then. I don't think I was capable of this kind of love before. Maybe I wasn't ready. But this is the right woman at the right time."

We were sitting on the deck of a reproduction Spanish galleon that the FounderCorps had built right next to the Ranch's main swimming pool. Red sails snapped in the breeze; the mast creaked. I half expected us to move, even though we were out in the middle of the desert, the keel fixed in sand, the hot orange sun shooting sideways across the dark horizon as it set. Jefferson looked at me. His four bodyguards in khaki FounderCorps uniforms looked at me.

Jefferson will never say exactly how the Founder communicates with him, if it's by letter or if they chat on the phone or if the Founder's whispers travel through the ether from a distant island or another dimension and find their way to his ears. Even oracles have their trade secrets. Blip journalists have tried more than once to tap Jefferson's phone, unsuccessfully because Jefferson has an uncanny knack for detecting and exposing spies. On the galleon, I first thought that Jefferson was blandly handsome, as harmless as a catalog model, but as he studied me, squinting against the sunset, something in me shifted and sank, like I had just received a black-mail letter.

"Billy needs a gal who can be a strong supporter," Jefferson told me in a voice that suggested we were negotiating an agreement, just the two of us. "Someone who doesn't want to get in the way of his faith. Are you that kind of gal?"

"Billy wants to make people's lives better," I said solemnly. "I think it's noble."

"She's something special," Billy said.

"I don't doubt it," said Jefferson. "Not for a second."

At the Ranch, our fantasies popped into reality like toadstools springing from the earth. If I mentioned a food I liked, it would appear in our refrigerator. If Billy admired one of Jefferson's motorcycles, a duplicate would arrive on a flatbed truck within days. Billy told Jefferson that we had joked about wanting to run through a field of wildflowers together and—poof!—two dozen FounderCorps members were out tilling and seeding the desert behind our villa, laying down rich, dark mulch on top of the sand. The next time we came back, we held hands and ran through a field of wild mustard to a spot where a picnic was waiting for us on a gingham blanket.

Billy pulled me down beside him and said, "If the truth is in the heart of the believer, then you're my truth. Do you believe in me like that?"

"Of course I do," I said. "You saved me."

"That's all I want," he said. "All I want is to help you."

OUT THE WINDOW an enormous moon has risen. We thump across ruts of air, and Middle Management crosses himself. New York buses have little stenciled notices by their doors that say: This Is a Kneeling Bus. When a bus stops to let people on, it lets out a long, sad, hydraulic sigh and lowers itself into the gutter. When I first noticed the sign, I thought it was so beautiful, so artistic how some bus bureaucrat had recognized the buses as kneeling.

I want to talk to the man in white. I want to find out what he knows, for him to help me. We are all on a funeral barge, and he is at the helm. When he leaves us, we will have arrived somewhere; we will have been transformed. In Jerome Shin's last movie, L.A. is the afterlife, although no one says so explicitly. I would have been in it, but Billy said no, Jerome was a Usurper. We watched it in our screening room at home. Billy and Quentin sat side by side, and I sat behind them, studying the dark silhouettes of their heads against the bright screen.

THE LAST TIME I was in bed with Quentin, he said to the ceiling, "Why isn't it working?"

I touched his chest, the wings of sparse black hair that spread from his sternum. "You don't think it is?"

"My whole life I've done everything they said. I've read every word the Founder ever wrote. I've treated Jefferson like a god. I've disengaged Usurpers—I disengaged my own mother. There shouldn't be a single degradon left on me. But I feel like my Esteem is just draining away, like I'm nothing but doubt."

"You have more Esteem than anyone I know."

"Is it working for you?"

"Have you talked to Jefferson? What does he say?"

"He told me I needed to adjust my attitude."

We were in my bedroom. One of Helena's nannies had taken her to ballet. Billy was away on location. The whole staff must have known what we were up to. Probably it was one of them who leaked the story to the tabloids. I hope whoever it was bought a nice house with the money. I hope they didn't feel too guilty when Quentin hanged himself.

"The first time I went to the Ranch," I said, "there was this FounderCorps girl who would come collect my laundry. She wasn't supposed to be around when I was in the bungalow, but one day she was late or I was early and we happened to meet. I had just started dating Billy, and I asked her if she liked being in the Church."

"What did she say?"

"She said she was born into it, and then she said of course she loved it, that she'd learned so much about herself. And even then I thought, *What self? What is there besides what they've taught her?*"

He looked at me, and I felt that whirlpool sensation, like I was being sucked into him. "That's what I mean," he said. "Exactly."

"Oh, God, sorry, I wasn't saying—you have a self. You're not like that. It's just—sometimes I wonder—"

"What?"

"My mother says it's wrong to think we're entitled to avoid bad feelings. She says they're part of the price we pay for living."

"No. No one deserves to live with doubt."

I shrugged.

After a moment he said, "Is she a Usurper?"

"I think Billy's gearing up to tell me so. It's okay. She probably won't notice if I disengage her."

He was silent for a minute. "But why isn't it working?" he said.

We lay in silence, two animals that had wandered into the same trap. At the time, I would have said pure lust had drawn me to Quentin, lust and our mutual urge to soil some corner of Billy's perfect world. But after he died I knew he had been my true love.

"Why don't you leave?"

"And be a blip?"

"You could do it."

"Easy for you to say. You've lived out there."

"People would help you. You could do it."

Again the vertigo of looking at him. "Really?" he said. "Someone who's spent most of his life on a ship or at the Ranch? Who's never been to normal schools? Who's never had a job that didn't involve Jefferson Morris?"

I didn't know what to say, so I told him about the glowing tiger and the dust that smothers everything else.

"EXCUSE ME." I flag down a passing flight attendant. "Would you give this to the man in white?"

She takes the small square napkin from me with her red talons and glances at it, reading the message. I can see she recognizes me and that she thinks she likes me. "I'll see what I can do." She starts to turn away, then turns back. "That poor boy," she says. "That poor, poor boy."

DURING HELENA'S BIRTH, I was asked to keep silent so as not to attach any degradons to her. She would encounter the despectulation of the world soon enough, but being born should not be traumatic.

"Did Billy eat the placenta?" my mother asked when I called to give her the news. "It says in the magazines that they eat the placenta."

"Can't you be happy for me?" I said. "Just this once? Just for giggles? And lots of people eat the placenta."

I think I remember when my parents were together, but I can't be sure. They never married, and they split when I was three, but I can picture my father in the kitchen of an unfamiliar house, pretending to tap-dance. My mother is facedown on the counter, one hand over her wild hair, one in a fist, laughing so hard the sound is crushed into silence. Her fist beats three times on the tiles, slowly, like an ominous messenger pounding on a door.

I CAN'T DECIDE if I understood the risk I was taking when I first found myself kissing Quentin in my bungalow at the Ranch. He walked in on me when I was alone and crying on the sofa, and his embrace, instinctive and meant to comfort, pushed us over a precipice we had not known we were standing on. I was crying because of Helena, because she had told me she would never love me as much as she loved the Founder, and I had realized I did not like my own daughter, that I disdained her infantile conceit, her parroting of Billy, her certainty of her place at the center of a convenient cosmology. I blamed her for her gullibility even though she was only a child, even though I had not been brave enough to warn her by screaming as she emerged from me. Tendrils of contempt wrapped around my love, and perhaps they made me susceptible to the dark gravity that bound my body to Quentin's. Or perhaps I was simply still the reckless girl who was pulled from swimming pools and prevented from jumping off balconies, who climbed unscathed from crumpled Corvettes, who lived at the center of a different convenient cosmology. Maybe I thought I could get fired from my life, take some time to watch the squirrels, and then present myself for absorption by a revised destiny.

SOMETHING IS coming apart. Grief bears down on me like a black wave that has traveled thousands of miles and now is nearing shore. I look out the window, but there is only the hugeness of the moon and a few lights scattered like birdseed over the earth. I wait for the naval officer to come and find me, but his bald spot stays where it is. I need to talk to him. I need someone to really look at me. I remind myself that Quentin is dead, but I press the orange plastic cube in the ceiling. The flight attendant leans over me, smiling.

"Did you give it to him?" I ask.

"I sure did."

"What did he say?"

"He said thank you."

"Will he come talk to me?"

Her smile freezes around its edges, and I can see she already likes me less than she did. "Well, I don't know. I didn't ask him that."

"Will you ask him, please?" I dig deep and come up with a gritty half handful of stardust that I fling at her. "Please?"

She tilts her head and walks up the aisle. I can see her back as she speaks to him, dipping apologetically.

The shrink I was seeing in New York gave me a mantra to replace the tiger: *I am not the center of the universe.* He sat back in his Eames chair with the satisfaction of someone who'd just laid down a royal flush, and I said, "You mean I should overcome my selfishness for the sake of my self?"

He beamed. "Exactly."

We're all on the same team, I wanted to tell him. We're all fighting a common enemy: bad feelings. But, unbidden, my mother's voice offers its two cents: "Self-doubt is not the plague of our time. People starve; the planet is dying; people have terrible diseases; people are wrongly imprisoned; people watch their families get murdered; people die because bits of someone else are decomposing inside them."

I know, I tell her. *Shut up. I get it.*

ALMOST SIX YEARS PASSED between the wedding and when I conceived Helena, and I could tell Billy and Jefferson were worried. They had equated youth with fertility, but my womb was still hungover from my teens, I think, and preferred to laze around and watch Billy's seed float harmlessly by. Now Helena is the age I was when Jerome Shin took me into the bathroom. But she is a girl who holds her father's hand and not the testicles of tragic film directors. When I see her picture in magazines, an excruciating bloom of love opens in my chest, threatening to break me from the inside. I believe she will come to me someday. I believe doubt will lead her to me.

"MA'AM, I WAS GIVEN a note saying I had a friend in this seat. Would that be you?"

"Yes," I say, staring up at him. "Yes."

"Is there something I can help you with, ma'am?"

"Can I do anything? To help you? I'd like to help."

"Thank you, ma'am, but right now there's not much for me to do but wait to arrive."

I nod. Middle Management is staring at me. His big vanilla head crowds my peripheral vision. "Do you recognize me?" I ask. What I mean is *Do you* see *me? Do you* know *me?*

He does. I can always tell. Disgust creeps through his serious, respectful mask, and I am filled with longing for my mother. "Ma'am, my duty is to see that Petty Officer Roberts's remains are treated with the respect they deserve and that they are delivered safely to his family. Now, if you'll excuse me, I'd better return to my seat."

"Wait," I say. He waits. He thinks I am a spoiled movie star. He thinks I want special treatment, to involve myself in something that has nothing to do with me. He thinks I'm jealous of the attention a dead man is getting. I begin to cry. "I'm just so sorry," I say.

The officer frowns but out of confusion and no longer disgust. "We all are, ma'am. You have my word I'll pass along your condolences to his family."

I lean against the window and cry. I fly through the air at five hundred miles per hour. I cry for Quentin, for the dead soldier, mostly for myself. The seat belt sign comes on, pinging a soothing tone. My mother tells me I am out of touch with reality. My glowing tiger prowls the aisle. Dust settles thickly on the other passengers, obliterating their faces, their T-shirts, their laptops, furring the ice cubes in their plastic cups. Sometimes, late at night, my father and I would find ourselves in the kitchen at the same time, and we would pour half-and-half over bowls of Raisin Bran.

We lift spoonfuls of dust to our mouths. Faster, I tell him, drive faster. A field of orange lights swings into my window, and I want to run through it and collapse on a gingham blanket. The landing gear squeals out from under the dead soldier. The buses of the world kneel and ask forgiveness.

Lambs

ROBERT YULEY (American watercolorist, 1958–2035) knelt on his
bed and leaned out the small square window of his cottage's loft
as the sheepman and his dim-looking teenage son and their avid
black-and-white border collie separated the lambs from the ewes.
They had herded the sheep into a round pen, and now, amid urgent
bleating, the son was scooping up the lambs one by one and passing them to his father, who set them down in a different pen, away
from their mothers. Grinning, the boy thrust a wriggling lamb
feetfirst at the sheepman, who dodged the flailing hooves and lost
his temper. While the father shouted, the son held the lamb against
his chest, gazing at the ground.

Beyond the pens was a flat shelf of grass and beyond that, down
some cliffs, was the North Atlantic, smooth this morning, with a
glossy gray mineral sheen. A smattering of low islands, partially
shrouded in a retreating bank of storybook Irish mist, added interest to the horizon. Robert worried for a moment about the lambs
being hungry, then realized there was probably no more need
for them to eat. He closed the window and descended a ladder to

the large room that was kitchen, studio, and living space. He put water in the electric kettle for tea and flipped the switch. Tea only appealed to him, for some reason, when he was abroad. At home he never thought to drink it.

A while later, after the lambs had been herded onto a trailer and the sheepman had driven them away down the hill, and after the empty trailer had bounced back up the road and gone down again laden with ewes, someone knocked on Robert's door. It was Sasha Kranz (American painter, 1988–2035), the girl in the cottage next door. She was young, cheerful, and scrubby, her roly-poly body swaddled in layers of paint-splattered clothes and surmounted by a vast and imperfectly knitted green snood from which her head popped like the round finial on a newel post.

"Sorry to intrude," she said, peering around him into his cottage, glimpsing stone walls and furniture similar to but not identical to the furniture in hers: a tired IKEA love seat covered with a tartan blanket, a peeling red wooden chair at a small table, a stove with a basket of peat bricks beside it. Charcoal drawings of sheep were clothespinned to strings that crisscrossed the stone walls. Robert stepped outside, blocking her view, and pulled the door shut behind him, confirming her earlier impression of his secretiveness. She reminded herself not to be nosy. "I just wanted to let you know we're doing a group dinner tonight," she said. "Potluck style, but you don't really have to bring anything. You can just show up if you want."

He leaned against the door and looked away. He wasn't one for eye contact, generally. The part of his face that showed between his bushy beard and straw-like bangs was weathered from time spent tramping around outdoors and, rumor had it, from hard living, and there was a wariness in his pale eyes that seemed somehow childlike, as though he anticipated being scolded and was preemptively resentful. His hands were as cracked as a miner's and black from handling his dry little plugs of drawing charcoal. Robert Yuley was famous in an insider-y, cultish way—one of Sasha's art-school teachers, Maxine Hill, had shown slides of his work—and Sasha had entertained a fantasy of them becoming friends, roaming around the hills together to sketch, maybe even having some roughhewn *en plein air* sex (Maxine would *die*), though it turned out he was *so* quiet she was baffled by the mechanics of how to connect with him. She found herself babbling to fill the silences.

"Some people are here," she went on, "apparently just for a couple nights. They're staying in number three. I guess the wife is a big deal, although I'd never heard of her. Bettina Ericsson?"

Robert frowned at the ocean. Ages ago, before he had decided to withdraw from the art world (and, while he was at it, most of the rest of the world), he had endured a drunken one-night stand with Bettina Ericsson. He doubted she would remember: She had been plastered and had never asked his name, and he had been clean-shaven then and much younger, and it had happened in chaotic nocturnal artistic New York, back when the city had seemed halfway to ruins.

"How do you know she's a big deal if you've never heard of her?" he asked. In his opinion, Sasha was talented but too credulous, too permeable, too easily impressed and wounded.

"Just from the way she acted, you know? She's kind of graaaand." Sasha put her fists on her hips and pulled her soft chin back into her neck with an expression of Napoleonic hauteur. "Have *you* heard of her? She does installations? I guess she writes poetry, too? And songs? She said she's published like five books, and apparently some opera she wrote was performed in Brussels or somewhere like that. Antwerp? I'd google her, but there's *no* service right now."

Robert deplored the studiedly offhand, roundabout process of insinuation by which artists established a pecking order and of which Bettina had been—and presumably still was—a master. With vague allusions and her graaaand manner, she convinced people that momentous, hush-hush-for-now developments were lurking in her near future. *Big things are in the works,* Bettina had said to Robert all those years ago. And then, holding her finger to her lips: *Shhhhh.* From what he heard, people mostly did this sort of thing on Twitter now, but most of the internet was an abstraction to him.

Bettina's unexpected presence was the kind of intrusion Robert hated. He had come to Ireland because a sculptor friend had recommended this artists' residency, praising its windblown austerity and lack of Wi-Fi and the charm of its cottages (restored from roofless, moss-covered pre-famine shells) and the starkness of its cliff-top location and the abundance of interesting ruins and ancient standing stones to be encountered on walks. The friend said one might also stumble upon the odd people the stones attracted, people with long loose hair and flowing robes who roamed the hills with knapsacks full of herbs and wine and candles and bits of bone, playing at paganism.

This description turned out to be accurate, even about the Druids, whom Robert had run across once or twice setting up their altars, but still the place didn't seem so different from his cabin on the shore of Lake Superior. He found himself wondering why he had come.

"Should be interesting, anyway," Sasha said. "See you later? Eight-ish?"

He wanted to say he was ill or too deeply into his work to do something as mundane as eat dinner, but if he refused, she would be hurt. Instead he gazed past her at the drooping barbed-wire fence, wisps of wool still clinging to it here and there, and the empty field beyond. "They took away the lambs."

Sasha spun around to confirm the absence of sheep. "They did? Shit, that is so sad. They were so freaking cute. I don't know if I'll be able to eat lamb after this. Do you eat it? Lamb?"

"No."

She gestured at the cottage's closed door. "Good thing you already did a lot of sketches since now your models are gone."

He continued to look at the field and plucked at his beard with thumb and forefinger. The sheep in his paintings were dingy wool cylinders with long, blunt faces, yellow eyes, and comically skinny legs. They had stained knees, shit-crusted fleece on their haunches, slashes of bright blue spray paint across their backs that identified which sheepman they belonged to. Robert liked to paint white things because of the pleasure he gleaned from leaving voids of dry white untouched paper, herding the loose-running paint around the edges. After Sasha left, he went inside and looked at his sketches, then at the stack of paintings on his table. What was the point of them? The animals he had studied, sitting among them for hours with his charcoal and drawing pad, were perhaps a bleating mass flowing into a slaughterhouse at this very moment. Surely a true painting of sheep would have some hint of collective doom. He had an impulse to burn his work, but he always did.

AT EIGHT-FIFTEEN, Robert left his cottage. It would not be dark until almost eleven. The wind had picked up, stippling the sea with whitecaps. Waves bloomed against the distant islands in silent puffs of spray. He opened the door to the communal cottage and peered into the gloom. A peat fire on the open hearth clouded the air with acrid, earthy smoke. From the kitchen came voices and a

wash of electric light, but the main room—thick stone walls, bare
rafters under a high peaked roof—was illuminated only by half a
dozen mismatched candles scattered on the long table and what
evening light came through the small, deep windows. At the end of
the table, Bettina Ericsson (Danish installation artist, poet, singer,
photographer, playwright, 1949–2023) sat staring at Robert.

"Which one are you?" she said.

"I'm Robert."

"Oh, yes. The other American." Her Danish accent, strong
when he last encountered her, had mostly fallen away. "I met the
girl already."

Her gaze was level, inert. She had concealed herself under a the-
atrically voluminous green loden cloak with frog closures at the
neck, but he could see she had become a large woman. The angles
of her face, once sharp, were vague and low-lying with fat and
age. She had lined her eyes thickly with black, and her long, pale
sheet of hair had been wrapped, turban-like, around her head and
secured with an excess of combs. She had never been beautiful, but
as a young woman she had been handsome—gaunt and regal, with
thick yellow eyebrows that at some point she had replaced with
skeptical arcs of brown pencil.

"I'm Bettina Ericsson," she said, thinking he was rude not to
ask. Probably he already knew who she was—in fact, he seemed
vaguely familiar, though so many people did. Such was one consequence of living a full life. People passed in a blur; she could
hardly be expected to remember them all. She added, "I'm an artist, poet, singer, and playwright."

"All of those?" Robert said mildly, wishing he hadn't come,
remembering how she had bared her teeth at him in bed, how he
had been afraid to kiss that fierce mouth. The whole experience
had been frightening, like being called upon to perform an exor-

cism. *Annihilate me,* she had commanded, gripping his jaw. *Make me sorry I met you.*

"A photographer as well, actually," she said. "Among other things. You know, you remind me of someone. I can't think who."

He lifted the bowl he had brought, his potluck offering, and tipped his head toward the kitchen. "I'll just take this in."

"I'd love a glass of wine." She spoke slowly, imperiously. "My husband's in there. Send him back with it if you prefer to hide. I can tell you're shy. What is your surname, by the way?"

"Not shy, just quiet."

"Excuses, excuses," she said, a hand emerging from the cloak to wave him away.

ZACHARY MOSKOWITZ (Irish art historian, 1954–2035), or O'Moskowitz, as he liked to joke, sat on the kitchen counter and drank red wine out of a jam jar while the American girl peered anxiously into the oven. When she bent over, the tail of the man's shirt she was wearing stretched over her ample ass. He thought she was careless to have let herself get fat while she was still young, though honestly the night turned him on. Sasha's broad ass, if he were to give it a friendly fuck right there in the kitchen, promised the kind of erotic thrill he most enjoyed: the opportunity to grip, clutch, cling to an abundance of flesh while at the same time savoring the enlivening tang of contempt.

"How long does it take to roast vegetables?" she asked. "I feel like these have been in there forever."

"Give them a poke and see," Zachary said, bouncing his heels against the cabinets.

Sasha found a fork and opened the oven, blinking against the heat, not wishing to bend down while this impish man watched her with the kind of jabbing, prodding, presumptuous lust that doesn't care if it's welcome. He was small and slight with curly gray hair and quizzical, wide-set eyes. She was trying her best to pretend she liked him. She wanted to be a good sport, always, especially at residencies, which were supposed to be about camaraderie and the free exchange of ideas. Robert came in with a bowl of something.

"Robert!" she said. "Will you look at these vegetables and tell me if you think they're done?"

"Shake hands first," said Zachary, hopping down from the counter. "I'm Zachary. Bettina is my wife."

Robert set down his bowl and shook hands. He accepted a fork from Sasha and bent obligingly into the heat.

"What kind of an artist are you, Robert?" Zachary said from behind him. "Not to ask the unanswerable."

"Watercolors." He jabbed at a parsnip. "Almost," he told Sasha. "A few more minutes."

"Watercolors! Brave man. I don't know how one controls the paint. Not sure it's worth it anyway—I've never liked them much, although I'm sure yours are good. Sort of anemic, usually. Or messy. I'm a professor of art history at Trinity, since you asked. When Emma offered us the cottage for a few nights, we jumped at the chance—you know, coming to the source of it all, submerging ourselves in art's primordial ooze."

"Ooze?" repeated Robert.

Zachary drew an arch in the air with one arm. "All of this. You lot. You people busy making things. Not to worry, though, I won't be peeking through your windows to critique. Really it's just a wee vacation for us. We've been trapped in cities for ages. Bettina never has much of break between her exhibitions."

He sounded Irish, but his diction had a confusing English bluff-ness that came and went. The accents over here tended to make

Robert anxious. He worried about misunderstanding and being misunderstood, and he knew that the natives were busily gleaning subtle, possibly incriminating information about social class and geography from one another's every word. The caretaker of the cottages had an impenetrably dense Kerry accent and deployed unreliably decipherable Irish words here and there, and Robert had taken to avoiding him to spare them both any more baffling exchanges.

He became aware that Zachary seemed to be waiting for him to say something, probably to ask about Bettina's many exhibitions. He would not.

"Incidentally," Zachary said, "what's your surname?"

"It's Yuley," Sasha said with something like pride.

Zachary drummed his fingers against his lips. "Yuley. Oh, yes, yes, yes. I believe I've heard of you. You're quite well-known, then, aren't you? Yuley. Watercolors."

Robert wrapped his hand in a dish towel and pulled the pan of vegetables out. From the main room, a burst of chatter suggested that the last two members of their small community had arrived.

"I'll just go see who that is," Zachary said and trotted off, nimble as a satyr.

BETTINA WAS WATCHING the doorway for Robert, and when he appeared behind the chubby girl, carrying a stack of empty plates, she said, "You forgot my wine."

"So I did," he said. No apology, nor did he offer to rectify the mistake. *Americans,* she thought.

"Too late now, anyway. These girls beat you to it." Several bottles of red wine, provided by the new girls, stood open on the table.

China Colleran (Irish printmaker, 1978–2035) had a shaved head, a floral garland tattooed around her neck like a ligature, and a severe manner; she cranked and rolled the various presses in the printmaking shed with the brusque industriousness of an assembly-line worker. Mädchen Hauer (German composer, 1982–2035) was ethereal and bland and usually holed up in her cottage with her laptop, keyboard, and headphones. Sometimes the other artists spotted her wandering down the narrow lanes, green Wellies crusted with sheep shit, clutching bouquets of wildflowers and grasses.

Having acknowledged Robert's neglect, Bettina found she wanted him nearby. Aloof people were a challenge. Sometimes, when she explained to them who she *was*, they became useful acolytes, or, if they refused to be convinced of her immortality, she enjoyed disdaining them. Also, she had decided she didn't know him but that he reminded her of someone. She was curious who. "Come sit by me," she said, draping her arm over the back of a chair.

He sat. She peeled the foil from a platter in front of her, revealing a set of dainty brown ribs garnished with a spiral of lemon.

"You did rack of lamb?" China said. "Just in the little kitchen in your cottage?"

"My wife is a fantastic cook," Zachary said. "Give her a knife and a fire, and she'll give you a feast."

"Cooking is my meditation," Bettina said to Robert, fixing him with her hard green gaze.

They passed around the food. "Where does this come from?" Mädchen asked about the watercress salad.

"Robert brought it," said Sasha, taking a slice of bread from a basket.

Robert had made a small pile of rice on his plate beside a small pile of Sasha's roasted vegetables. "I found it in the stream up the hill," he said.

"Foraged!" declared Zachary. "So picturesque! I hope you washed it. We should have insisted this be an entirely foraged meal. Bettina and I should have plucked our lamb from across the road. Someone else could have gone down and prised mussels off the rocks."

"My husband is a Jew, you know," Bettina said to Robert while she sliced her lamb. "He loves things that don't cost money. He pretends it is an aesthetic choice, but it is a genetic compulsion."

Sasha, who was listening without being included, thought the way Bettina was talking about her husband's Jewishness had a weird salaciousness to it, like someone confessing a fetish. Sasha's father was Jewish, and yet she could manage to get through a conversation without regurgitating stereotypes in a tone of dark candor. She always felt an aura of discomfort, a lowering memory, when Europeans talked about Jews and Jewishness, and now she glanced at Mädchen for no reason other than that she was German.

"There aren't any lambs for you to pluck anymore," Robert said. "They took them away today."

"Away?" said Zachary. "To slaughter?"

"No, for a holiday at the seashore," said China.

"They were already at the seashore," said Mädchen.

"The landscape seems different now," said Sasha. "I feel different when I look at it. Sorrowful."

"You'd rather your meat be shrink-wrapped, stamped with the golden arches, nothing to do with an animal?" Zachary said.

"No," said Sasha. "It's not like that." She looked at Robert for help, but he appeared occupied with eating. Already she was ashamed of her desire to make these people like her. Obviously they could not be bothered. Sometimes when she was with a group of artists, especially after a few drinks, the conversation took on a thrilling freedom. They spoke about their preoccupations and emotions with a candor derived from a communal trust that they were not ordinary, that they all led similarly obsessive, elevated lives. It had been a mistake to think this would be one of those gatherings. They had already dismissed her. They assumed because she was young and friendly and American that she could not be a good artist. But she was—she would be—and if they trusted surfaces so easily, then they could not see the truth of things and therefore could not be good artists themselves. Reassured, she took some lamb.

"You feel sorry for the lambs then, Sasha, but you still eat them," China observed.

Sasha blushed. "I'm thinking about becoming a vegetarian."

"No, don't do that," Zachary said. "There's nothing better than a bit of meat on the bones." He smirked. As a reflex, she laughed as he clearly wanted her to, then immediately felt ashamed for appeasing him.

"Are *you* a vegetarian?" Bettina asked Robert when he passed along the lamb platter without taking any.

"Yes."

She settled back in her seat, and when he dared glance at her, he saw she was studying him. There was something expectant about the way she looked at him, as though they were a pair of spies tasked with passing secrets over dinner. "I wouldn't have thought. You seem like the red-blooded American man. Strong and virile."

"My wife is a bit of a slut," Zachary said cheerfully. "But there's a great deal to be gained from that, for the brave."

Robert had the disorienting sense Bettina had mistaken him for someone else. Maybe that had happened the first time, too, when she had beckoned him to her table in that dingy bar and instructed him to buy her a whiskey. After that, his pitiful supply of cash exhausted, she had bought the rest of their rounds and made vague boasts about her imminent artistic glory until she abruptly instructed him to take her to his apartment, which he had done, silently leading the way up four flights while she sang an aria, pausing on the landings to savor the echo of her own voice in the grimy, urine-smelling stairwell even after a woman stuck her head out and told her to shut the fuck up. Naked on the mattress on the floor of his barren studio, grasping his shoulders, she had bared her teeth, reminding him of a stoat or a mink, some fierce, soft animal. Her exposed incisors, stained and slick, had been somehow more intimate than any confrontation he had with the damp mess of blond curls that flourished unchecked between her legs.

"How do they kill them, the lambs?" Mädchen asked.

"Cut their throats, don't they?" said China. "Or is it like cattle? With a bolt gun?"

Bettina was looking up at the ceiling. "Real thatch," she remarked. *"Très authentique."*

Robert was thinking about the lambs. How *did* they kill them? Could the lambs see the others being slaughtered? Could the ewes hear the lambs? How did people bear it, killing such small, innocent things? Gutting them one after another after another? He used to have dogs, but with his last dog, from the time she was a puppy, he had been bothered by the fact that she would die. Too often, scratching her back or putting down her bowl of food, he would be reminded she would die and would think about how she did not know. Which was better, innocence or knowledge? He couldn't decide.

The others were talking about Tessa, a shared acquaintance, who had just had a big solo show in London.

"I'm not sure it did what she wanted it to do," Zachary said in a mournful tone, glee simmering underneath. "I'm afraid it was a bit of a reality check."

"Is the work good?" Sasha asked.

"You don't know it?" Bettina said, shocked, setting down her knife and fork. "She is quite well-known, quite talked about. You can't be so provincial, dear."

"It doesn't matter if it's good," Zachary said. "Tessa has lots of rich friends who will buy."

China, glaring, reached out to break a piece of dripped wax off a candle. "I like her work," she said. "There's something about the way she applies paint that I find very moving."

Moving, Sasha repeated to herself, momentarily distracted from her outrage at being called provincial. Yes, paint could be moving, as a medium. *Medium:* the viscous colors she squeezed from metal tubes but also a spiritualist figure, the one who bridges the gap between the living and the dead. Her paintings were disembodied visions, rappings and tappings brought over from the other side by her beckoning brushes—the other side being not death but a flickering dimension inhabited by images and colors she could never translate to paint the way she wanted to. Paint was the medium of both her hope and her disappointment.

Bettina gave Robert a conspiratorial look. Americans were always fascinated by the aristocracy. He would enjoy a few tidbits about Tessa. "She's terribly, terribly posh," she said, slicing lamb as she spoke. "She's one of those people who says she lives on a farm but means she lives in a castle. Her husband says he's a soldier, but he means he's a general. In the reserves. She's close to the Middletons." Watching him for a reaction, she snapped a bite of meat off her fork. He stared back at her warily, and she began to wonder if he wasn't a little simple.

Zachary rolled his eyes. "Useful for discounted party supplies."

Jaysus, they were a pair of snobs, though, weren't they, China thought, poking bits of hardened wax back into a candle's molten cauldron, watching them soften, turn transparent, and disappear. They were the kind of people to say whatever nasty thing was nearest at hand and assume it was clever because it was nasty. Zachary's thigh was against hers, pressing, but she didn't bother moving away. She thought about being in the printmaking cottage, rolling out sticky ink, heaving over the press's heavy lever.

"Build up the fire a bit, would you?" Bettina said to Robert.

He rose, less out of obedience than a desire to be away from her. As he placed a new peat brick on the fire, brown and heavy and dense, the ones already burning collapsed and broke apart, and he had to snatch his hand out of the sudden blaze. The chunks of glowing orange peat looked almost transparent, like a bed of crystals, and rippled with light. At the edge of the hearth was a basket of kindling and newspaper. The paper on top had photographs of a sheepdog trial, and Robert took a page and set it on the fire, where it vanished immediately into black flakes of ash. What he wished he could capture in his paintings, but never would, was flames eating through the paper.

Bettina was looking again at the cottage's thatched and raftered summit, dim with candlelight and full of smoke. She lifted her hands, and everyone looked up, too. "This is Valhalla," she said. "It really is Valhalla."

"My wife is Danish," Zachary explained to no one in particular. "Norse mythology has had a heavy influence on her."

"Have you been up the road?" China asked. "To see the monastic cells? A thousand years old. Likely more. You could barely call them huts. More like caves. You can't believe anyone could have lived there. The monks must have been so cold, chilled to the bone absolutely all the time."

"What does that have to do with Norse mythology?" Bettina said.

"Nothing. I just wonder if prayer ever gave them any pleasure."

"Is it supposed to?" said Zachary.

China shook her head. "You would hope it might offer some comfort."

"I think it was all one and the same," said Zachary. "The more miserable they were, the more smug they were about their holiness. Hope their cocks froze off."

"I know who you remind me of," Bettina said to Robert, so loudly and triumphantly that everyone fell silent. "You remind me of the loneliest man I ever met."

"Who was he?" said Sasha after a moment.

"You don't have to ask, dear Sasha," China said. "She's going to tell us anyway."

"SOME YEARS AGO," Bettina said, pausing to stare into each of the others' faces in turn, "maybe four or five years ago, I traveled as far north as I could for a project, to the high Arctic, to islands where there is nothing but ice and snow. You always have to be on alert for polar bears. People carry guns, but I would not. I refused. Walruses lie on icebergs. Glaciers are everywhere, bright blue, creeping down to the sea. Sometimes where they meet the sea they collapse, and you can be killed by flying bits of ice.

"My project had nothing to do with the place specifically, though. I cared only about the remoteness. I was to communicate telepathically with a group of artists in Antwerp." She stared around the table.

"You're a psychic as well then," China said.

Bettina nodded. "It is the greatest of my gifts. So. At appointed times on appointed days, I sent messages to the artists, and they would be waiting to receive them and to do what they sensed I was asking. I learned later it worked quite well, really, that they heard me quite clearly—something to do with the polar regions' strange effect on magnetism—but that is not the point.

"I arranged to visit an abandoned town where there had been a coal mine. The mine belonged to Russia, although the islands themselves did not. There are so many abandoned places in these islands. The place is too harsh—people have grand dreams, but the cold wears them down. The hardness. The mining town was made up of big buildings in a Soviet style, blocky, you know, all on stilts because the ground is frozen, enough to accommodate more than a thousand people, although now only one man lives there."

Bettina cast a significant glance at Robert. "This man walked down to meet me at the dock. He was wearing a long coat with brass buttons on the front and a tall black fur hat, like a hussar or a Cossack or I don't know, and he had a rifle over his shoulder. For the bears. He had long hair and a high-pitched giggle. He had once been a professor of political science at a university in Novosibirsk. Before he came to the Arctic, he was planning to kill himself because his wife had cheated on him. One day he had his bottles of pills and vodka assembled in his desk drawer at the university, and he had been surfing the Web, wasting time until everyone else left and he would be free to die, when he stumbled upon an advertisement for a job as a guide to this ghost town. So instead of dying he decided he would come to live alone in this ruined place. Every few months a helicopter brought him supplies, and he had a small generator, just for his rooms. Otherwise, nothing.

"He led me up the road to the town. Where the buildings were, there was a grassy field and a huge bust of Lenin at one end. The grass had been imported from Ukraine, Alexei said, as well as the soil in which it grew. If they had not brought the soil, too, the grass would not have grown. The mine was above, on the mountainside. There was a sort of covered tunnel leading up to it. The miners had to climb to the opening and then be lowered down again, into the dark.

"One of the buildings was an aquatic center. Alexei left me alone in there—I asked him to. There was an empty swimming pool of green tiles. On the level below the pool it was very dark with many small rooms and narrow corridors. I went through with a flashlight. The darkness made the most ordinary objects seem terrifying. Things like a doctor's scale or a boot or mattress.

"It was all I could do not to run out of there, but I did not. When I left, I felt I was covered in ghosts. Like perhaps I was halfway to being a ghost myself, I went to sit by Lenin to recover myself, and as I was sitting, I saw a curtain move in a building across the grassy square. There was a figure in the window, a shadow, and then it was gone.

"I will admit I was frightened. Or thrilled. I don't know if I can always tell the difference. The point is I was coursing with adrenaline. I felt I was accessing a new plane. The Arctic regions, you know, things are strange there. Compasses don't behave. There is the aurora. The sun does not set, and then it does not rise. You are always in danger of being devoured by a bear." She shrugged. "It's strange. But it makes sense to me, because of my Norse blood. So I thought, yes, I am afraid, I am electric with fear, and even though it is not the appointed time, I will try to put this feeling to use and communicate with Antwerp. I closed my eyes and centered myself like I do, and that is when I had my great vision."

She surveyed the table, waiting.

"Well," China said wryly, rising, "it's time for bed. Good night and sweet dreams." She made a small bow and left. When the door closed behind her, a gust of cold wind made the peat flare almost white. A candle blew out, but Mädchen relit it from one of the others.

"What was the vision?" Sasha asked.

Bettina leaned back into the shadows. "The end of the world," she said. "I know it is coming. Not tomorrow, you know, but not in too long, either. I saw the planet sweeping along its orbit without any life on it. I saw other things I can't describe. Or perhaps I will not allow myself to describe them."

"Unfortunately, her vision didn't tell *how* the world would end," Zachary said in apparent seriousness. "So we don't know what to warn against. Not that anyone would listen."

"I think it will be quick," Bettina said, "if that's any comfort. I saw a white flash. Fire."

Sasha nodded, eyebrows politely raised, relieved the vision was so mundane, so unimaginative.

"That's who you remind me of," Bettina said to Robert. "Alexei. Not in the way you look. Just something. It was him, if you wondered, in the window. He liked to do that as a joke when people visited. Spook them."

"I'm not lonely, though," Robert said.

Bettina seemed genuinely surprised. "No?"

"No."

Mädchen, who was holding a pale hank of her own hair to her nose and dreamily considering whether she would wash it after dinner to get the peat smoke out or wait until the morning, had nothing to say about Bettina's vision. A bodhran was lying on the windowsill behind her, and she picked it up and began to tap out a rhythm. When she stopped, a tapping continued. They all looked around, surprised. "It rains?" Mädchen said.

"Must be," said Zachary.

The tapping became more forceful.

"Sounds like hooves on the roof," Robert said.

"Still on about the lambs, are you?" said Zachary.

"Like hooves," Bettina repeated. "Hooves. Yes. The simile holds. You know I have written three books of poetry."

"It's the ghosts of the lambs," Zachary said, "come to take revenge on us. They'll be coming through the windows to slit our throats."

"There is something terrible, isn't there," Bettina said, "about watching them with their mothers, knowing what's going to happen to them when they themselves don't know."

"Would it be better if they did?" Robert said, thinking of his old dog, how before it died it had raised its head and closed its eyes and seemed to suckle at the air. Had death conjured its mother's teat?

"Innocence is pitiable," Bettina said.

"Knowledge is pitiable, too," said Zachary.

An obscure, unbearable confusion had welled up in Robert. "Why do they feel fear?" he asked. "The lambs? Before they die."

"What do you mean?" asked Bettina.

"I mean, if they don't know they're mortal, what do they think they're afraid *of*?"

"They don't *think*," Zachary said, exasperated. "They just act on instinct. You're missing the entire point of animals."

"Fear helps them survive," said Sasha, "run away at the right times, whatever. It's an adaptation."

"When the mothers try to protect their babies," Robert said, "what do they think they're protecting them *from*? When the baby gazelles or whatever get eaten by lions, what do the mothers think has *happened*?"

"It's not as though we know much more than they do," Bettina said. "We know we should be afraid. That's all."

After a silence, Mädchen said, "Is there pudding?"

Sasha jumped up, started clearing plates. "I brought an apple pie."

"Just like mum makes," said Zachary.

"PERHAPS I SHOULD SING," said Bettina, pouring the dregs of a wine bottle into her glass. "Many of my poems are meant to be sung. My husband will accompany me."

"On what?" Sasha asked, but Zachary was already reaching for a guitar that had been propped in a corner of the room, hidden by a bookshelf. Robert smiled to himself. Of course they had come prepared.

Zachary dragged a ladder-back chair up to the hearth and sat with his legs crossed, cradling the guitar, tuning it. Bettina, in her long cloak, came and stood beside him. She went through a series of vocal exercises, alternating duck call sounds and arbitrary high notes.

"The smoke is not good for my voice," Bettina announced. Then she said, "Look at Zachary with his guitar. Like Bob Dylan. Another sexy Jew."

To Sasha's disappointment and Robert's relief, the song was beautiful. Bettina's voice was raspy and soulful, Zachary's accompaniment minimal and sweet. Mädchen joined in with the bodhran, and the rain kept up its percussion.

Robert, who had been drinking wine with great purpose during Bettina's story, closed his eyes and thought of the Arctic. He would like to go there, to see the snow and ice which he might paint by not painting, by leaving the paper blank. He thought of the white bears, the black water.

Sasha wished the song were not so lovely. Its loveliness was making Bettina's vision more credible, more frightening. She wondered about the white flash, if anyone would even have time to understand what was happening.

Mädchen tapped the bodhran and thought of the standing stones, of the people who sometimes came striding up the hills in long robes. She gave them flowers for their altars.

WHEN ROBERT LEFT the dinner, the rain had stopped but the wind still blew. The dense mat of clouds was breaking apart into rafts of piled-up billows lit silver as they sailed past the moon. The sound of the ocean surged and diminished, surged and diminished. In open channels between the clouds, stars grazed their black field.

Walking back to his cottage, Robert swung his flashlight over the hillside. Two ewes and three lambs huddled there in the damp grass. Their eyes flashed green in the light. One of the ewes, startled, lurched up and gave a protracted, woeful bleat. It was such a futile sound, Robert thought, such a strange groan. They called their babies with that sound, complained about the wind and rain, expressed alarm and warning and happy anticipation of the feed pellets the sheepman dumped out of fifty-pound sacks every morning. These five must have been off somewhere when the others were taken. Sheep were always escaping their fields, brainlessly squeezing out through gaps in the fence and wandering over forbidden hillsides that were no different than the ones they'd left behind. Did these sheep wonder where the others had gone? He thought they must. He opened the door to his cottage and stood there for a moment looking out, almost inviting them in, almost offering them shelter.

The lucky few. The lonely refugees in the dark. The sheepman would find them, Robert supposed. They might have only won themselves one extra night. They would give themselves up in the morning in exchange for pellets. He hummed Bettina's song to himself as he lit a peat fire in his stove and fed his paintings into it one by one. They flared into light, then blackened, their edges curling over, the sheep disappearing.

When the fire comes, the white flash, he is an old man. He is ready for it, sitting waiting on a folding chair on the shore of Lake Superior with his pad of paper and a piece of charcoal in his trembling hand as the sky changes and then is gone.

The Great Central Pacific
Guano Company

AT FIRST, we were many. Forty men, a dozen women, ten children. Most of the children were born on the atoll, but one was born in France, another in Saigon, another at sea. Ships brought the wood and bricks that made our village, the corrugated sheets of tin for our roofs, the panes of glass, the kerosene, the pots and pans, the bottles and jars, the cloth, the shoes, the soap, the schoolbooks swollen with humidity, the year-old ladies' magazines for the Governor's young wife, the sweets for the Governor's son, the flour and sugar, the dragonfruit and rambutan and pineapple and mangosteen.

We had barrels to catch the rain that fell in brief, passionate fits in the afternoons. We set out clay jars and coconut shells to collect more, rows of them around our houses like open mouths. The lagoon stank of seaweed and too much sun, and when we bathed in it, tiny swimming lice stung us. A huge colony of seabirds nested on its southern edge. They thrust up sharp wings and beaks and chattered all day, their conversation rising in a crescendo at sunset until darkness brought down an exhausted silence. We had bristly pigs that slept under the coconut palms, brushing the sand with their stringy tails as they dreamed, rousing themselves to chomp down any land crabs that happened by. We had many millions of crabs: small, bright orange cannibals always in a grim hurry. They hurried across the empty sand. They hurried to tear one another's limbs off. They hurried to devour anything fleshy and helpless. We fashioned low fences around our houses with dead palm leaves to keep them from devouring our babies. When we killed a pig, a mass of crabs picked its bones clean.

Our village was at the northern end of the atoll, on the largest islet, in the shelter of our mountain. Not really a mountain—just a tooth of rock left from a dead volcano but the only thing taller than a palm tree and so a mountain to us. We had a long barracks with an armory and hammocks for the garrison. We had fifteen little cottages, basically huts, and one fine house, up on stilts, where the Governor lived with his wife. The Governor wore parade dress with braid and polished buttons and a bicorne hat, his face always sheened with sweat. His wife had a gramophone with a mahogany base and a shiny brass horn scalloped like a flower. She was as pink and delicate as a beautiful child, barely five feet tall, with a waist a man could close two hands around. To make herself grand, she wore pearls and petticoats and powdered her face, even though the rest of us had run out of powder long ago and were as brown as natives, even though her face was cakey and streaked by lunchtime. Freckles showed through across the tops of her cheekbones. She dressed her son in velvet knickers and let his hair grow long.

On the edge of the lagoon a mile down the beach stood two shacks: one small and one large but both rough and crooked. In the smaller lived the Director of the Great Central Pacific Guano Company, and in the larger were his sacks of guano. No one knew who owned the atoll. It was a time when countries were scrambling for every islet like hens pecking up seed. The Governor and the garrison were French, but the Director was American and claimed the island was, too, under an American law allowing Americans to claim any island that had been shat upon by seabirds. The Director said representatives of the Great Central Pacific Guano Company had been on the atoll before anyone else—except for some natives who had left their bones in a shallow cave halfway up the mountain—and because the previous Governor had died suddenly and the garrison was always being reshuffled, no one could be certain of the truth.

The Great Central Pacific Guano Company was a shoestring operation, nothing like the mines Madame Fournier had seen when she was young, with hundreds of toiling men and huge pits and vast drying platforms and iron tracks for carts that carried the phosphate rock to waiting ships. No, for workers the Director had only five natives who slept crowded into one house on the edge of the village, and the deposits they worked were soft and of low quality. We saw little of him, but on the occasions he came into the village, we found reasons to cross his path, to look at him. He was a very tall, dark-eyed man who had a studied, deliberate way of moving. Beneath his frayed straw hat, his face was not weathered like our husbands' but smooth and clean-shaven like the boys who had bestowed our first kisses in the shadowed gardens of houses where waltzes played and our friends danced, before we could even have imagined this place. We traded romantic fictions about him. He had fallen in love with a married woman and been driven to sea by her husband; he had gambled away his fortune; he had committed a murder; he was mourning a great loss; he loved us secretly and from afar.

The natives dug with rusted shovels, standing up to their knees in pale sludge at the far end of the islet, spreading the guano on rocks to dry until it could be scraped into sacks they carried over their shoulders to the Director's storehouse, where he sat in the shade and weighed each man's take. Our supply ships were poor ships, small ones, willing to take the Director's meager cargo, nothing like the mighty vessels Madame Fournier had seen. "Everything on them was white with the guano dust," she said. "The decks, the masts, the rigging. My father told me they were ghost ships and the terrible smell that hung around them was the stink of hell." When our supply ships came, the sailors battled through the waves in boats to bring us our meager goods and take away the sacks while frigate birds looked on from the Director's roof, plastering it with fresh smears of treasure.

"I ADVISE YOU to evacuate," the Englishman said, standing on the beach, his trousers soaked up to his thighs. "There is a disruption—a military disruption—and the supply ships will be delayed indefinitely. They might not come at all."

The doctor translated, and the Governor stood with one hand tucked into his jacket, head bowed, watching three crabs investigate his boots. Meditatively, he lifted a toe and held a crab against the sand, bearing down until its shell cracked. Its comrades hurried to eat it. At anchor beyond the reef, the English ship puffed impatient clouds of steam. On their way through the breakers, the sailors had nearly capsized the dinghy, and the Englishman, young but done up in a captain's jacket, had panicked and leapt into the water and sloshed ashore.

"Why," asked the Governor, "did the colonial authority not send word?"

"In Saigon, I was asked as a favor to convey this urgent message to you on behalf of the French government. We can take twenty passengers as far as Brisbane, and from there you'll have to make your own way."

"Only twenty?" asked Madame Berger, who spoke English. "What about the rest?"

"The decision rests with me," the Governor reminded her sharply.

"We will send an appeal so other ships know to come," said the Englishman. "Everyone will be able to leave, but we will take families first."

The Governor's face, burned red and with a hooked nose, twisted into a scowl, and he reached up to adjust his bicorne, pulling it low. "Pardon me, monsieur, but you are not the governor of this atoll. You are not the governor of any atoll." The doctor was translating more rapidly now, speaking over the Governor as though they were having an argument. "I know nothing of you. You know nothing of us. If there were a real need to evacuate, a French ship would have been sent with official orders. I will not abandon a fortified colony because the boy captain of a toy ship heard a rumor in Saigon. Perhaps your people run from responsibility, leaving their territories for the scavengers"—here he flung out an arm toward the Director's encampment and the doctor, faithful mimic, did the same—"but my people do not. And so I wish you a good day and a *bon voyage*."

The Governor strode away to his house. His wife dawdled after him, pulling their son by his hand and looking back over her shoulder. The Englishman pressed his lips together and shook one wet trouser leg and then the other. "Anyone who wishes to leave, this may be your only chance," he said. "I strongly urge you to evacuate."

As she repeated his words for us, Madame Berger lifted her daughter to her hip and stroked the little girl's hair. We wanted to go, but our husbands said we could not disobey the Governor. We could not be deserters. They said this Englishman might be setting a trap, trying to steal our atoll. Let him have it, we said. The Governor knows best, they said. But the children, we said. For France, our husbands said. Our destiny is here, they said, as is our duty.

Only the Director's five natives left. They came running from their crowded house with their belongings in sacks over their shoulders and said they wanted to go to another atoll, not all the way to Brisbane, just to another island with a proper town, it didn't matter which. We asked if someone shouldn't tell the Director first, and one of them spat in the sand. When the Englishman agreed to take them, the natives relieved his sailors of their oars and rowed cleanly, rapidly away through the waves. Later, when that day had become the subject of wonder, we talked about what might have happened to them. We said the captain had turned them into English sailors because they knew the islands and were strong with the oars. We said they were digging guano someplace else. We said they were in Australia with wives and families. We said the ship had sunk and they were all drowned.

BEFORE, our atoll was a volcano alone in the ocean. A reef grew up around it. But the volcano died, and rain washed it away bit by bit until the crater sank lower than the reef and became a lagoon. There were places in the lagoon where the shallowness gave way, and we found ourselves looking down into nothing, pure depth. We wondered if lava would someday shoot up through these holes, if strange beasts were hiding in them, if they were tunnels through the earth, if we could swim through them and emerge in France.

Long ago, natives had come to the atoll in canoes and left their bones behind. We had asked the Director's natives about the bones, but they shrugged and said they didn't know about those people. They were not their people.

THE MEN DIED more easily than we did. Their gums became livid. Their teeth wiggled in their sockets. Blood pooled in purple lakes under their skin. They indulged their lethargy; they suffered; they ranted and raved. We tended the children and rationed the coconuts and guarded the pigs and stole the seabirds' eggs. In the afternoons, the men took to their hammocks, and we sat with the children, doing lessons and listening to the rain and the warbling gramophone and the clamor of the birds. The Governor's wife played Bizet and Offenbach and marches by Sousa, whose band she had seen in Paris at the Exposition. The Governor himself seldom appeared, but when he did, his hat was askew and his buttons unpolished and unfastened. His trousers sagged. He watched our efforts without interest, preferring to skulk around the barracks, peering in through the cloudy windows at the dying soldiers. He sat on the beach like a man who has fallen off a horse, legs flopped wide, staring at the empty horizon in surprised consternation.

The first to go was Monsieur Fournier. He had always seemed frail with his pince-nez and bald, burned scalp and tortoise neck. He had kept a little shop for us. Its shelves stood empty for months before his death, although we suspected him of putting aside a cache for Madame Fournier and their children, who were plumper than the rest and whose gums were hardly red at all. But Monsieur Fournier had become mottled with bruises and raged with fever and tremors and died one afternoon during the rain. The doctor went down the beach to see the Director and returned with borrowed shovels. The healthiest men dug a pit near our mountain, out of the reach of high tide, knowing it would not be our last grave. Madame Sauvage, who was Madame Fournier's bosom friend but hardheaded, shielded her eyes with one hand and looked up at the mountain, saying, "We could do like the natives and let the crabs pick the bones clean. Then we would only have to bury those. Seems more practical, no?"

After that, Madame Fournier was not her friend anymore.

THE CRABS WERE poisonous for us to eat. The birds were stringy, almost not worth the effort of netting, plucking, and roasting. Their eggs had a rancid taste, but we ate them anyway. We fished in the lagoon, but the larger, better fish were out at sea, where we could not catch them without a boat. We did not dare take the garrison's only boat (upturned under the palms, a cathedral for the crabs) through the waves. The pigs were precious gods, and their deaths—strictly scheduled, the flesh shared out in tiny portions— filled us with bloodthirsty ecstasy and the urge to dance wildly around our cooking fires. We dreamed about mangosteen and pineapple and the hairy red rambutan with its sweet pink-white inside like a scallop. Perhaps we were hardier than the men. Or perhaps we gave ourselves larger shares of the coconuts, which fended off the scurvy. Perhaps we did, in secret, drink a little pig's blood. Perhaps we were more determined to live. We did not all live, but the day the Governor emerged from his house, thrumming with purpose and decision and with his buttons shined and his hat pulled low on his brow, a year after the offended Englishman had steamed away, ten of us still lived and six of our children but only thirteen men.

The Director lived, though we did not include him in our number. We saw him from a distance, fishing the reef from his small boat or sitting in the shade beside his shack. Madame Lemieux said she had seen him knocking a whole young coconut from a tree just for himself but had been too timid to stop him, to explain how we must share, how we felt as much devotion to the coconuts as mother birds nurturing their eggs.

Sometimes when we gathered eggs, a mother frigate bird or gull would swoop, crying out that we were murderers, pecking at our heads and hands, and though we understood her anguish, we had no mercy to give. Our own young were as stringy and stunted as the brown and tufted hatchlings, no longer cherubic darlings but yawning mouths atop straining throats. We had given extra food to the children who died, but it made no difference. They had surrendered, teeth falling from their gums in a parody of old age, eyes drying out as they gazed at the sand and water that would be their only world. How lost those children must have been when they arrived in heaven, how bewildered by the gardens and lakes, the cobblestone streets and grand buildings, the sweets, the high mountains, the snow.

The men must have been half mad to go with the Governor, to believe in his ship. Or they were entirely mad, and we were too half mad to stop them. "A ship!" the Governor had declared, speaking to us from his porch, washed and shaved and combed but shrunken inside his uniform, his pistol tucked into its knotted belt. "I have sighted a ship!" He pointed to the clean blue seam. "We must reach it. The time has come."

"I saw it, too," said one of the soldiers, so yellow with jaundice and sunken with hunger that he resembled a goblin. "I saw broad sails. A magnificent ship. We must go after it. They will save us."

"Only sails?" asked another soldier.

"There was a smokestack," said the Governor. "I saw clouds of steam."

"Hunger is giving you visions," we told them.

"There is no ship," we told them.

The Governor roared at us, jabbing a finger at the barren horizon. "I am the Governor of this atoll, and I say there was a ship!"

The boat was righted and carried to the water, and the men rowed through the waves. They all went willingly except the doctor, who was forced in at gunpoint by the Governor while his wife wailed and clutched at the Governor's sleeve. "You killed my children," she cried, "and now you are taking my husband to his death."

"Not to death, madame," he said. "To salvation."

AND SO THEY abandoned us. After all our toils we had not expected this shamefaced exodus made with haste, with something like relief. They took nothing with them. No food, no water, no weapons besides the Governor's pistol. As they rowed through the swells, disappearing over each crest and then climbing up only to slide away again, an embarrassed silence came over us. The Governor's wife, small and stalwart, had shaken her husband's hand and presented their son for a goodbye kiss, but once he was gone she began to weep, pressing her fists to her eyes, her son embracing her legs. We stood and watched until we could not tell the boat from the shadows in the water.

Madame Travert claimed she saw it capsize. She had climbed up the mountain for a better view so indeed she might have, though she did not mention seeing any such thing until two days had passed, when we were beginning to understand the boat would never return, let alone any magnificent ship. "No," said Madame Porcher, "they were only blown off course. They are rowing back. They will be here any minute." But we had seen so many men die.

To die seemed so simple, the most likely outcome of any day. They had slipped away, out of the blue noose in which we lived.

"A great black shape came out of the water," said Madame Travert, "like the shadow of an enormous bird, and overturned the boat."

"Maybe a devilfish," suggested Madame Lapointe, braiding her daughter's salty, sticky hair. Her husband had been one of the early deaths, and now the departure of the rest seemed not to bother her. We were gathered in the Governor's house, indulging in a lit lantern. Usually when the sun set we went meekly to sleep.

"Or a whale's fluke," Madame Adenot said, setting a new disc on the gramophone and turning the crank. There was a blank rush like water and then the first notes of "The Habanera": a soprano voice, all alone, sinuously descending a staircase.

The Governor's wife looked more like a child than ever, her face unpowdered and blotchy from crying, her freckles stark. Her hair had come loose from its pins and stood out from her head like burned feathers. Her son draped himself over her back and locked his arms around her neck. "My God," she whispered. "It was the devil. He sent the phantom ship. He reached out of the sea and took them."

"Devil*fish*," said Madame Lapointe. "The manta."

"If it was the devil," hissed the doctor's wife, "then your husband was the one he chose to talk to. Your husband was the one who was listening."

The Governor's wife began to cry again. She was a noisy, guttural crier, a fishlike gulper of air. Her son clung to her, riding out her tortured rocking like a monkey in a windblown tree. "What will we do?" she asked. "He will take us as well. We should throw ourselves into the sea."

"Whatever has happened is your husband's fault!" the doctor's wife was shouting. "He made us stay here. He took my husband away. He drew his pistol!"

The Governor's wife clutched her hands together. "It was the *devil*!"

There was a knock at the door. We looked at one another. Madame Porcher leapt to her feet. "They have returned!"

She pulled the door wide, and there, just barely touched by the lantern light, was the Director.

WE HAD FORGOTTEN about him, this last man. His voice was steady, measured. He spoke like someone whose words had been kept for a long time, stacked up like his bags of guano, endlessly assessed and shifted. He knew our names; he knew which children belonged to each of us; he knew what had happened to the men. He told us how he had watched us, seen the lights of our fires and lanterns, heard the cries of our babies, marveled at the good fortune of our men to have wives and families and compatriots. He spoke some French; we spoke some English; Madame Berger translated when there were gaps. "I have been very alone," he told us. "I felt like I was gazing through a window at you, unseen and unwelcome. You had men of your own and didn't need me. But now, let us keep one another company. Let me protect you."

"From the crabs?" whispered Madame Sauvage. "From the birds? He can protect us from the waves? From the scurvy?" He paused, looking at her, not seeming to understand, but Madame Berger did not translate. He was handsome in the lantern light but melancholy, like the ghost of a poet.

"When the ship was here," he went on, "no one came to ask if I wanted to leave. You sent my natives away. With no one to help me dig, I have no livelihood, no purpose. You have made me a beggar."

We tried to protest that we had not sent them away, that they had fled. We tried to blame the men. He shook his head. "What matters now is that we survive. Let me protect you from disorder, from your female weakness. I will be father to you all, brother to you all"—we knew how his sentence, our sentence, must end— "and husband to you all."

We didn't know how to be women without men. If we turned him down, told him to go back alone to his shack, one of us would steal down the beach, try to take him for herself.

Gracefully, again the hostess, the Governor's wife went to the gramophone, put on a disc, and turned the crank. A march by John Philip Sousa trooped jauntily out of the brass blossom, reminding us to bear up, go forward. The Director listened until the tune was over, and then he bade us good night. We did not know until later that he went through the dark to the barracks and threw all the rifles into the lagoon, save one.

THIS IS the part of the story we do not tell, not to the men from the newspapers, not to our new husbands, not to our mothers or sisters. To them, we say, "With the gun he was like a god. The gun always in one hand, a child always in the other—what could we do? We were slaves, prisoners. We feared for the children." To one another, we say nothing. We pretend we left our bones on that island. We are all dead, our flesh parceled out among the crabs. To ourselves, in our thoughts, we admit this: We were a mostly willing harem. Seduction was a pleasant alternative to grief, to the memories of our cowardly husbands with their bleeding gums.

And for a time, we desired the Director. At least we desired not to be outshone by the others. Or we desired the fish he caught and was willing to barter away, his bluefish and king mackerel.

For the first time in a year, we were not hungry, not lethargic. The fish healed our bodies. In the barracks, he lifted hanks of our salty hair and sniffed as though inhaling sweet perfume. He asked us to tell him stories (we had begun to speak our own pidgin) while he fiddled with our bodies, plucking at our nipples while we recited the same fairy tales we told our children. "I am a fisher of women," he said to each of us as though the joke had just occurred to him.

"I detest him," Madame Sauvage said, "but I can't give up the fish."

"Liar," said Madame Lemieux.

"I will share my fish with you," offered Madame Fournier, "if you stop going to see him."

Madame Sauvage shrugged. "That will only make him angry."

"You flatter yourself," said Madame Adenot.

Madame Sauvage shrugged again. "We must all flatter ourselves to survive."

The children were always hanging from him, missing their fathers. They fought for his attention. They begged for stories about places he had been: New York City, San Francisco, Quito, Macau. They sat with him while he whetted his razor on a leather strap and shaved with a broken mirror and a bit of hoarded soap. He told them he had killed a bear in Alaska and a lion in Tanganyika, and he said John Philip Sousa had once asked him to join his band, on clarinet. He told them that he had seen a mermaid. He sent them up the mountain to watch for ships. He had them steal eggs and cut new thatch for the houses and patrol around him while he ate, driving away the crabs. He took them with him when he fished, and he told them about sharks.

Only the Governor's wife refused him. When we gathered in the evenings to listen to the gramophone, she treated him with lofty hospitality, inquiring after his health and his success on the reef that day as though he were a minor bureaucrat she was obliged to entertain until her husband returned home. She watched our gambits for his attention with indifference, high above the fray in her stilted house. Cold infanta, she accepted the fish he brought with only a nod, just as she accepted his wild stories—a dip of her narrow chin, nothing more. To his flattery—his barbs, his boasts, his prophecies—she gave the same nod and a flicker of her eyes under their pink lids, always puffy from crying.

Without her, we might have gone on peacefully, polygamously forever, or for as long as we needed. She meant to discourage him with her airs and her sadness, but she was only inflaming him. We could see his agitation in the way he stared at her. We could feel it in the way he touched us, groping at our unsatisfying flesh for some trace of her.

ONE DAY he caught an enormous silver fish with fat, frowning lips. Glaring proudly out from under his straw hat, he carried it slung over his shoulders to the Governor's house, climbed to the porch, and went inside without knocking. In a minute the fish flew out the door and over the porch and landed in the sand. We did not dare take it, and long before he emerged again, the crabs had picked it to nothing.

————

WE DO NOT TELL how after that she became a shade, drifting behind the windows of her fine house. Birds nested on her porch. Her little boy lolled among them, sapped by her grief. We combed his long, wispy hair. We gave him clothes left by dead children and burned the grimy velvet knickers he had outgrown.

We were innocents, really. We had known chaste garden kisses and then our husbands and then the atoll. How could we have guessed that hate and desire could breed each other, consume each other? He stopped summoning us to his barracks. He stopped fishing. He touched no one but her. In the evenings, he liked to sit regally in the Governor's cane chair with one leg stretched out. He would give a little roll of one hand when he wanted us to start the gramophone, an emperor signaling for a concert to begin. The boy who had polished the horn was long dead, and a green patina covered the brass blossom like mold. The crank turned reluctantly, with a whine and a catch, and the discs were so scratched that a whooshing like waves almost drowned out the broken music, notes that sounded so faraway they might have been distant echoes from the Paris Opéra or of jaunty drums being beaten in New York City.

"Can't anyone make her stop crying?" he demanded about the Governor's wife.

"We have tried," we said. And we had. We had held her and kissed her and bribed her with the sweet ribs of a pig. We had reasoned and pleaded and warned and threatened and entreated. "Think of your son," we said. "Be strong for your son." We had taken her into the ocean to baptize the sorrow out of her. But still she wept.

"Stop crying," he told her. She sat on the floor with her son clinging to her back and peered down into a sadness as bottomless as the holes in the lagoon. She did not move. A tear dripped from

her chin. He rose and crossed the room. "Stop it." He prodded her
with the butt of his rifle. "Stop crying and never start again."

The Governor's wife drew a long, choking sob. She lifted her
head and looked up into his face. "You made me this way."

"You're ungrateful. You still think you're high and mighty, but
you're only a whore."

"You are a buffoon," she said. "You are dirt."

"Get out," he told us quietly, tapping the rifle once against the
floor.

Madame Fournier bent to help up the Governor's wife, but he
pushed her aside. "She stays," he said.

"Let me take the little boy then," Madame Fournier said.

"Leave him," he said.

SOME TIME PASSED before we saw the Governor's son playing
alone on the beach, picking up crabs and flinging them into the
sea. We went to him, wanting to embrace him, but he spooked and
fled like a wild animal. When his mother and the Director finally
emerged from the house, it was evening and the sea was glazed
with lavender. The little boy ran to his mother and clutched at her
skirts. She, no longer weeping, her hair loose and wild, kept walking as she pried her son's grip loose and pushed him away. He came
back, howling, and she disentangled herself again, pushing him so
roughly that he fell down. When he came back a third time, the
Director grabbed him by his arm, and then it was the Governor's
wife who howled and clutched. Seizing her son, she lifted him up
to her face and whispered something before she flung him away.
He sat in the sand, legs wide, and stared after his mother with the
same look of betrayal his father had once given the wide-open
ocean. Calmly, the Director ushered the Governor's wife into the

small boat, and she went without protest, gazing back at the beach while he rowed them out beyond the reef.

WE DO NOT SAY that we let him take her or that we had, at times, imagined we would be glad to be rid of her and her tears. But when she was gone, we knew how the men must have felt. The weight of our mistakes was too much to bear. The terror of making more, worse mistakes was too much to bear. Fear saturated us. Fear of the gun, of the razor caressing its strop, of the devil who could leap out of the sea and pull us down.

He told us they had spoken in her house for a long time and come to what he thought was a cordial understanding. To solidify their newfound peace, they had agreed to go fishing and bring everyone a treat for dinner. Then, to his everlasting shock, just after they reached deep water, the Governor's wife had leapt from the boat and sank without struggle, dragged down by her heavy petticoats.

"Her troubles are over," the Director said, sitting on her porch, now his porch, and wearing one of the Governor's bicorne hats. "In heaven she will have nothing to cry about." The children no longer wished to go near him, but we were afraid and nudged them onto his knees, where they perched grimly, like gargoyles.

Before we came to the island, we had not known it was possible to believe a thing and its opposite at the same time. But we came to believe we would die on the island and also that we would be rescued. We believed the Director was a murderer; we believed he wanted to help us. We knew the world was a sphere, that the sea was an endless surface with no edges, but the planet had become a flat circle of water with our bare ring of sand in its middle like the hole at the center of a gramophone disc. We believed our island was the only place left on earth, and we believed everything else was still there: Saigon and Paris, America, houses made from stone, cities and bathtubs and theaters and greengrocers, people we had once known.

As schoolgirls, we had spun painted plaster globes, closing our eyes and putting our fingers on the places we would live. If our finger landed out in the seemingly empty blue, we would say, "Doesn't count! Spin again!" We might have covered our island with our clean, soft, childish fingertips, obliterating it without knowing.

THE DIRECTOR SUMMONED us to his fine house on stilts, but he could find no satisfaction in our bodies anymore. We worked to please him. We tried with more fervor than before because our greatest terror was where he would look next for succor, for tears and a small body.

He resumed the operations of the Great Central Pacific Guano Company. At first we protested, but, rifle slung over his back, he carried one of the little boys under his arm toward his boat until we ran after him and promised to dig. We worked barefoot, standing up to our knees in a slick, chalky ooze. The preserved bodies of birds surfaced in the muck, mummified by their own shit, and we tossed them aside. We worked accompanied by the grainy, slicing sound of the dull shovels and our singing. We sang songs we remembered from our childhoods, and we sang what we'd heard a thousand times on the gramophone: "The Habanera" and Rossini and Verdi and Sousa. We spread the guano on rocks to dry, then we scraped it into sacks and carried the sacks to his storehouse. He was unhappy with what we harvested, and we were told to go into the bird colonies and take the guano-spackled nests, dumping out the eggs and hatchlings. And so we did.

Madame Lemieux became pregnant and then Madame Porcher. They dug with furious determination, not singing, and they would not rest even when we begged them. "They are trying to dig their own graves," we whispered behind their backs.

The Governor's son turned into a vicious little demon. He broke crabs into smaller and smaller pieces to see how long they stayed alive. He captured a gull, breaking its wing in the process. When the gull refused his proffered morsels and did nothing but shriek its misery, he set it on the beach for the crabs.

The Director ate our pigs, our coconuts. We did not try to stop him. We could not protect the pigs. We tried to protect the children, but even a tiny islet can be too large for the shepherds of such skittish, slippery creatures. The Director burned our kerosene. We began to suspect one another of collaboration. We helped Madame Lemieux and Madame Porcher through their labors, but when we bathed their newborn sons, his heirs, we thought of drowning them for the sake of our own children.

A CHILD WITH CHILD. The body thin and compact, no breasts to speak of, the faintest wispy blond down under the arms and between the legs, the face and arms and calves gone brown, the rest still white and soft, the belly small but unmistakably domed. She did not know what we saw as she bathed, and she splashed in the lagoon with the other children, too accustomed to the stings of the swimming lice to complain. The girl was only eleven. She had become quiet and furtive, but we had hoped to blame her age, her need to have secrets, even here. We did not tell her what we saw in her. We did not want to frighten her. But we clutched hands, our fingernails biting into flesh. Our fear broke under the weight of our failures.

As we explained, the end was an accident. The one who did it did not mean to come up behind him while he inspected our half-empty sacks. She did not mean to swing her shovel back behind her shoulder, nor to release it—and release is the right word because it sprang forward like a beast cut from its leash, pulling her in its wake—nor did she mean to turn it just so, finding an angle through the air that let the sharp iron edge meet his skull just above his ear where the bone would be most easily cracked. He staggered to one side, his handsome mouth opening in puzzlement. He watched us pull his rifle from his hands and seemed as startled as we were by how easy it was to disarm him. We circled around. The shovel came down again, and his blood spattered our faces and then, after he had fallen and the shovel came down again, our skirts and our guano-caked shins.

We were tired of digging. We left him for the crabs. Thousands came to his funeral feast, a mountain of them, marking his grave with an orange tumulus. The way we tell the story, a miraculous coincidence brought the cruiser that very day, as though the swing of the shovel had been an escapist's trick, the compression of a hidden spring that set us free. But the truth was that we had already seen the ship's gray silhouette rending the blue from the blue. The child keeping watch on the mountain had come running to tell us while we dug the guano.

Madame Fournier had saved a little kerosene. For kindling we used the thatched roof of the Director's shed. The flames ran in orange frills along the spines of the dry leaves, catching the white droppings of the frigate birds with hungry pops. The walls of the storehouse were whitewashed with guano dust, and the fire leapt and pounced as though amazed by its own good fortune. We ran down the beach, shouting like children, and we turned to see a balloon of fire rise from the storehouse as it exploded, a cracked black husk around a blinding sun. We ran from the ash and the smoke and the searing ammoniac reek of the guano, away from the blackening, collapsing ribs of that wrecked ghost ship, and we ran to stand on the beach and wave to the other ship, the ship of the living that was turning in from the horizon.

Backcountry

WHEN INGRID WAS twenty-five, she lived for four months in a big house on the edge of an unfinished—never to be finished—ski resort. This was in Montana, on Adelaide Peak, twenty years ago. Richie, her much older kind-of boyfriend and the mastermind of the whole sad enterprise, had borrowed against his land to build the house, a baronial place full of grandiose touches like antler chandeliers and stone fireplaces and a drawer that warmed plates. It was the only structure on the mountain. After Richie went missing and Ingrid was left alone, all his expensive possessions started to seem foolish, and a careless contempt for them would steal over her—for him, too, who had been dumb or weak enough to probably die.

Richie liked to say the house was ski-in, ski-out, even if skiing out took some work since there weren't any lifts. If they wanted to go down, they had to climb up, earn their turns. After the search was called off, Ingrid hiked or skinned up Adelaide on the days when the weather allowed and skied different routes down, looking for some sign: a ski tip poking out of the snow, Richie's blaze-orange beanie snagged on a branch. Truthfully, though, she wasn't looking very hard. Going up, she often lost herself in the rhythmic jab of her poles, the cold air cycling through her lungs, the crows caw-cawing in the trees. Coming down, she got to thinking about her technique and line and sometimes forgot all about Richie until she was back at the house. Then the sight of it, stone and timber, dark and empty, reminded her he'd be spending another night out there, somewhere, either dead in the cold with the night creatures or, less probably but still possibly, alive and safe somewhere else, somewhere like the Cayman Islands, having abandoned her and his other problems with one tidy disappearance.

BEFORE SHE MET RICHIE, Ingrid had been with Wesley, the man she would eventually marry. They'd gotten together one winter in Breckenridge, when they were both working in a ski shop, a clattering dungeon that smelled of socks and wax and steel edges fresh off the grinder, and had dated for some months, into the summer. When he left her, Wesley disguised the leaving as a simple departure: He was going backpacking around the world, seeking something vague yet important. To be fair, he invited her along, but he'd known she didn't have the money.

Ingrid had grown up on Lake Tahoe—her parents owned a bar and grill, a taxidermy-and-neon kind of place—and as soon as she finished high school, she'd taken off without any plan beyond drifting through the mountain states. The people she hung out with were seasonal people like herself: lifties or instructors or patrollers in the winter, rafting or fishing guides or dude-ranch wranglers in the summer. In the shoulder seasons, they tried to get jobs waiting tables or working cash registers, and they ate ramen and canned

chili from the discount store while they waited for the snow to finish melting or start falling.

Seasonal people are always in and out of versions of lust and
love, and why not? Everyone's fit. Everyone's drunk on nature
and cheap beer. When seasonal people spout off, without irony,
about mother nature and the purity of the mountains and how love
should be shared freely, all you have to do is keep saying, *Yeah,
totally, I know what you mean,* and eventually you're kissing someone. So when Wesley left, Ingrid was sad but not devastated. She
decided she'd go where the wind blew her.

First it blew her to Keystone, where she got her first real instruc-
tor job and burned through a succession of amiably stoned quasi-
boyfriends, and then it blew her to Idaho for the summer (rafting
gig), and then, in October, to Jackson Hole to teach ski school.
Before the season started, before there was even any snow, she went
to a party in a crash-pad cabin that reminded her of so many others
she'd seen over the years—not squalid, exactly, but improvised,
with towels for curtains and sleeping bags on bare mattresses—
and that was where she met Richie.

At first she'd assumed he was somebody's father, or maybe one
of the lifer instructors who eventually get as craggy and weathered
as the mountains themselves, but he was a stranger who'd been
visiting a friend next door and heard the merriment and decided
to investigate. He was a friendly guy—he said so himself—
and seemed to assume he would be welcome everywhere. When
Ingrid went to get a beer, he buttonholed her near the refrigerator
and started telling her about the resort he was building outside Yel-
lowstone, how it would be world-class, a real destination. Then he
switched topics abruptly.

"I must seem like an old geezer to you," he said, "but the thing is, I can sell ice to an Eskimo. I can sell brimstone to the devil. I *know* I can talk you into going on a date with me."

"So what you're saying," she said, amused, "is that I need a date with you as much as an Eskimo needs ice."

"Hell, you can never have too much ice," he said.

As happens to fair-skinned outdoorsy people, his face had been scorched and abraded by the elements to a deep, mottled pink, and he had a hard, round whiskey gut like something out of a mold pan. A gold watch sat in a nest of crispy blond fur on his wrist. He was too old for her and too swaggering and slick, but she figured if the wind blew her out to dinner with some rich divorced guy (he told her he was divorced) and then, the next weekend, up to his lonely house on Adelaide Peak and never quite blew her out again, so be it. By the time he confessed he wasn't divorced but separated, from a woman who lived in the nearest town, called Witching, Ingrid had not only given up her ski-school job but had started to think of herself as someone whose plates should be warmed in a drawer, who should be able to open a set of French doors and step out into killer backcountry. He seemed surprised by how little she cared about his bombshell. Your marriage is your responsibility, she told him. It doesn't have anything to do with me.

"Her name is Adelaide," he said. His wife's name.

"Did you name the mountain after her?"

He laughed, an actual guffaw. "Someone named the mountain a long time before I came on the scene, honey. It's a coincidence. But maybe I attached too much importance to it back in the day, when I was a romantic idiot." His tone was indulgent and paternal, which she found irritating since she didn't think of Richie as her superior in any way, except maybe on skis. She had been surprised, when the snow finally came, to discover he was a grade-A ripper, fearless and stylish, his big body quiet through the tick-tock swing of his poles and the graceful genuflections of his Telemark turns.

Five years earlier, Richie had inherited six thousand acres of land—the lower reaches of Adelaide. His father never built anything on it besides a few rickety hunting camps, preferring to live in Witching, in a modest A-frame with Richie's mother. After she died, Richie's father moved to a tiny cabin on the shore of Lake Witching that Richie described as a stupid fucking freezing-ass gnome house—typical of his father, who had never known how to have a good time, or even an okay time, or how to let anyone else have an okay time, forget about a good one.

A few debts came with the land, mostly tax-related, but Richie, who'd been dreaming since childhood of skiers swooping down Adelaide and clomping into a magnificent lodge to linger over beer and fondue and make impulsive offers on overpriced condos, had no intention of cashing out prematurely. He didn't doubt he could cajole the government into selling him use of the much vaster parcel of public wilderness that extended uphill from his land to the top of Adelaide and, to the west, encompassed the eminently developable Mount Gust. Of *course* they would let him build lifts and restaurants and crisscross the place with access roads and boundary ropes. He couldn't imagine they would mind if he cut down trees, dug out boulders, piped in water for the snow cannons, sent patrollers up with dynamite to clear avalanches from the high bowl. Richie was so confident everything would fall into place that before the Forest Service even laid eyes on his proposal he'd started cutting runs on his land, treeless strips that fanned out down the slopes like veins. In Witching, he set himself up with an office full of letterhead and glossy trail maps and sweatshirts monogrammed with *Ski Adelaide!* that he gave away indiscriminately and 3-D renderings of the base lodge, complete with sun-deck and ticket windows.

The first night he brought Ingrid to the house, she had played up her youth, marveling at everything with such rapture that she worried he might think she was making fun, but he radiated pride, started pointing out custom-made cabinets, gave a demonstration of the ski room's boot dryers. "No fucking way!" she said about the den with a pool table and carved cherry bar backed by smoked mirrors. "Get out of town!" she said when he flipped a switch to illuminate the Jacuzzi on the deck, even though she had known, from the moment she stepped into the house, that there would be a Jacuzzi.

"How about a dip?" he said, handing her a glass of wine. She could almost have mouthed along with the question, she saw it coming from so far away. She felt a patronizing amusement at the power he seemed to ascribe to this glowing turquoise lure, kept snug under a vinyl lid and faithfully fed chlorine pellets in exchange for the hope that women might want to lower their bod-ies into it.

Sitting in her underwear in the roiling water, she let her head loll back. "Great stars," she called over the jets.

"Wait till you see this place in the morning." He moved stealth-ily through the maelstrom and was suddenly close, one hand on her thigh. With a dripping, steaming arm, he gestured to the cold-smelling darkness. "Ski-in, ski-out. You'll have to imagine the snow."

"What makes you think I'll be here in the morning?"

He leaned in. Booze and chlorine, a faint gaminess she attrib-uted to his being over fifty. "Just a hunch."

She'd had a sense of déjà vu, like she was reenacting a movie she'd seen but couldn't quite place, and what followed in his big bed on his lamé red sheets had that same stale sense of role-playing. It occurred to her that maybe all flirtation is hackneyed and hollow, maybe all romance nothing more than biology gussied up in a tacky figure-skating costume. He called her *baby* and asked if she was a good girl and did lots of instructing and demanding in an alert, rapid, encouraging way that made her think of a jockey talking to a horse.

He didn't crave her pain or humiliation, just her submission, her malleability, her assurances that she *did* like it when he did that, that she *was* a good girl. He needed her to submit to the idea of him as a happy-go-lucky ass-slapping good-ol'-boy huckster always half a step ahead of trouble. She was happy enough to oblige. She believed in the power of lowering herself, and she believed she deserved to be celebrated for the accomplishment of not yet having lived too long.

THERE WERE TRACES of Adelaide, the almost ex-wife, scattered around his house. The pair of black cotton underwear balled between the washer and dryer got tossed in the trash, though Ingrid kept the tea tree oil and lotion and tampons she found under the bathroom sink, as pleased as if they had been left for her as gifts. She ignored the name scrawled in certain books she pulled off the shelves. She hung her necklaces from the delicate brass jewelry tree that stood, wintry and denuded, on a shelf in the cavernous master closet.

In their first couple of weeks together, Richie would make a big show of cuddling and kissing and whispering little endearments after sex, but before long he started going right from clutching and grunting to being an inert, snoring mound on the other side of the bed. Back in her teens, Ingrid had learned that ejaculation sometimes emptied men of a certain animating humanity. The energies they used to attract women in the first place—attentiveness, empathy, vitality—were commandeered and diverted by their bodies toward the essential project of replenishing their testicles, and they became lumpen and taciturn. Usually she found this transformation annoying, symptomatic of a childish self-indulgence that men (generally speaking) managed to wield somehow as a strength, but in Richie's case the shutdown was the only part of their whole arrangement that made her feel seedy and ashamed, less like a captivating, irresistible minx and more like a generic vessel required for an ancient but discredited ritual. She would slink out of bed and go clean up, dawdling in front of the mirror before she switched out the light.

Once the snow came, it kept coming. A couple of feet had accumulated when, early one morning, she heard a snowmobile and then a shrill human racket. Through the leaded-glass window by the front door she saw a tall woman in a black snowmobile suit with a fur-lined hood screaming up at the bedroom window. Her machine was slewed at an angle behind Richie's truck. As she hurled something at the house—a rock?—Ingrid finally understood her cries. *Richie! Richie! Richie!* Another rock. Glass broke. Only then, running up the stairs to get Richie out of the shower, did Ingrid realize the woman had to be Adelaide.

Ingrid followed as Richie charged out into the snow in his bathrobe and slippers, steam rising cartoonishly from the top of his damp head, skinny ankles flushed salmon pink. He grabbed Adelaide's cocked arm and forced it down.

Her hood fell back.

Ingrid had imagined Richie's wife in various incarnations—mousy, sexy, rugged, frumpy—but always as a woman, whole and recognizable as such, not as anything like this bewildering being.

The skin of her face resembled papier-mâché not yet completely dry, rippled and rutted with long, tender pink ladders showing where she had been sewn together, all of it off-kilter, pulling down to the left. She appeared to be missing an ear. Short, sparse dark hair sprouted chaotically from her furrowed scalp. Twisting in Richie's grasp, she dropped to sit in the snow, legs bent under her. She looked at Ingrid. "You don't belong here," she said. "This isn't your place."

For a confused moment, Ingrid wondered if Richie, still gripping Adelaide's arm, had been the cause of her injuries. But, no, this woman had been savaged by something else. Atop her ordinary body in its snowmobiling suit, her mangled face and wild, patchy hair had the effect of a headdress, a mask.

Richie said, "Ingrid, quit staring. Go inside."

He didn't stay out long. Ten minutes. Ingrid watched from upstairs. The contortions of Adelaide's face must have been painful. Eventually she scooped up handfuls of snow and pressed them against her cheeks.

Richie came inside after the snowmobile had gone revving and growling away. "I was meaning to tell you about—" He stopped and stared into space, then said, "Anyway, now you know about her. Now she knows about you." He sounded both grave and sardonic. "Now everybody knows about everybody."

Ingrid asked what had happened.

A mountain lion had attacked Adelaide while she was jogging in a canyon, he said. She'd surprised it. It must not have been very hungry or determined because she'd managed to fight it off with a branch and rocks, and then she'd walked two miles to get help, knocked on someone's door basically flayed, holding one of her eyeballs in place with her hand. She was tough, he'd give her that.

"Was that before or after you separated?"

"After," he said. Then, "Damn it. Before. There's the truth."

But things had already gone wrong between them, he said. *That* was a fact, even though, okay, maybe he couldn't deal with it: her drooping eyelid, the pucker at one corner of her lopsided mouth, how her left ear was just a hole in her head. She'd been under bandages for so long, had so many surgeries, he'd held out hope she would emerge, at the end, looking more or less as she had before. Silly in retrospect.

He said he would tape some trash bags over the broken window so they could get out and ski, enjoy the fresh snow, the bluebird day.

IN LATE JANUARY, the Forest Service put the kibosh on Richie's plan. They denied his application to develop the upper reaches of Adelaide Peak and all of Mount Gust, citing elk habitat and restrictions on land use and, infuriatingly to Richie, local opposition. "Don't they want jobs?" he demanded of Ingrid as though she were a delegate sent by the people of Witching. "Don't they want to sell their shitty little houses for a fortune?"

Money dried up fast. A few days after his main investor pulled out, Richie left the house before Ingrid woke. His skis were gone, but she didn't think to look for tracks until late in the afternoon, when snow was already falling. Everyone had known a big snow was coming, expected to last two days, and she couldn't explain to search and rescue why Richie would have stayed out so long or why he didn't tell her where he was going. There wasn't much the guys could do until the storm passed, and then there was so much snow, so much mountain. After ten days, they called off the search.

"The truth is," Leroy, the search boss, said, sitting on one of Richie's rustic leather couches, "we probably won't find him until spring. And even then . . ." He hitched a thumb over his shoulder, at the mountain out there, the great secretive bulk of it. "He could be anywhere."

Ingrid suspected Leroy didn't have the heart to suggest that Richie might have gotten lost on purpose—Richie's troubles were no secret—and she didn't have the nerve to voice her theory that his missing skis were a red herring and he'd slipped off to some tropical haven with whatever money he'd managed to sock away.

"I'm going to keep looking for him," she told Leroy.

"Just do me a favor and make sure we don't have to come up there after you," he said.

Ingrid thought she would get some communication from Adelaide, who was probably the owner of the house if Richie was presumed dead, but no word came. She figured Adelaide must have decided she'd rather let her squat than deal with kicking her out. In any event, she stayed.

SOMETIMES SLUGGISH WASPS appeared in the house, usually one at a time, wandering sleepily out of a hidden nest somewhere, drawn to the wall of windows where they would land and walk slowly up the glass as though crossing a frozen pond, a whole sideways world of sky and snow and mountain beneath their barbed yellow feet. She watched them glumly, mesmerized, wanting neither to kill them nor to live with them.

She hadn't met many of Richie's friends before he disappeared, but now gradually she did. They came by the house, or they introduced themselves in Witching. She could tell they thought she should leave but were also impressed, in spite of themselves, that she kept searching. Richie's life, as she pieced it together from their stories, had been a steady undulation of grand plans and ignominious failures. He had tried to start a bison ranch in Wyoming, but his animals caught a virus and died. He partnered in a restaurant in a transitional Denver neighborhood that transitioned the wrong way. He invented a new kind of ski binding he was sure would change the sport until he broke both of his ankles demonstrating the prototypes.

Adelaide (the human Adelaide) had been another grand plan. Ingrid found a box of mementos in a cabinet: yellowed wedding invitations and obscure souvenirs and photos of Adelaide with her original face, which had been on the flat side, with high cheekbones and wide-set eyes and determination lying like bedrock under all her expressions. There was a journal in which she and Richie had written sappy notes to each other before they married.

Sometimes I think of you, and it stops me in my tracks as though I walked into a wall. And I just have to stand there and think about you some more before I get back to myself enough to go about my business.

Richie had written that. Ingrid recognized the handwriting but not the man.

You are the axis of me, Adelaide wrote. *You are my sky and my skin.*

Ingrid put the journal away, faintly revolted. She couldn't imagine being willing to lower herself for Richie in a way that was not a game, not tawdry role-play meant to squeeze the final twinges of sexual novelty from a humdrum life. She supposed there were men she'd beg not to leave her, whom she'd throw herself on the ground for, but she thought they would have to be extraordinary in some way, misty Hollywood ideals. Richie was just a guy, just a puffed-up old rooster guy, though the fact that Adelaide loved him so much raised his stock a bit for Ingrid. Poor Adelaide. No matter how ferociously she had insulted or berated him, how eloquently she had denounced his disloyalty, how incisively she had exposed the futile vampirism of his horniness (he would still die one day, no matter how young his lovers), she had been helpless to make him feel the shame she thought would balance out her suffering.

Ingrid resolved never to be so powerless. It did not occur to her that such resolutions are in vain, that the potential for destruction is built into love as fundamentally as into atoms of uranium.

NEAR THE END OF MARCH, when Richie had been missing almost two months, a late snow came: almost a foot at the house, more up top. Ingrid stood at the wall of windows, wearied by the sight of it. She wanted springtime. Sun and rain. If Richie was on the mountain, she wanted meltwater to sluice him down, for some hiker's dog to sniff him out. She wanted permission to take up her life again. Finding Richie would change nothing, she knew that, but still she felt bound by some garbled, residual obedience to her promise to search for him, like a flustered, prideful child alone in a gathering dusk, the other hide-and-seekers gone home laughing.

Out she went into the fresh snow. As she skinned up, her mood improved. Squeaking, coppery smelling powder made a nice change from icy, dirt-patched crust. The sun was full on the slope, and by the time she got to the clearing where the upper terminal of Lift B was to have been, she had shed her layers down to a long-sleeved wool T-shirt. At the base of the ridge that led up to the bowl, she paused to drink from her water bottle, then went on, her tracks the only thing marring the smooth snow.

The wind had accumulated a blue-white cornice below the summit, a thick lip of snow she eyed as she climbed. At the top, she stopped well back from the edge. Far below, a narrow road ran through the valley beside a river still frozen along its banks. To the east, Lake Witching was a flat plain of white interrupted here and there by hedgehog islands. All around were mountains: snow and rock and black masses of trees clinging on like mussels. She had the sensation of having lost track of scale, like she was looking down into something beautifully crafted but not quite real, a model world in a glass case. A passenger jet skated over the empty blue sky, pouring out skinny, parallel clouds. Probably someone was looking back at her through an oval window up there, though neither could see the other, only the plane, the snowy peak.

She pulled on her shell and zipped it, straightened her goggles, tugged her hat low, did all her little rituals, her systems check, her superstitious adjustments. Gingerly, she stepped closer to the edge and jabbed with her pole. Solid snowpack. She inched farther, jabbing until the pole slid into the cornice. She lifted one ski, turned it sideways, and, leaning away, delivered a firm, flat kangaroo kick and then another until the snow gave way, shearing off in a crumbling hunk and sliding away down the bowl, a cloud of crystals billowing up in its wake. She watched it go, reassured by the way the fluted face held firm under the sluff. Climbing, she had heard some troubling creaking, the mountain grinding its teeth.

She tapped her poles together—another ritual: *clink, clink*— then dropped in. She made only two turns before she realized a buckle on her left boot was loose and stopped, cranky at her carelessness. The face was steep, and she had to dig her edges in hard as she reached down.

A sandpapering roar, a glittering fog.

She hadn't told her friends or parents about Richie. No one knew where she was. After she'd settled in at his house, she'd called a girl she knew in Jackson Hole and made a vague excuse about having to quit her ski-school job and go away suddenly for family reasons, a story that was accepted with little resistance, as seasonal people were always disappearing and reappearing. See you when I see you, the girl had said.

Later, among other skiers and boarders, Ingrid would some-times occasionally mention she'd had a close call with an ava-lanche, though she fudged the circumstances, just said she was in the backcountry in Montana, foolishly alone. By the grace of some motherfucking miracle, she said, when the slab gave way she had barely moved, slid just a few feet, like the mountain was grabbing at her but couldn't quite hold on. After things settled again, she was standing on the edge of a mini-cliff, just above the fracture. Literally inches above it, she said. Downhill, the snow was still moving, white and churning, sweeping along like an ocean wave. It wasn't a big slide, but big enough. The sound of it grew fainter. Mountain people knew what she meant. Close calls were never really clean escapes. They introduced you to your own ghost.

After the avalanche, she stood for a while and waited for some-thing else to happen. When nothing did, she sidestepped cautiously down below the fracture and made a few turns. The snow held. She continued on, skirting the place where the avalanche had petered out in a jumbled mess of snow and rocks and branches, where she could easily have been buried, contorted under the snow, packed tight like a fossil. When, farther downhill, she paused to catch her breath, there was silence except for the crows, the meltwater drip-ping from the trees. Maybe she'd skied right over him somewhere and never known.

When she got back to the house, she packed up her stuff and left.

She went to Jackson Hole and got lucky at the first restaurant she tried. A bartender had gotten busted selling coke, so she was hired. A few weeks later, she read in the paper that Richie's body had been found. Some snowboarder kids had come across him on

Mount Gust, sitting against a tree, still half-buried in snow, 9 millimeter in his hand, hole in his head. Ingrid had been looking on the wrong mountain.

She thought one of the search and rescue guys might have called to let her know he'd been found, but then she supposed she'd surrendered any claim on Richie when she left. Maybe they'd gone to the house, found it empty, and decided she'd gotten bored and had taken off to look for a new benefactor. In the article, Leroy was quoted as saying that Richie had been irresponsible not to leave a note. "Guys risked their lives out there looking for him," he said.

Adelaide, asked what she would do with the land, said only, "Nothing."

Toward the end of the season, Wesley slid onto one of Ingrid's barstools. He'd planned to travel for a year but had ended up being gone for three. "One thing led to another," he said. "I kept meeting great people who were on their way somewhere, and I'd go along."

He never apologized for leaving, but he did say he was sorry if he'd treated her badly. She said she didn't think he had.

"I had some stuff to get out of my system," he said.

She wondered if he expected her to ask if he had succeeded, if all that indefinable, corrupting *stuff* had been successfully jettisoned over the world's beaches and mountains, dispersed among its temples and hot springs, its hostels and nightclubs. There was no point. She didn't think the impulse to be wild, if you had it, could ever really be purged. You tamped it down and let your life settle on top. Right then and there she decided she didn't need to know everything about Wesley.

This was another foolish resolution, made in mockery of her future self, who became chaotic with fury after she found pictures of Wesley's twenty-six-year-old mistress on his phone, all smooth skin and pointed breasts and heavy eyeliner, though even in her shock Ingrid noticed that the girl's face was plain under all that makeup, with a nascent shrewish sharpness. This hint of ugliness both consoled and embittered her. She raged at Wesley. Then she begged and pleaded with him, not so much so he would stay but so he would somehow not do what he had already done.

AFTER INGRID AND WESLEY leave their marriage counselor's office, they pick up their younger son from a friend's house and their older son from his soccer game and drive to a pizza parlor where his team is having a party. It is a hot, low-ceilinged place with a red-and-black-tiled floor and a claw machine full of plush animals waiting to be grappled up and away as though from the embassy in Saigon. The tables are crowded with pepperoni pies and pitchers of soda and amber plastic cups and boys in green jerseys bent to the work of eating, their hair still damp with sweat at their napes.

The humid, noisy place comes as a shock after the concentrated hush of Dr. Rivkoff's office, its cocooning misery.

"It's over, and I'm sorry," Wesley had said. "Isn't that enough?"

Dr. Rivkoff had fixed Ingrid with a game-show host's keen but impartial gaze. She is not a Jungian but dresses like one, in long beaded necklaces and expensively minimalist layers of draped linen. "Is it?"

"I'm so tired of talking about myself," Wesley added before Ingrid could say anything.

Skepticism had flickered under Dr. Rivkoff's neutral expression. Therapists were like astronauts, Ingrid thought, striking off through the infinite vastness of people's willingness to talk about themselves.

Ingrid sits in a booth with some other moms. Wesley is with the dads at a table on the far side of the boys, all of them angled to watch basketball on an enormous flat-screen. A young waitress in a ponytail and short shorts brings them a tray of beers, and they eye her and smile. Ingrid wishes there had been time with Dr. Rivkoff to discuss how, the other day, she had walked in on her older son masturbating to an actual, physical Victoria's Secret catalog that had come in the mail for some reason ("Old school!" Wesley had said when she told him, forgetting for a moment that he was still supposed to be monkishly contrite and nonsexual), and while she knows this is natural and inevitable and something her son will do frequently and forever, she can't help but blame her husband. He has invited the serpent into their house.

"I don't know what's enough," Ingrid had said to Dr. Rivkoff. "I want him to be embarrassed about being such a cliché, the aging doofus slobbering over the pretty young thing." She paused, corrected, "Well, the *young* thing. But I can tell deep down he's proud of himself, like, *Still got it!* I'm not saying he doesn't feel bad. I just don't believe he genuinely regrets what he did."

"I can't control what you believe," said Wesley.

"You could make more of an effort to be convincing."

"So," interjected Dr. Rivkoff, "Ingrid, you're saying you're frustrated because Wesley doesn't seem to feel what you want him to feel. But that's life, isn't it?"

Ingrid had stared at the strange, spidery air plants that live in a glass bowl on Dr. Rivkoff's coffee table without benefit of soil or water. She had never told Wesley about Richie or Adelaide. Finally, she said, "The problem is, I remember being young. I think I can imagine what went on between them *too* clearly."

"So I'm supposed to be responsible for your imagination now as well," Wesley said.

"I just mean," she said, "that I'm not sure I can pretend not to be haunted by this."

"I'm afraid we don't get to choose what haunts us," Dr. Rivkoff had said.

Ingrid's older son tips his head back and lowers the point of a pizza slice into his mouth, tongue extended to meet it, eyes closed, being silly, though she can't help but see lasciviousness. They are virginal, these boys, but no longer innocent. Their minds are already churning with muddled fantasies; they can't possibly imagine becoming bored with a woman's body, and yet that capacity is already in all of them, buried under their narrow, hairless chests and downy cheeks and briny pubescent odors. Maybe it's in girls, too, but Ingrid doesn't think so. Not in the same way.

All at once the cheese separates from her son's pizza and lands flat on his face, red sauce–side up, slick and shiny, grotesque. The boys laugh. Ingrid thinks of Adelaide in the snow. She thinks of her young self standing and watching the other woman and feeling almost nothing: mild pity, faint embarrassment. She should have been afraid. She should have understood that even a life lived properly, lived better than she was living, could bring so much grief.

Acknowledgments

These stories were written over the course of more than a decade, under wildly varied circumstances. Some took multiple turns under a workshop's scrutinizing lens and some were written in solitude and received little feedback. I'm grateful to everyone who offered their thoughts at the Iowa Writers' Workshop and at Stanford, especially to my teachers who led the conversations around "The Cowboy Tango," "La Moretta," "Angel Lust," "In the Olympic Village," "You Have a Friend in 10A," and "The Great Central Pacific Guano Company": Lan Samantha Chang, Tobias Wolff, Elizabeth Tallent, and the late John L'Heureux. Thanks to Bread Loaf and to the Cill Rialaig artists' residency in Ireland.

My beloved agent, Rebecca Gradinger, has been a part of my writing life since before any of these were published. Working together on stories was how we got to know each other and found our collaborative footing, and I've learned so much from her over the years. Thank you to all the usual suspects at Knopf: my remarkable editor Jordan Pavlin, Reagan Arthur, Emily Reardon, Sara Eagle, Paul Bogaards, and, well, everyone. Enormous thanks

Acknowledgments

also to Jane Lawson, Larry Finlay, Bill Scott-Kerr, Tabitha Pelly, and the team at Transworld and Doubleday UK.

Many more people were involved in the publication of these stories in journals and magazines than I ever knew or communicated with, so I would like to express my general gratitude to all the staff, readers, and benefactors who hold up the world of short stories in this country. At *VQR*, where three of these stories first appeared, thank you to Ted Genoways, Paul Reyes, Jon Peede, Allison Wright, Molly Minturn, and Aja Gabel. Thank you to Richard Russo and Heidi Pitlor for including "The Cowboy Tango" in *The Best American Short Stories 2010*. Thank you to Karolina Waclawiak at BuzzFeed, Meakin Armstrong at *Guernica*, Halimah Marcus at *Electric Literature*, David Leavitt at *Subtropics*, Rob Spillman at *Tin House*, Jillian Goodman at *Mary Review*, and Jill Meyers at *American Short Fiction*. I know some of those fine people have long moved on since we emailed story drafts back and forth years ago, but I so valued and benefited from our editorial relationships. I am also forever indebted to all for their willingness to read and publish my work, especially when I was a whippersnapper just starting out.

Lastly, thank you to my family and friends who have supported my writing career in more ways than I could list or even fully grasp. This book, for me, is rich with memories of attempts and failures, of stinging criticism and small breakthroughs and uncertain experiments, of frustrations and of thrilling, longed-for acceptance emails. That is to say, this book came out of years spent learning to be a writer, a process that will never be complete.

A NOTE ABOUT THE AUTHOR

MAGGIE SHIPSTEAD is the *New York Times* best-selling author of the novels *Great Circle, Astonish Me,* and *Seating Arrangements. Seating Arrangements* was the winner of the Dylan Thomas Prize and the Los Angeles Times Book Prize for First Fiction, and *Great Circle* was short-listed for the Booker Prize. She is a graduate of the Iowa Writers' Workshop, a former Wallace Stegner Fellow at Stanford, and the recipient of a fellowship from the National Endowment for the Arts. She lives in Los Angeles.

A NOTE ON THE TYPE

Pierre Simon Fournier *le jeune* (1712–1768), who designed the type used in this book, was both an originator and a collector of types. His types are old style in character and sharply cut. In 1764 and 1766 he published his *Manuel typographique,* a treatise on the history of French types and printing, on typefounding in all its details, and on what many consider his most important contribution to typography— the measurement of type by the point system.

Composed by North Market Street Graphics,
Lancaster, Pennsylvania

Printed and bound by Berryville Graphics,
Berryville, Virginia

Designed by Cassandra J. Pappas